Sisters Lie

Shary Caya Lavoie

DEDICATION

To Twyla Virginia Gordon Caya. For all those sisters.

DFTRM

CONTENTS

ACKNOWLEDGMENTS

As the youngest of a rather large family, the majority of these family members being sisters, let me stress here and now, this book is a work of fiction. Pure fiction. Let me also point out that the creepiest things I currently have tucked away in the deep, dark corners of *my* closet are a plastic pentagram, a red clown wig and an expired suture removal kit. They have probably been there for over twenty years, but that's a story for another time.

I would like to acknowledge the many people who played roles in bringing this book to publication: Kailyn Lavoie, Michele Vachon, Izabella Lavoie, Morgan Bernier, Leah McMahan, Magan Tatrn and Jess Lavoie. Of course, this list would not be complete if I didn't include my husband, Bert Lavoie, for cooking many extra meals, picking up a lot of slack around the house, and answering so many 'which sounds better' questions, while I worked diligently on my writing.

PROLOGUE

CHRISTMAS DAY

Chelsie stood up and cleared her throat. She wasn't comfortable speaking in front of everyone, not even her own family, but this was important. She looked around the crowded living room and tried to make her voice heard over the ubiquitous talking and laughter. "Excuse me, everyone. Excuse me. Please, can I have your attention?" No one paused their conversation. No one turned their head in her direction.

In an effort to get her family to focus on her, she stepped up on the large, brick hearth of the wood-burning fireplace next to the sparkling Christmas tree. Her small frame was lost among the evergreen branches and twinkling lights, the warm fire crackling in back of her. She again spoke out to her family and again was ignored. Fortunately, her Uncle Jack noticed her unsuccessful attempts to get her family's attention as they continued to enjoy the Christmas party. He stepped up next to her on the hearth and put his arm around her shoulder. Then he whistled loudly. It was a shrill, piercing whistle that caused everyone to immediately stop what they were doing and look up at him. Once the room was quiet, he smiled and said in his deep voice, "I think Chelsie needs our attention." Chelsie smiled at him gratefully.

"I'm sorry to interrupt, this will only take a minute." She nervously twisted the ring on her finger as she spoke. "I know that we are all missing Nana Caroline this Christmas. It's hard to believe that she and Grampy David have only been gone a few weeks. I was thinking of a way that we could honor her this holiday season and I found this site called GeneScreen online. They do DNA testing. I was thinking that maybe her daughters, Aunt Beth, Aunt Jody, Aunt Delaney, and my mom, Samantha to the rest of you, could send their DNA samples into GeneScreen and we could learn about our heritage. You know, now that Nana isn't here to tell us more about our family history. I thought it would be fun. I ordered kits for everyone, and to get us started, I made this family tree…"

Our Family Tree

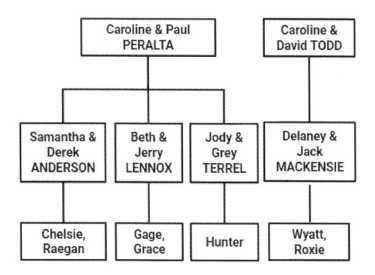

1 JODY

No matter how long Jody stared at the email, the results didn't change. Neither did the amount of shock she was feeling. How could it be? How could what she believed for the last forty-two years not be real? They say DNA doesn't lie, so it must be true, right? But this time, it was her DNA, and the results were right there in front of her.

She already knew that Delaney was her half-sister, no surprise there. Delaney was born four years after she was, which was years after her parents divorced and her mother married David. But Beth was her half-sister, too? How could that be? Samantha, Beth and she all had the same mother and father. At least, that's what she had always believed.

Jody put her tablet on the counter and wiped her thick, dark hair away from her face. She was surprised to find she was sweating. It wasn't warm inside her house. It was only March, there was still snow on the ground in the small town of Cayne, Maine. Still, her forehead was damp. She walked to the sink and washed her hands, staring out the window into the large, wooded backyard, but not really seeing it. Her mind was still reviewing the DNA results that had come from the GeneScreen email she had so cheerfully opened not five minutes ago.

It had sounded like such a fun idea when Chelsie had talked everyone into doing this last Christmas—sending their DNA to GeneScreen to learn about their heritage. Jody was sure no one ever expected to learn that Jody, Beth and Samantha were not full-blooded sisters.

She had been excited when she first saw the email sitting in her inbox. She had ignored the other emails and clicked on her touchpad to open this one first. It started off with a section explaining that her ancestors were from Ireland, Scotland, England, and to her surprise, Italy. "We get around," she had muttered under her breath. Then she continued to the list of other relatives who had also submitted their DNA to GeneScreen. She recognized a few of the names. Margaret Canton was her mother's younger sister, and she was pretty sure Eliza Canton Ellison was Aunt Margaret's oldest daughter. There was a Brady Gladstone that she thought might be a distant cousin, but she wasn't sure. There were two names she wasn't familiar with, Maria Carver and Antonia Bernicia. GeneScreen indicated they were second cousins. She figured she would ask Beth about those names later. The next name that popped up was Beth. Beth Peralta Lennox. This wasn't unexpected. She and Beth spit in their respective tubes and sent their samples in at the same time. What was unexpected was their relationship. They were not sisters. GeneScreen listed them as half-sisters. Their DNA wasn't close enough to be sisters. It was only a twenty-two percent match. That's what had her freaking out right now. It was pretty obvious. She and Beth had different fathers.

But how could that be? Beth was only two years older than her, and Samantha just a year older than Beth. They were sisters. They were so close. When they were little, they always played together. Their mother dressed them alike. They walked to school together. They shared a room until they moved to the house on Old Cottage Lane. Even after their parents divorced and their mother remarried, they continued to be best friends. When Delaney was born, she joined them and they grew from three to four. Now, after all these years, with the receipt of one simple email that Jody stared at on the tablet she held in her hands, she saw it was all a lie. She didn't fit in quite the way she thought she had. How could her mother have deceived her this way? How could she not have told her that the man she grew up believing was her father, the man she had loved her entire life, was not her real dad? And why didn't he tell her? Did he even know the truth?

That thought sent a chill down Jody's spine. Did he know she wasn't his daughter? Her mind shifted to thoughts of him. His name was Paul. Paul Peralta, but even now, as grown women, she and Beth and Samantha never called him anything but Daddy. Not Father or Dad, just Daddy. He had been such a big part of their childhood, even though their parents divorced when they were quite young, and he continued to be to this day.

Paul was tall with warm, brown hair, now graying at the temples, and clear, gray eyes. He had a perpetual tan, partly because that was the skin tone he was born with, and partly because he loved the outdoors. When he was young, his forestry job kept him outside more often than not. Now, at least once or twice a day, he liked to walk the trails that surrounded his home.

Jody pictured his face with ruddy red cheeks, his nose that was a little too big for his face, and the small, half-moon scar that was just above his left eyebrow. The scar didn't usually show, even now his shaggy curls would cover it, but when he pushed his hair back, or when the wind blew just right, she could see it. For years, whenever she asked him what happened, he would make up stories about how different fantastical creatures had flown down from the sky and tried to bite him, or how he had to battle great dragons or one-eyed monsters to save his girls from their evil clutches. Many years later she learned that he actually got the scar when he and another forest ranger were tearing down an illegal hunting cabin in the middle of the woods and he caught himself in the head with a crowbar.

Jody always thought of her father as a gentle giant. She remembered giggling while she and Beth and Samantha would climb on him like he was their personal teddy bear. He would grab all three of them in his long, muscular arms and pick them up while at the same time yelling, "Gotcha!" Sometimes he would take turns throwing them into the air one-by-one. This was always accompanied by his frequent, baritone laughter.

Jody walked to the closest cabinet and grabbed a glass. She filled it with water from the dispenser in the refrigerator. Then she gulped it down, refilled it, and drained it a second time. She reread the DNA results. They hadn't changed. It was clear that the man she had called Daddy her entire life wasn't her father.

She again wondered if he knew, or if that had been only her mother's secret. She wished she could ask her mother, but that was no longer possible. Her mother, along with her mother's husband, David, had died in a car crash only three months earlier. A wave of sorrow rushed through Jody, but it was short-lived. It was quickly replaced with a flash of anger because she couldn't go to her mother now and ask her why she had kept this terrible secret. Why hadn't she told Jody who her real father was?

Jody slumped in a chair at the kitchen table and rested her head between her hands. Memories of her childhood ran through her mind, of all the good times she had with her father. She found herself thinking about one October when she was nine or ten. Her mother had dropped her off to spend Halloween with him. Neither Samantha nor Beth wanted to go that year.

"Daddy, Mom made me wear this stupid princess costume. I don't want to be a princess when I go to Jenna's party. All the kids are going to make fun of me. I look like a big, pink powder puff!"

Paul chuckled as he watched his daughter drop onto the couch, the sparkling pink netting of her dress flaring out around her. Her mouth was drawn downward and her arms were folded tightly across her chest. "I don't know if you look like a powder puff, but I wouldn't be surprised one bit if you sprouted wings and flew off to a magical fairyland."

"Daddy, this isn't funny! It is very serious!"

Paul tried not to grin at the intense look on Jody's tiny face, her eyes narrowed and her lips pursed. "Okay, Honey. I get it. You are too old to be going to Jenna's house as a princess. So, tell me, did Mom specifically say you had to wear that costume to the party?"

Jody thought for a few seconds before a smile played across her lips. "No, she never said I had to wear it to Jenna's. All she said was to put it on before I left the house."

"I think that may give us a little wiggle room. What would you like to go as, if you weren't going as a glittery, pink princess?"

"Gee, Daddy, I don't know. Maybe a killer vampire? Or a blood-thirsty monster who likes to stab people to death? What about that zombie thing with red eyes and long, black hair? You know, the one with pointed ears and big, sharp teeth?"

"That's quite a stretch from a fairy princess. We don't have much time; let's see what we can do." With that, Paul removed the majority of the pink netting that was the princess costume. Cooking oil and cocoa powder turned Jody's hair from soft, shiny brown to dark, dirty and stringy looking. Then he applied various items from bottles found in the garage to the remaining pink netting of Jody's costume. She now emerged looking like a blood-soaked zombie with a comically large plastic knife seemingly implanted in her stomach. This was quite a change from the fairy princess that *had stood before them only minutes earlier. The grin on her face was priceless.*

As Jody thought back to that time with Daddy, she felt certain there was no way he knew she wasn't his daughter. Her mother must have kept that secret from him, just like she kept it from her. She sighed as she pushed this memory from her mind and again looked down at the tablet. No matter how many times she read the email, it could only mean one thing, Beth was her half-sister. When Samantha got her DNA results, she would show up as her half-sister, too. Jody felt like her entire life had been a lie.

She walked across the kitchen and stepped down into the living room. On the mantel over the red-brick fireplace was a picture of herself along with her three sisters. Samantha, the oldest, was three years older than she was. Like Jody, Samantha had thick, wavy brown hair, but that's where their resemblance ended. While Samantha was tall and thin, Jody was shorter with a more muscular build. Samantha had hazel eyes that people often referred to as 'doe-eyes,' Jody's eyes were a rich, chocolate brown, and more almond-shaped. Samantha's nose flared and her lips were full. Jody's features were small. Still, the most noticeable difference between the two of them was their skin tone. Samantha's skin was fair with a pink hue. She always wore big hats to avoid freckles. Jody had skin of a deep olive-tone that seldom burned. As Jody studied the picture, it was easy to believe they weren't full sisters.

Then her attention turned to Beth. Beth was the second-oldest in the family. She was two years older than Jody, fourteen months younger than Samantha. Like Samantha, Beth had big, hazel eyes, but unlike her sisters, her hair was blond—almost a golden color. She was the same height as Jody, which was several inches shy of Samantha. Beth was tiny, not at all muscular. She probably never wore bigger than a size two her entire life. Beth had pale skin but visited tanning booths frequently, so she almost always had a golden hue about her.

Lastly, Jody looked at Delaney. At first glance, Jody thought Delaney looked the most different of the four of them. That was to be expected because Delaney had a different father. Delaney was tall, almost as tall as Samantha. She was thin with long, strawberry-blond hair. Her hair was wavy when it was long, curly when it was short. Both the color and the curls were natural, not the result of a perm or hair dye. She had big, green eyes and medium-size features. She didn't look like any of her sisters, she favored her father.

As Jody continued to stare at the picture, a thought crossed her mind. She realized that she didn't look any more like her sisters than Delaney did, especially with her olive skin and brown eyes. It's funny how she never noticed that before.

She backed away from the picture and sat on the couch that was directly across from the fireplace. As she sank into the soft leather, she grabbed the square, orange pillow from near the armrest and pulled it close to her.

The clock on the mantel indicated it was a few minutes after 3:00. Hunter, her son, was out of school, but had soccer practice so he wouldn't be home for another hour or two. Grey was picking him up on his way home from work.

Grey. She had to call Grey. She needed to talk to someone and she wasn't ready to share this information with Beth, although she knew it was quite possible that Beth had already received her results from GeneScreen. She reached in the pocket of her black yoga pants and pulled out her cell phone. Her hand only shook a little as she opened her contacts list and pressed the button next to Grey's picture. He answered immediately.

"Hi. I'm heading over to the soccer field now. I finished up early and I thought I would catch Hunter's practice. What's up?"

"Hi." Jody gripped her cell phone tightly, staring blankly in front of her. She knew her husband was expecting her to talk. After all, she called him. She was having trouble finding the words she wanted to say.

"Jody, are you there? Is everything okay?" Grey's voice was monotone, not registering annoyance or concern.

"I'm here. It's just that I got some news today. Not really news. More like, information. And I'm surprised. You might say shocked."

"What is it? Are you okay?" This time Jody could hear the concern that edged into her husband's voice.

"Yes, I'm fine. Everyone's fine. I got my results back from GeneScreen."

Several seconds passed and Jody didn't speak. "And?" Grey questioned with a hint of impatience.

"The results aren't back yet for Delaney or Samantha, but they are back for me and Beth, and they show that Beth is my half-sister. We are only twenty-two percent connected, and according to GeneScreen, we are half-sisters. Not whole sisters like we always thought. That means Daddy isn't my father. I don't know who my real father is. Grey, my whole life is a lie. I don't even know who I am anymore."

Now that the words were out, there was no denying it. Jody began shaking from hearing this revelation aloud. She started to cry. It was not a gentle cry where tears just pooled in her eyes and ran down her cheeks. It was a loud, agonizing cry, filled with anguished gasps. This went on for what must have been several minutes before she finally wiped tears from both eyes and snot away from her nose with the hem of her sleeve. She then focused her attention on her cell phone. She could hear Grey calling to her.

"Jody, listen. It's going to be okay. Listen to me. Are you there?"

"I'm here," she managed to say between her last remaining sobs. Then she added, "Grey, it's not just that I don't know who my father is. Think about this. Does Daddy know that I'm not his daughter? I mean, if he finds out, is he going to take me out of his will? I know I shouldn't be worried about that, but Daddy is a very wealthy man. We could be losing millions if he finds out I'm not his real daughter."

"Do you think he would do that, Jody? Assuming that he doesn't know and that one of your sisters tells him, do you really believe he would disinherit you now? After all these years of believing you were his?"

"I don't know. I mean, it's possible. DNA doesn't lie."

"The GeneScreen test, it shows that you and Beth are half-sisters, right?"

"Yes," Jody replied meekly, her crying having now subsided to a whimper.

"Is that all it indicated? Did it give you any more information?"

"No." She answered, but waited in silence, wondering what Grey was putting together in his mind. What was he going to say next?

"Jody, are you sure that Paul isn't your father? Or is it possible that he isn't Beth's father instead?"

2 SAMANTHA

Samantha sat at the kitchen table alone. She tried to focus on the leftover meatloaf she had heated in the microwave, but it tasted bland. She wasn't sure if it was the meatloaf or simply her mood. Nothing in her life gave her much pleasure these days. With Chelsie away at school, Derek at the office again, and Raegan, who knew where she was these days, Samantha's life seemed as tasteless as the slab of colorless meat that lie flat in the center of her plate.

She attempted a few more bites but realized it was useless. She rose from her chair, grabbed the plate and fork from the table, and carried them to the sink. She discarded her barely eaten dinner down the drain and rinsed her dish. Then she carefully loaded everything into the dishwasher, ensuring the gold sunflower on the edge of her plate was facing up and to the right, just like the gold sunflowers on the other plates that were already in the dishwasher. She slammed the door shut and went in search of her cell phone.

She grimaced when she saw she hadn't missed any calls, but seriously, what was she expecting? Did she think her husband would call? She wished Derek would be considerate enough to let her know that he was going to be working late, but that was unlikely. He worked late pretty much every Thursday night and he never bothered to pick up the telephone and let her know. He would consider that small gesture to be a wasted effort. He wouldn't be home before 10:00 or 10:30 tonight.

She was more disappointed that it wasn't one of her daughters calling. They were the only two people who truly cared about her. Her husband sure as hell didn't. Her sisters said they cared, but did they really? No, they only said the words, but they never wanted to spend time with her. She knew they talked about her behind her back. She could almost hear their comments. *Samantha stresses me out. Samantha is so difficult. Samantha is always such a bitch.* Why would she want to hang around with them, knowing that's how they felt about her. She didn't need them. She didn't need anyone. She was fine being alone. As long as she had her daughters.

It was difficult, of course, with Chelsie being away at college. Chelsie left in September for the University of Maine, almost one hundred miles away. She would call as often as she could, but she was so busy with classes and clubs and working part-time in the school's dining hall, that the calls were far and few between. She missed Chelsie.

That left Raegan, her youngest daughter. Raegan was the only one left to spend time with her. She did her best, but like any 17-year-old, she had her own life to live.

Samantha checked the clock. She had a few hours before Raegan would come bounding in, yelling something about softball practice or getting held up at the library. Then Raegan would go on about how she had a ton of homework to get done before school tomorrow. She would check to make sure Samantha was okay—she was a good daughter and always looked after her mother—but she wouldn't have time to sit and chat. She would run up the stairs, jump in the shower, and later, there would be muffled sounds of music, or more likely, gaming sounds, from her computer. How that girl managed grades that kept her on the honor roll, Samantha would never understand.

Thinking about her daughter made Samantha smile. Raegan was so much like she was at that age with her dark hair, big eyes, and freckles that popped up every summer, staying until the leaves began showing signs of gold and red. But even more similar was Raegan's personality, at least how Samantha's used to be when she was younger. Raegan was not afraid of anything. She was smart and daring and she had boundless energy. She was always ready to take on new adventures. Raegan was a little pushy, a little funny and a lot nosey, all rolled into one. She treated life like it was to be conquered; she was taking it head-on.

Unfortunately, all this energy meant that Raegan had lots of interests and almost no time for Samantha. Sure, Raegan would ask how Samantha was doing, and she was always watching to make sure Samantha was okay, but as far as actually spending time together? That didn't happen. Raegan's senior year was spent running from school to softball to the library and of course, all the time she spent on that damn computer. Samantha could not understand Raegan's love of gaming, but she did understand that Raegan would be locked away in her room for hours on end glued to her computer screen. All this left very little time for Samantha. Samantha wasn't surprised that she was being taken for granted, but she didn't have to like it. So here she was, sitting in her kitchen, crying and alone.

Samantha thought back to her past and wondered what happened to the happy, outgoing girl she used to be. When did she lose her and become this quiet, lonely woman with no one to love her? She hadn't been that way when she met Derek. She was sure of it. Part of the reason he fell in love with her was because she was so lively, so fun. She thought back to the first time he laid eyes on her.

It was the summer before she started her senior year in college. She was studying to be a teacher and he was working on a dual-enrollment degree in marketing and computer science. It was a week before school was to start, what was known as the dog days of summer. It was hot and humid with no breeze to cool the air.

Samantha thought it would be fun to head to the old quarry on the east side of Raven Mountain. Most people didn't go there to swim, the water was too deep and too cold to be safe, but Samantha was daring and after all, what could go wrong? Within an hour of calling a few friends, she was parking her Ford Explorer in the dirt lot next to several other cars belonging to kids who attended her college. She slipped through the gate and walked down the overgrown path through the pines until the quarry opened up before her.

Samantha immediately recognized several others from her school. Then her attention was drawn to the gang of new people just arriving. Some looked familiar, but several she didn't know. One in particular caught her eye. A male. He was tall and thin, but not scrawny. His well-defined muscles clearly indicated he worked out. He had brownish-blond hair and the bluest eyes she had ever seen. She tried to look away before he caught her staring at him, but she couldn't. He was mesmerizing.

When he looked over and met her gaze, she felt her cheeks turn bright red. That was unusual for her; she didn't embarrass easily. He grinned and oh, shit, was that a wink? Samantha was a sucker for a hot guy and a wink. Stumbling backwards, she turned and joined her friends, but not before she saw him laugh.

It wasn't long before he came over and introduced himself to her. His name was Derek Anderson and like her, he was a senior. They spent the next hour talking before Derek noticed that no one was swimming. "So, what do you think? Should we get this party started?"

Samantha looked at him and grinned. Despite the eating, drinking, and music, she knew exactly what he had in mind. She kicked off her Converse sneakers and pulled off her sundress, exposing a simple white bikini. Then, without waiting for Derek to respond, she ran toward the water yelling "Race ya" over her shoulder.

As she was getting ready to jump into the cold water, after

all, the quarry was deep and even in late August, deep water in Maine is cold, Derek shot by her and let out a loud, Tarzan-like holler. There was a splash and she was soaked before she even jumped in. The two of them bobbed around laughing and splashing for a few minutes before they were joined by several other swimmers. Derek leaned in close to her and whispered in her ear, "Now this is a party."

After their swim, Samantha's initial shyness, totally out of character for her, was gone. She chatted with Derek like she had known him all of her life. They ate lunch together, played on the same volleyball team, even laid next to each other on the same blanket. The attraction she felt for him was clearly mutual. By late afternoon they had made plans to see each other the next day. Derek was going to pick her up for an early morning hike by the ocean, followed by lunch at the best lobster shack in the entire state, at least that's how Derek described it. Back then, Derek didn't disappoint.

Samantha glanced around the shiny white kitchen as she stuffed her cell phone in the pocket of her oversized sweater. There was a smile on her face as the memory of her first meeting with Derek lingered. They were so infatuated with each other. It didn't take long before that infatuation turned to love. But now it all seemed so long ago. When was the last time Derek looked at her like that, she wondered. Ten years ago? Twenty? She couldn't remember. Sometime before the girls were born and she got caught up in motherhood. Sometime before she traded her adventurous ways for the responsibilities that came with caring for tiny little humans.

She remembered all the times he wanted her to leave the girls with her mother and fly to Paris, or go skiing in Colorado, or take any of a hundred other exciting adventures, but she never could. The girls needed her and she would not just up and go because he felt like it. Things change when you're a mother. Why couldn't he understand? He told her she wasn't fun anymore, that she worried too much. She told him he needed to grow up and be a responsible father. Sure, he supported them financially, but he continued to take the same risks he took when he was younger. She sighed just thinking about it.

It took a few years, but eventually he calmed down. He started working more. He quit asking her to go on vacations and instead he started taking business trips alone. He seemed to focus all of his attention on work. He grew distant, but honestly, Samantha was too preoccupied with the girls to worry. Now it was too late to worry and she couldn't let her mind go to thoughts of what he might be doing to satisfy his adventurous side. It was easier to ignore the signs that were right in front of her and pretend everything was fine. Most of the time she could do that, but sometimes, when she was alone at night, the doubts she tried so hard to push into the darkest parts of her mind would find a way to work themselves into her conscious thought. This was one of those times.

Samantha's cell phone buzzed and she was torn away from both her happier thoughts of the past as well as the gray void she was slipping into. She glanced at the phone's screen. It was nothing, only a notification that she had received an email. Good. She didn't want to talk to anyone. Other than her girls, the people who called her had nothing interesting to say. They mostly wasted her time. She wandered into the living room and sat in the recliner, tucking her legs up underneath her. She started to reach for the remote control to the television but decided against it. Silence felt like a better option for the mood she was in. She fiddled with the hem of her shirt, eventually smoothing it out as she lay her head against the soft fabric of the chair. She closed her eyes and thought of Chelsie.

She missed her oldest daughter. Chelsie was the quiet, studious type. The easy child. She was the one who always had time to sit and chat with Samantha after school. They would share cups of tea in the winter or ice-cold glasses of lemonade in the summer and talk about, well, nothing. It was nice, the time they spent together. Samantha missed that. It was probably selfish of her to encourage those times so much when Chelsie was in high school. A better mother would have pushed her daughter to make friends and hang out with them, but Samantha wasn't a better mother. She enjoyed that time with Chelsie, only now Chelsie was in school studying pre-law and cheering on the Maine Black Bears, all while Samantha sat home drinking her tea alone.

Samantha's phone buzzed again, this time indicating an incoming call. It was Beth. She wasn't surprised. After all, Jody and Beth must have received the GeneScreen results by now. Screw them. They only called when they wanted something. She let the phone drop onto the chair next to her, unanswered. She could feel it vibrating against her leg. She didn't feel like having that discussion with Beth. Beth would hear the lack of surprise in her voice and it would just lead to an argument. When it came to her sisters, everything led to an argument and she didn't have it in her to deal with one of them tonight. She was upset enough with being deserted by her own family; she didn't need to get yelled at by the likes of Beth. Especially since Beth and Jody were probably reeling from the results of their DNA tests.

Samantha thought of the surprised looks that would be on their faces when they realized that one of them wasn't a full-blooded sister. They would, of course, be shocked. First, they would deny it. They would think GeneScreen made a mistake. Then they would be angry. How could their mother never have told them the truth?

Samantha wasn't sure how the bargaining stage would come into play, but she definitely could see depression setting in. Maybe not actual depression, but at the very least, they would probably be sad. Finally, they would both come to accept it. Beth would call Delaney and talk it through with her. She was always closest to Delaney. Jody would start doing other research, and of course, that would lead to bigger things. Things Samantha didn't feel like thinking about right now.

Her cell phone buzzed again. Beth was trying to call her a second time. Samantha sighed as she swiped the red tab. She didn't want to talk to her sister. She was tired and not up for the stress tonight. Plus, this was a call Samantha was dreading because Beth would want to know what her DNA results indicated. Then she would have to explain that she never bothered to submit her DNA to GeneScreen. After all, she already knew what to expect.

3 BETH

The entire kitchen smelled like chocolate chip cookies. Maybe even the entire house. Nothing wrong with that, Beth thought as she swallowed the gummy she had just popped into her mouth. She was hurrying to get the last batch of cookies out of the oven before the twins got home. Knowing her kids, they would dig in and undo at least a half-dozen of all her hard work. They wouldn't care that these cookies were for tonight's bake sale at the school, and not to fill their own never-ending appetites. At least Gage's appetite. Grace didn't eat nearly as much as her brother. Especially lately since she was on a healthy eating kick. Beth recalled her saying something about her new whole-food plant-based diet and how much better it was for her body, her mind, and for the environment. Mostly what Beth heard was blah blah blah. She managed to stay healthy and keep her weight down just fine eating the way she did. She didn't need her 16-year-old daughter telling her any differently. Plus, Beth understood that was Grace's diet this week. Next week it would be something else. Teenage girls, she thought to herself as she plopped the final tray of cookies on top of the stove to cool.

Beth meticulously wrapped another dozen cookies in the small, clear bags she purchased on Amazon, two cookies per package. All that was left was the tray that she had just pulled out of the oven. Seventy-two cookies, or thirty-six packages, each selling for one dollar. Heck, she thought, it would have been so much easier if I had just sent the school a check for thirty-six dollars. I could have saved myself a lot of work.

Beth sighed and picked the spatula up from the granite counter. She scooped each of the last twelve cookies off the pan and placed them on the cooling rack. No sign of the kids yet and it was still too early for Jerry to be home. Then she caught site of the mail she had brought in and tossed on the corner of the kitchen island. Brushing a stray blond hair away from her forehead, she reached for the mail. Junk, junk, car insurance, but the fourth piece caught her eye. GeneScreen. "Oh," she said aloud. She realized the results of the DNA test she and her sisters took just after Christmas had arrived.

She picked up the envelope and only hesitated a moment before tearing it open. She was curious about her heritage. It seemed that no one was quite sure exactly which part of Europe their ancestors hailed from. She skimmed the letter, too excited to read it all in detail.

As she glanced at its contents she noticed words like Ireland, Scotland, England, Poland and Germany.

No real surprises there. Then she jumped down to the next paragraph. Here is where they linked her to other family members. At the very top of the list was Jody. Again, no surprise. Jody was her sister. But wait, according to GeneScreen, she and Jody were only twenty-two percent connected. That seemed odd. Shouldn't sisters have a higher DNA connection than twenty-two percent? Beth wiped her eyes and read that section slower, more carefully. She hadn't made a mistake. What she read was correct. Not only that, but GeneScreen did not list Jody as a sister. It listed her as a half-sister. "Oh my God," Beth said. "How can that be?"

She reread the entire letter from top to bottom. She had understood it correctly the first time. The only new information she gathered was a few additional family names; three she knew, two she didn't. The two names she wasn't familiar with were both from relatives who were born in the 1800s. Those names didn't interest her. The only one that did was Jody, her half-sister. That meant that they didn't have the same father. Paul was father to only one of them. But which one, she wondered.

She continued to stare at the letter trying to decide what to do next. Had Jody seen these results? What about Samantha? And Delaney? Did they know, too? Delaney probably wouldn't because she would already show up as a half-sister, but surely Samantha would see it.

She scanned the letter a third time but didn't see a connection to Samantha or Delaney listed on her family tree. She wasn't surprised. They probably sent their DNA samples in later than she and Jody had. Neither one of them seemed very excited to find out about their heritage. Especially Samantha. Of course, Samantha was never excited to participate in family events. Her life with Derek had to be miserable and it clearly affected Samantha's mood. She was always so unhappy, so difficult. Beth felt sad for Samantha and her daughters. Chelsie was relieved when she left for college, and as for Raegan, Beth felt sorry for her. That girl still had another year at home with a non-existent father and a clingy, depressed mother. That was no way for a 17-year-old to spend her senior year of high school.

Before Beth could decide what to do, she heard the front door open and the sound of two noisy teenagers bursting into the living room. She quickly folded the letter and stuffed it into the front pocket of the flowered apron she wore over her favorite Mickey Mouse sweatshirt. Listening to her children's easy banter as they pulled off their coats and wet boots, she quickly grabbed the small brown bottle out of her purse and downed one of the pills without bothering with water. Then she grabbed a spatula and dispensed two cookies into each of the six remaining cellophane bags before Gage could get his hands on them. Still shaking, she managed to plaster a fake smile on her face. "Hi, kids. How was school?"

"Why do parents always ask that?" Gage said with a playful glint in his eyes. "It's like we have nothing else to talk about, nothing else in our lives, except school. We are more than just juniors in high school, you know."

"Excuse me, Darling Son. I apologize. Let me rephrase my question." Beth laughed and decided to play along. "What exciting venture crossed your path today in the thrilling, joyous, adventure that is your life?"

Gage grinned at his mother. "You know, Mom, just the usual. School." He grabbed a banana from the iron fruit bowl on the island and started to head upstairs to his room. "You didn't forget that I'm going to the hockey game tonight with Matt and Travis, right? They're picking me up around five. We're going to grab pizza before the game."

"I didn't forget." Beth smiled at her son and threw him one of the packages of cookies. The school would get by with thirty-five dollars instead of thirty-six.

"You spoil him, Mom," Grace said, rolling her eyes as she opened the refrigerator and rummaged around the leftovers looking for a snack.

"You can have a package of cookies, too, Grace."

"Ugh, no way! All that refined sugar. And you know I can't eat anything with eggs in it. You know that, Mother. Plus, I absolutely have to lose an entire pound before prom. What if Jaxon asks me and I can't fit into my dress? Then what? I mean, I would just die if I had a date with the hottest guy in school and I couldn't go because I didn't have a dress to wear."

"I didn't realize a cookie would make that much of a difference, but what do I know?" Beth said sarcastically to her daughter. "Clearly I have forgotten how difficult it is to be sixteen."

Grace grabbed an apple out of the refrigerator and sat at the island. "I'll drop the cookies off at the bake sale on my way to drama club tonight. I'll have to leave around five to get there on time. Can I use your car?"

"Yes, since Gage said Matt is picking him up and I'm not going anywhere, that's fine. It's just Dad and me at home tonight. Probably nothing more exciting than popcorn, television, and maybe hot chocolate in front of the fireplace."

"Mom, ew."

"Ew? Ew what? What are you talking about?"

"You and Dad in front of the fireplace. Gross. I know what that means. Get a room, why don't you." Grace finished her apple in silence and wondered how she would have delivered the damn cookies for her mother if Gage had needed the car. He always had dibs on her mother's car. She wished her family could afford to buy a third vehicle for her and Gage to share. It would make things so much easier. But who was she kidding, even if they could, it would belong to Gage, not her. It was always Gage first. She loved her mother, but just once, she wished her mother would love her best. She scooted her stool back and slid out of it. She tossed her apple core in the trash and, like her brother, disappeared upstairs, leaving Beth alone in the kitchen.

Beth had just started to pull out the things she would need to prepare dinner when the telephone rang. It was Jerry. He wasn't going to be home until late. He would just grab something out of a vending machine. He wasn't all that hungry anyway. He loved her and he would see her tonight.

Beth sighed and put the already defrosted chicken back in the refrigerator. No use cooking for just me, she thought. Gage was going out for pizza and Grace wouldn't eat an entire dinner, let alone something that wasn't plant-based. Plus, she had just filled up on an apple. No need to worry about her daughter being hungry.

She may have stopped worrying about Grace, but that didn't stop her concerns about Jerry. He was staying at the garage late again and eating food from a vending machine. That wasn't healthy. It would be better if he was home where she could make him a hot meal. So what if she had cleaned the entire house and baked cookies all day. She still would have preferred to serve her family a wholesome dinner. That was her responsibility. She didn't like it when they weren't around for her to do this.

Jerry being at work reminded her of when they were first married and he always used to stay late at the garage. Of course, it was different then. He was just starting his own business and he had to work almost every night to establish himself. He explained to her that he couldn't afford to turn away customers; he certainly couldn't risk having unhappy clientele. There was no money to hire a second mechanic, so he stayed late, sometimes seven nights a week. By the time he came home, he was tired and dirty and wanted nothing more than a shower and a comfortable bed.

Beth had been so upset back then. All she wanted to do was make him a nice meal and spend a quiet evening with him, but he was always tired. This made her feel like a failure. All she had was being Jerry's wife. She never had any desire to have a career of her own. She didn't want to go back to school, she was content with a high school diploma. She had no interest in working outside of the house. It was fine if other women chose that path in life, but it wasn't for her. She didn't care about world events, politics bored her, she didn't have a desire to travel. Beth's greatest joy was taking care of her husband. It's what she wanted, what she was good at. With Jerry at the garage so much, it left her feeling like a failure. What if marriage wasn't all that she had anticipated?

Those months were tough for Beth. She was lonely and she felt like her world was turning gray. She would find herself crying for no reason. Some days she wouldn't want to get out of bed. The only thing she was good at was being a homemaker, and with Jerry gone so much, her role was starting to seem irrelevant. Not knowing what else to do, she talked to her family physician. It turned out her condition was not unusual, and it was entirely treatable. Her doctor prescribed an antidepressant to take on a daily basis, plus a strong benzodiazepine when she felt like she was having a sudden bout of extreme worry. These pills worked like magic for Beth. So much of her anxiety was gone and she could relax. It no longer felt like her world was ending.

Finally, she understood that Jerry needed to work to get his new business off the ground. She was actually relieved that he was working so hard, not like Samantha's husband, who should have been working, but instead had all kinds of shenanigans going on.

Eventually, the shop took off, business stabilized, and Jerry was able to hire additional help. He didn't have to work such long hours. He was home every night for supper. She took care of the house; he took care of the expenses. They took care of each other. Once the twins were born, her life was perfect. She had everything she ever wanted. She smiled as she thought about the fairytale life she was living, but she continued to fill the prescriptions that her doctor provided to her.

Leaving her memories behind her, Beth remembered the letter in her apron pocket. She pulled it out and flattened it against the kitchen island. Carefully reviewing it, she came to the same conclusion. She and Jody were half-sisters. Since it was unlikely they had different mothers, they must have different fathers. But which one had a different dad? And did Daddy know? Was he aware that only one of them was his daughter? How could they find out?

Beth must have sat there staring at the paper longer than she thought, because soon she heard both kids coming down the stairs. For the second time that day, she stuffed the letter back in her pocket, the same letter that was about to change everything she knew about her life. Who would have thought on that

Christmas Day when Beth and her sisters, Jody, Samantha and Delaney, had all agreed to take the DNA test, that it would come to this? This wasn't exactly the family discovery any of them had expected.

Gage and Grace walked into the kitchen. "What's up, you two?"

"I'm leaving now, Mom. Remember? Pizza and a game?"

"I remember, Gage. Have a good time, but be careful. Make sure Matt drives safely."

"Yes, Mother," he called as he was putting on his jacket.

"Wait, young man. You come here and give me a hug. There's no reason you can't hug your old mom before you run out of the house."

Gage sighed and trudged across the kitchen floor to where Beth was standing. He wrapped one arm around her and kissed her on the top of her head. Then he hurried back to the living room. Seconds later Beth heard the front door bang shut, followed almost immediately by the sound of a pickup truck driving away. I hope he had time to buckle his seatbelt, she thought.

"I'm going too, Mom. Are the cookies ready?"

Beth turned her attention to Grace. "Yes, they're all set. Now remember, they should sell for one dollar a package. And here's the list of ingredients if anyone asks. No nuts, but there is gluten in them."

"Thanks, Mom. I've got to run. Wish me luck. I'm trying out for the part of the queen in the school play."

"Good luck. I'm sure you'll be wonderful! Wait, I take that back. Not the wonderful part. You will be wonderful. The good luck part. I think I'm supposed to say, break a leg."

Grace laughed, hesitating to see if her mother was going to say anything else, maybe hug her goodbye and tell her to drive safely. When she didn't, Grace lowered her eyes and said, "Got it, Mom. See you tonight."

The door closed and Beth was alone. She walked into the living room, turned on the light, and sank into the large, sectional sofa. Almost immediately she felt Topper, their ridiculously large German shepherd, start nuzzling her hand. How can a dog so large be such a big baby, she thought as she gave him a few quick pats before gently pushing him away.

She again pulled the letter out of her pocket, but this time she didn't need to study it. She knew what it said. There was no denying it. Either she or Jody was not the daughter of Paul Peralta. She also knew it would be pretty easy to find out which one of them it was. All she had to do was call Samantha. Samantha was taking the GeneScreen DNA test, too. Whichever one of them matched Samantha would be Paul's daughter. Simple. Simple, but not something she was looking forward to. Samantha was not the easiest person to talk to and this wasn't the easiest subject to talk about. Maybe she would have a hot bath first. She could even enjoy a glass of wine since she was going to be home alone for the next several hours. A little me time, she thought. It couldn't hurt to relax and have a little buzz going before calling Samantha.

Maybe she would even call Delaney to see what she thought before she made that call. She was always closest to Delaney and trusted her opinion. Delaney might know a better way to deal with this situation. At the very least, she will talk me into calling Samantha, Beth thought. Then Beth smiled, feeling better about her decision to wait before doing anything. She locked the front door and headed upstairs to her room.

4 DELANEY

Delaney was rushing to get home. She knew Jack would have everything under control, but it would be the third night this week he had to make dinner for the kids and that didn't seem fair. Of course, the kids wouldn't complain, dinner was better when he cooked. The best she would have done was canned tomato soup and grilled cheese sandwiches. Still, she wanted to get home. Today wasn't supposed to be this busy, but she ended up showing three houses instead of two, and she had to pick out the tile for the Forest Heights colonial. Plus, she had to figure out the design for Jack's new project house in Lewiston. Luckily, tomorrow her calendar was light.

Delaney loved working with Jack and never regretted giving up her nursing position shortly after they were married. Jack's construction business was going strong and he appreciated her knack for decorating, so when he suggested she join him full-time, she jumped at the chance.

It started when he flipped a few houses in

addition to the regular job he was working. The flips were so successful that soon a few houses turned into many. Now they had a major construction business designing and building houses all the way from Bangor to South Portland. Sometimes they would have as many as ten or twelve projects going at the same time. Of course, there were other times when they would only have three or four to deal with. These times were the entire reason why Delaney picked up her real estate agent license. They usually had a healthy income and enough work to secure their future, but they could never be too careful, especially when they had two children to put through college. It didn't help when she and Jack also had a taste for the finer things in life.

As Delaney drove home, she thought about both of her children. It was hard to believe that Wyatt was 14-years-old. Tall with dark hair like Jack, he was already a legend on the basketball team of his middle school. The coaches at Cayne High School were hounding him about joining the team next year.

Then there was Roxie Rain. Roxie was three years younger than her brother. She was petite with long, wavy brown hair and huge green eyes. Roxie was a people pleaser, always willing to give into her brother to avoid arguing with him. Not that there were many occasions when they argued. They actually got along quite well with each other. Roxie had tried all kinds of different after-school activities: gymnastics, softball, dance, basketball and Girl Scouts. So far, she had not found her passion. Hopefully, she would find something soon that she wanted to stick with for more than one season.

Thinking of her children made Delaney smile. They were both incredible. And then there was Jack, her husband of almost sixteen years. She hit the jackpot with him. Pun intended, she giggled to herself. He was the classic tall, dark and handsome type. Top that off with him being a hard worker and a good provider, as well as an awesome dad, and she had no complaints. She was a lucky woman.

Well, she was mostly lucky. There was the incident with the Clover Lane house in Winthrop. She had picked out the kitchen cabinets and counters for the deluxe house in Augusta that Dr. Spangler was building at the same time she made the far less expensive choices for the Winthrop house. She wasn't sure if the mistake was hers or if Annie, the sales person at Apex Kitchens, made the mistake, but somehow the Winthrop house ended up with an eighty-five thousand dollar kitchen— more than double what it should have been. While she and Jack were doing fine financially, at least on the surface, this was not the kind of mistake they could afford. To make matters worse, this was the second time something like this had happened in less than a month. She knew when Jack found out he would not be happy. He wouldn't say much, he would just get that look of disappointment on his face and retreat to his office, sighing and shaking his head. That was worse than if he would yell at her. At least then it would be out in the open. But he wouldn't even give her a chance to explain.

He would just assume the errors were hers.

She swallowed hard as she drove, her cheerful mood being replaced by a sick feeling in her stomach. How could she make him listen to her?

She had just turned right on Mill Lane when her cell phone rang. She glanced at the screen in the center of her Lexus. It was Beth. She pushed the button on her steering wheel. "Hey, what's up?" she said, the speaker, mystically placed in the vehicle, picking up her voice.

"Hi." Beth's voice sounded distant, not because of the car speaker system, which was stellar, but because of Beth. Something was wrong.

"What is it? Are you okay?"

"Yes. I'm fine. It's just that I got the results of my DNA test today. Have you heard? Have you talked to anyone else yet? Jody, or Samantha?"

"Seriously? You think Samantha would be calling me? Get real. So, what did the test show? I take it you're not royalty?"

"No jokes. This is serious."

"Okay. Seriously. What's wrong?"

Beth sighed. The tension she was feeling carried across the phone. "It appears that you aren't the only half-sibling in the family. Jody and I are half-sisters, too."

"What? How can that be?"

"According to GeneScreen, Jody and I are only twenty-two percent connected. We are half-sisters. I would guess we have different fathers."

"I'll be damned," Delaney muttered without thinking. "Do you know which one of you is Paul's daughter?"

"No, I have no idea. I was wondering if you knew anything. After all, Mom always talked to you more than the rest of us."

Delaney stayed silent for a moment, thinking back to her conversations with their mother. Never once did she mention that her sisters had a father other than Paul. There was one time that she said something about taking a secret or two to the grave. Delaney had suspected there could be a half-sister situation, but her mother had never admitted to it. Finally, realizing she had been silent too long, she turned her attention back to Beth. "No, sorry, Mom never said a word to me about it."

"I figured as much, but I thought I would ask. I guess the only way to know for sure is to ask Samantha. God, I hate calling her. No matter what I say, she finds a way to twist it into something negative."

Despite her foul mood, Delaney had to chuckle. That was so often the thought process when one had to call Samantha. She could be such a bitch. Then Delaney responded to Beth. "You don't have to call her. You could just see who else shows up on your GeneScreen profile. If some of Paul's relatives show up on your family tree and not Jody's, that would indicate that Paul is your real father. Or vice-versa if they show up on Jody's. Have you talked to Jody about it? Does she know?"

"I haven't called her yet, but I will. I'm still trying to absorb all of this myself. I assume she received her results today, but I'm not sure."

"I am sorry you have to go through this. Who would have thought that I'm not the only half in this family? Is there anything I can do?"

"No, I just wanted to see if you knew anything. I need some time to think about it so I'm going to hang up now. I'll call you tomorrow, okay?"

"Yes, of course. Don't worry. It will all work out."

"Easy for you to say. You don't have to call Samantha."

"This is true, Dear Sister. This is true. And Beth, being a half-sister isn't so bad. I can vouch for that. And I am here if you need me."

"I know. Thank you."

"You're welcome. Goodnight." Delaney hung up the phone. Fuck, she said to herself. Fuck. Fuck. Fuck. She couldn't believe this was happening. And now, of all times. Why couldn't this happen in a few more weeks? Or even better, a few more months.

Her hands started to tremble against the steering wheel, enough that she decided she needed to pull over. There was a Target just ahead so she put her blinker on and eased into the right lane. She pulled into the parking lot as far away from the front of the store as she could. She needed to think.

She put the car in park and hung her head in her hands. Suddenly the chill in the air intensified. She reached over and turned the heat up a couple of notches. She had suggested to Beth a way to tell if Paul was Jody's father, or Beth's, but she didn't need a way. She already knew. All those years of studying to be a nurse had taught her many things, and those things included basic genetics. Mom had green eyes. Paul's eyes were gray. Jody had dark brown eyes. Jody also had dark brown hair and olive-colored skin. There were many periods in Jody's life when she died her hair blond, but she could never change her skin tone. She never looked quite like any of her sisters. It was a pretty safe bet that Paul was not Jody's father. That's what made the most sense. Delaney had always suspected Jody might be a half-sister based on her appearance; this wasn't a surprise. Usually, she just pushed that thought from her mind, never truly believing it would become reality.

Delaney felt bad for Jody. It must be hard to get this kind of news, especially this late in life. Sadly, her empathy for Jody wasn't what was worrying her right now. It was the timing of Jody finding this out. Once Jody realized that Paul wasn't her father, she would also realize that she wasn't eligible for the big inheritance she was in line to receive when Paul died. Right now, his money was going to be split three ways; it would go to Samantha, Beth, and Jody in equal shares. Once he found out that Jody wasn't his, that money would most likely be split only two ways. Jody would be out cold. That meant that the arrangement the four sisters had agreed on with regard to the recent inheritance following their mother's death would probably be out the window.

When their mother died just before Christmas, the three oldest sisters had agreed to let Delaney inherit

44

her estate. It wasn't a huge sum, but it was decent enough since it would be going to one sister and not four. They did this because it would be the only inheritance Delaney would ever receive. On the other hand, the three of them would be sharing a rather large estate when Paul died. It was very generous of them and Delaney was thankful. It also made sense since the sum she would receive did not compare to the large amount they would each get, even though their inheritance would be split three ways.

But now, since the paperwork wasn't complete, that could all change. Jody would want half of their mother's inheritance since she would no longer be eligible for Paul's. If this GeneScreen thing had come up a few weeks later it would have been too late, the paperwork would have been complete, but Delaney didn't think there was any way she could push it through in time now. Now, when she needed the money the most. Those errors at work were going to cause some real financial problems. It would have been nice to have her inheritance so she could pay them off before Jack found out about them. Now, not only would she have to share the inheritance with Jody, but re-doing all of the paperwork would slow the entire process down. There was no way to take care of this mess before Jack found out. At least if it was Beth who was not Paul's daughter, she may have had time to push everything through before Beth even tried to claim half the inheritance. She didn't think about money the way that Jody did. But with Jody, not a chance in hell. That will be the first thing on her mind.

Delaney turned the heat up another notch and glanced at the clock. It was too late to worry about dinner with the family now, that was a lost cause. Instead, she put the car in drive and headed in the opposite direction of her house. Dinner no longer mattered. She had something much more important to take care of before she could even think about heading home.

5 JODY

Grey and Hunter had been home for supper, eaten, and were back out. How ironic I made spaghetti, Jody thought, seeing as just today I found out I'm Italian. She tried to smile at her joke, but it was too soon. Discovering that Paul may not be her biological father was painful, and her emotions were too raw to find any amusement in the situation.

Jody had hoped to spend time with Grey tonight. She needed someone to talk to, but it wasn't in the cards. Hunter wanted to go to the school's hockey game and he had begged Grey to take him. At 16-years-old, Hunter didn't have a lot of friends, and since Grey loved hockey, he was happy to oblige. If truth be told, Jody liked how close the two of them were. They were so much alike. They even looked alike—same eyes, same hair color, same build. Since his recent growth spurt, Hunter was even the same height as Grey. As Jody had stood there, seeing the pleading look in both of their eyes, what else could she have done? Talking with Grey would wait.

Instead, she had laughed and told them to go and have a good time. After all, she had waited all afternoon to talk to Grey. What difference would it make if she had to wait a few more hours?

Jody decided to take an early shower and change into warm, fleece pajamas. Then she headed into Grey's office to pay a few bills. Money wasn't exactly tight, but she did like to keep close tabs on their spending. Since Covid, she had only been working part-time at her bookkeeping job, and Grey's salary as a history teacher could only go so far.

She went into the office located at the very front of the house and switched on the small desk lamp. Grey had totally made the room his own, which was why Jody seldom spent time in here. Usually, she just retrieved the laptop and worked in the living room in her recliner, but tonight she opened it on the desk between the two monitors. She wasn't sure what inspired her to stay in this room, maybe she felt closer to Grey in here, surrounded by his favorite belongings. She looked around and had to smile at what she considered to be rather childish décor. The bookshelf in the corner contained several statues of dragons in varying colors— purple, green, dark blue and gold. They were either flying, breathing fire or protecting treasure. The books on the shelves were mostly fantasy, although a few looked like they might fall into the mystery or crime categories.

Hanging on the wall behind her was Grey's pride and joy, a large collection of knives and swords, all fitted into a display case that he built himself. There were medieval knight swords and crusader swords and one called a serpent breath sword that she remembered because she had been angry that he paid several hundred dollars for it. Above the swords was a collection of medieval weapons. If she remembered what he taught her, there was a mace, a war hammer, two battle axes, and a variety of daggers. Off to the side was a crossbow and maybe a longbow. She couldn't quite remember that one. Every now and again she would find him in here playing with these deadly weapons as if they were toys. At those times, he would smile sheepishly and put them back on the rack.

She sat in the black, faux-leather chair at his desk and pulled the laptop out of the top drawer. She was careful not to disturb either of the two flatscreens that were currently displaying rather vivid games, both being run by a multitude of blinking lights on towers that constituted Grey's computers. Geesh, she thought, my husband really is a geek. What kind of grown man is this immersed in fantasy computer games?

The first screen was a dark, bluish-black scene. She could see tiny peasant workers entering a cave with wooden wheelbarrows, while other workers were exiting the same cave with wheelbarrows filled with chunks of gold. At the top of the screen, the gold count was steadily increasing. Apparently, Grey had this game set to collect riches while he was away. If only it was that easy in real life, Jody thought.

The second screen, ablaze with reds and oranges,

was more active than the first. This screen had armored knights battling against creatures that were not human. Jody watched and it seemed that no matter how many creatures the human knights killed, more kept attacking them. Again, at the top of the screen, a tally was being kept to show how much stronger the human knights were becoming. Grey had this game set so they would win the battle and get stronger while he was away. That didn't seem quite fair since he wasn't even here. Jody didn't like this game.

It was 7:00; she still had time to update the checkbook and make some tea before her television show started at 8:00. She turned her back on the weapon rack and focused on the computer.

Jody had barely started paying bills when she heard the doorbell ring. She wondered who it could be. They seldom had visitors in the evening. She wrapped her robe tightly around her and walked to the front door, her furry slippers scuffing the floor as she made her way down the short hallway. She flicked on the outside lights and peeked through the sidelight to see who was standing on the porch. When she saw who it was, a look of surprise momentarily crossed her face. She unlocked the front door and pulled it open. "Hi," she said. "C'mon in. What a pleasant surprise."

6 THE VISITOR

Jody quickly pushed the door closed in back of me. Even though her robe was thick fleece, she looked cold from the winter air that blew in. "I'm sorry I'm in my pajamas so early," she said. "Gosh, what time is it?" She asked this as she glanced at the clock on the foyer wall. "Just after 7:00." She answered her own question. Then she continued. "It's early. I'm usually more of a night owl. It's just that with Grey and Hunter gone, I figured it didn't matter if I got ready for bed a bit early. But please, I'm rambling. Come in."

I entered the large, modern ranch house, shivering from the cold. "Here, let me take your coat. You can put your hat and gloves on the heater vent so they'll be warm when you leave." Jody smiled as she pointed to the vent on the floor. "I was just working on some bills in the office. Why don't you come in there with me while I write the last couple of checks, and then we can go in the kitchen and I'll make us a snack. How does that sound?"

"Fine," I replied as I removed my black watch cap and placed it gently on the heater vent. I hadn't responded to any of her other comments. I wasn't in the mood for small talk.

"Good. As long as you're okay waiting a few minutes to talk about whatever you came over for. I don't imagine you ventured out in the cold without a reason. Are you sure you don't mind waiting while I finish up what I'm doing?"

"I don't mind." I said the words, but I had to fight the urge to wring my hands together, even though they were still tucked inside my gloves.

Jody led us back to the office. She never noticed that she did all the talking. She was far too focused on finishing the task at hand. If she hadn't been, she would have seen the anger flaring from my eyes, or been aware of my considerable fidgeting.

"Why don't you sit over there," Jody suggested. She indicated a chair in the corner of the office behind the desk, opposite the bookshelf, and next to the medieval weapons rack. "I'll only be a minute. I hate to be rude, but if I don't get this done, I'll totally forget my place. Lord knows I can't skip paying the electric bill."

I couldn't believe how she had nonchalantly put me in the corner and then turned her back on me. How could she have not sensed my need to talk to her? At the very least, she should have felt my agitation, if not my anger. Instead, she sat there and reloaded her checkbook on her laptop. She said something about having only a couple more bills to pay and she would be through. Then she could fully focus on me. Bullshit. It was obvious that she wasn't happy to see me.

"Just one more check to enter," Jody advised, as the music from the nonstop swordfight and gold harvesting played from the computers. As I watched her, I didn't believe she was that concerned with her finances. She could have easily taken care of them after I left. I think she sensed my anxiety and she needed time to figure out what caused it. She was trying to decipher why I was there. She knew this visit wasn't going to be pleasant and she was using the extra time to steady her nerves.

I felt my anger build inside of me until I couldn't stay quiet any longer. "I can't believe you are turning your back on me." I watched as Jody froze, her fingers hovered over the keyboard. She didn't turn, she just sat there and waited.

"You know why I'm here, don't you? You know the truth." Jody still hadn't moved. I understood that she didn't know what to do. "Are you just going to sit there and ignore me? What the fuck is wrong with you?"

I'm sure Jody sensed that I had stood up and started pacing behind her, but she remained frozen in place as our conversation continued. Finally, she turned the chair toward me. Her voice was meek and barely audible. She whimpered, "Why are you so angry? What do you want?"

I stopped pacing and looked at her, flabbergasted. She was acting like she didn't have a fucking clue what I was talking about. Angrier than I had been since I arrived, I reached down and grabbed the arms of the office chair. She looked so small sitting there, but I didn't let her size fool me. I brought my face close to hers and watched as her brown eyes filled with tears. She looked confused. I remembered that she didn't like confrontation, so perhaps the tears were real. But by then I was far too enraged to let her timid, helpless 'little girl' look stop me. I got my face only inches from hers. She cringed when she felt my hatred.

I watched her when the confusion left her face the same way the color drained from her cheeks. She was scared when she sensed the anger, the hatred, in my voice. "You knew and you never said a word. You never told me. I had a right to know and you never told me. I expected as much from him, that fucking loser. But you? I expected more. What kind of horrible, self-centered bitch are you? You ruined everything. I fucking hate you."

Jody shivered and I imagine the skin on her forearms prickled. I almost felt the hair rise on the back of her neck at the same time a chill ran down her spine. Her mind was churning. She thought I loved her, but then she learned the truth. She knew how much I loathed the very site of her. Still, she muttered, "I don't understand. What are you talking about?"

More words were said between us. I had to yell to make sure she heard every word. Her face darkened. She looked confused, but that expression didn't last. Something clicked in her mind and suddenly she didn't look like a frightened little girl. She looked pissed. She started to say things that made no sense. Then she started to threaten me. She actually told me that she would tell everyone if I didn't leave her house and mind my own damn business. Just who the hell did she think she was?

I rose to my full height and glared at her. I think she knew she had gone too far because her eyes widened and she stopped talking. The room suddenly felt cold; I didn't know if it was my anger or a dark fear that swept through Jody's heart. I stared into her eyes until she clenched them shut. I noticed her hands, previously folded together on her lap, were now grasping the arms of the chair. I knew she felt the climate of the room shift. It was dark and dangerous.

She opened her eyes and stared at me. She must have noticed my face was contorted with pure hatred. My eyes were narrowed into slits. My nose was flaring and my mouth was set in a hard, stern frown. I saw the terror on her face. Her legs shook as she tried to back the chair away from me. I had let her go, but only a few inches. Just far enough so she could turn toward the desk. I wondered if she knew it was too late.

My right hand was raised. Jody never had a chance to scream before the authentic replica of the fourteenth-century dagger sliced clean through the blood vessels on the left side of her neck. Her head lulled forward. Copious amounts of blood pulsated out of her body and poured down her arm, running off her fingertips. The blood soaked into her heavy nightwear, turning it from pale blue to crimson to almost black. It drained downward in a steady stream. I actually saw the blood pool on her beautiful hardwood floor. It's funny what thoughts go through your mind when you kill someone. When I watched Jody's blood spread across the floor, I remembered her talking about how she had just paid over a thousand dollars to have the floors in the house refinished. All that money she spent--for nothing. But it was a fleeting thought. Mostly what went through my mind was the comment that she made, that she didn't know until I had just then told her.

7 GREY

Grey's headlights hit the front of the house as he swung into the driveway. While he waited for the garage door to open, he was surprised to see the outside lights were not turned on and the house was dark. It looked like only his office light was on. That was odd. Jody maintained her childhood fear of the dark and usually had every light in the house burning when she was home alone.

As soon as he pulled into the garage, Hunter jumped out and headed inside. "Thanks, Dad. That was fun."

"You're welcome, Son. Anytime."

Grey followed Hunter into the house. He loved spending time with that boy, more than Hunter could possibly imagine. After all, there was a time when he wasn't sure he would be lucky enough to become a father. There wasn't a day that went by that he wasn't grateful for his son. As he stood there in the dark hallway, he thought back to a time sixteen years earlier.

It had taken him and Jody a long time to conceive, long enough that he was thinking it might never happen. They had stopped using birth control, anticipating the start of a large family. When nothing happened, they chalked it up to bad timing, or bad luck. Eventually Jody talked with her doctor and was advised it often takes months, or even a year, for a couple to get pregnant. They shouldn't worry. A year went by. Then another. Grey suggested to Jody that they go for testing, or genetic counseling. She said she would make an appointment, but she never did. Then she quit telling him she would try. She wouldn't even talk about it.

Not knowing what else to do, Grey made an appointment with his doctor. He was desperate to become a father and he couldn't watch more time go by doing nothing. He didn't tell Jody; he just had himself checked. He was fine. His sperm count was slightly above average. He wanted to tell Jody this so she could talk to her doctor. They needed to discuss options. He tried to bring it up, but she didn't see it as him wanting to find a way for them to have a baby together. She saw it as him blaming her for their inability to conceive. As desperate as he was to become a father, he didn't mention it to her again. These were the loneliest months that Grey could remember. Luckily, they didn't last very long.

Six months later, he came home to a dinner table set with their best dishes. She served his favorite meal. Her eyes were shining, her cheeks were pink. She was having trouble concealing a grin on her face. When they were done eating, she didn't let him bring the plates to the kitchen. Instead, she reached under her chair and pulled out a small, gift-wrapped box. Again, that ridiculous grin was on her face.

"What's this?" Grey said as he smiled at his wife.

"Open it. You'll see."

Grey tore the paper off and separated the white tissue. He couldn't believe what he was seeing. One tiny yellow baby rattle was tucked inside. It was little, but the promise it held was big. He looked at Jody, hope filling his heart. "Are you...?" He couldn't get the words out.

"Yes, my love. I'm pregnant. We're going to have a baby."

Grey realized he was still standing in the back hall smiling to himself at that memory. Hunter had already gone to his bedroom. Grey hung his keys on the hook and walked into the kitchen. "Jody?" he called, flicking on the kitchen light, again surprised that the house was so dark.

He went through the kitchen to the living room, pausing only to turn on the lamp next to his chair. "Jody?" He called her name, but this time with the slightest hesitation. Something felt off. The house was too dark. Too quiet.

Grey noticed the light coming from his office at the front of the house, just like he noticed it when he was pulling in the garage. That wasn't like Jody. She didn't particularly like his choice of décor, nor did she understand his love of gaming. He slowly walked in that direction, looking around him as he moved forward. "Jody?" He called her name, but softly now.

Still no response. The only noise was the sound of his computer games coming through the half-open door to his office. Grey had an uneasy feeling. He could feel the hair prickle at the back of his neck. Little beads of sweat popped up on his brow and he absent-mindedly wiped them away with the back of his hand. He approached his office cautiously. He could see the light atop his desk was on. In addition to the background music of his games, he could now hear the hum from his computers. And what was that metallic smell he was sensing? His mind was running wild. Where was Jody? Had she fallen and hit her head? Could she have had a stroke? A heart attack? What was it his aunt's friend died of—some type of aneurism? "Jody?" His voice was barely a whisper.

He put his hand on the doorknob and pushed the door fully open, slowly stepping into the room. As he looked around the corner where his desk sat, he gasped and jumped back, his hand going over his mouth to stifle a scream. He only partially succeeded and a muffled groan escaped his lips. There was Jody, slumped over the side of his chair, arm and head dangling almost to the floor. Even with the short glance he had taken, he could see where blood had dripped down her arm. No, dripped was not the right word. Blood had gushed down her arm and pooled on the floor beneath her. Her long hair was dark and matted, so drenched with blood it was almost black. The neckline of her robe was glossy where the blood had saturated it before spreading out to a deep crimson along her chest and down her sleeve.

He couldn't see her face. Her head was hanging too low, her hair too thick. And the blood. God, there was so much blood. When he dared look closer, he could see her hands. Jody had tiny hands, almost child-sized.

Through the blood he could see them, one hanging to the side of her, the other still on her lap. He noticed the one on her lap, now blue, had polished red nails. Everything about her was unmoving. Lifeless. Grey gagged as he backed out of the room, trying to prevent himself from throwing up the French fries he had eaten earlier at the hockey game.

"Hunter." At first his son's name came out as a whisper. It was barely audible. Grey cleared his throat. Then he screamed. "Hunter!" He could hear his own voice. He sounded like a bobcat in heat. "Hunter!"

"Dad?" Grey could sense more than see his son running down the hall. Clearly Hunter had heard the fear, the urgency, the absolute terror in his father's voice. "Dad, what's wrong?"

Grey had backed out of the office. Seeing Hunter, his face white with fear, brought Grey back to his senses.

"It's Mom. We need to call the police."

"What is it? Dad, you're scaring me. What's wrong?" Hunter felt his stomach lurch as he took a few steps closer to the office, trying to peer around his father.

Grey threw his arms tightly around his son and said, "I'm sorry. I'm so sorry. She's gone. Mom is gone. She's been killed."

Grey could feel Hunter stiffen in his arms, but he held his son tightly, refusing to let him go. He could hear Hunter's sobs. "What happened? Let me go. I want to see her."

"It's too late. She's gone. We need to call the police."

This scene carried out for several minutes before Grey was able to calm Hunter down. While he didn't go into detail, he did tell Hunter enough so Hunter knew his mother was dead and there was no hope of saving her. Grey then dialed nine-one-one and within minutes there were blue flashing lights and red flashing lights and the entire house was crawling with people in uniform. Two police officers arrived and entered the office. One immediately pulled out his radio and called for homicide, an evidence tech, a medical examiner and a wagon. The other took Grey and Hunter into the living room and had them sit on the couch, not allowing them to move away from that spot. Then there were more officers. EMT personnel arrived and wrapped both men in blankets and took them to the waiting ambulance. Although they both said they weren't hurt, the paramedics insisted they go outside with them. A different police officer accompanied them.

From the ambulance Grey could see more police cruisers arrive. There were also unmarked police cars in the drive. Someone was wrapping yellow crime scene tape around the house. Another car arrived and a woman of about thirty stepped out carrying a suitcase. *Forensic Unit* was printed on the jacket across her back. Then another person came over to the ambulance. "Mr. Terrel? I'm Detective Ronan Holmes." Detective Holmes paused only for a moment, quickly realizing that Grey was far too shaken up to make the association about dealing with a detective with the last name of Holmes, so he continued. "I would like to offer my condolences about your wife. I'm sure this is a very difficult time for you and your son."

Grey just stared at the detective like he was a total moron. *I just found my wife covered in blood in my office chair and you're sure it's a difficult time. Aren't you the brilliant police detective,* he was thinking to himself.

"Again, Mr. Terrel, I'm very sorry for your loss. I am here to tell you that we are going to find out who did this. In that regard, I do have a few questions for you. Do you think you're able to come with me?"

Grey looked grimly at Detective Holmes, his face void of expression. "I don't want to leave my son."

"We're just going to go to my car, right over there."

"It's okay, Dad," Hunter said. "Go. Answer his questions. We need to find out who did this to Mom. Help him find out who did this."

Hunter's voice cracked as he practically begged his father to go with the detective. Grey could feel his son's pain and looked back at Detective Holmes. He nodded his head and mumbled "Yes."

Cold, but no longer shaking, Grey followed the detective to his car. He sat in the front seat staring out the window. Holmes sat next to him in the driver's seat. Holmes was a big man, late-forties, with brown hair that was graying at the temples. The look on his face wasn't unkind, but it did indicate he wasn't there for small talk;

he meant business. A fleeting thought passed through Grey's mind as he waited for the detective to speak—I'm glad I was at a hockey game with hundreds of other people tonight.

"How are you holding up, Mr. Terrel? I understand this is a bad time." Holmes' voice was deep, but not at all gruff like Grey expected.

"I don't know. I can't believe this is happening."

"I'm sorry to have to ask you these questions now, but I'm sure you know, the sooner we start asking questions, the sooner we can find who did this."

"I understand." Grey pulled the blanket tightly over his shoulders, no longer cold, but feeling exposed as he thought again of Jody, her dead body dangling over the side of his office chair. He didn't even realize that his eyes had again filled with tears.

"Tell me about your night, Mr. Terrel, from the last time you spoke with your wife until you returned home and called us. Don't leave out any details. You never know what might be important."

Grey told Detective Holmes everything he could think of, from giving Jody a quick kiss goodbye when he and Hunter left the house, to the hockey game, and then returning home to a dark house. He could hear his voice crack when he got to the part about finding Jody, but he did manage to get through the story without crying.

"I'm curious, who won the game?"

Grey snapped his head up and glared at Detective Holmes, anger flaring in his eyes. Seriously, his wife lie murdered in his house and this asshole is interested in sports?

Detective Holmes caught the look on Grey's face and decided it would be best to further explain his line of questioning. "I don't mean to sound insensitive, Mr. Terrel. I just need details to assure you were actually at the game."

Suddenly it clicked in Grey's mind. Holmes didn't care about the game. He was trying to rule him out as a suspect. "I didn't kill my wife, Detective Holmes. I loved her. We were happy. I could never do that. Never." Grey said these words while looking directly into Detective Holmes' eyes, never wavering, never even blinking.

"I understand. Now, who won the game?"

"Blue Devils won. Six-four. Tied at the end of the first. They were ahead four to three at the end of the second. Dionne finished his hat trick in the third and they won."

"Thank you. Did you see anyone that you knew there? Talk to any other parents? Kids? Make any purchases on a credit card?"

Grey only hesitated a moment before responding. "I paid cash for our tickets. I have them here in my pocket." As he said this, he let go of the blanket and dug into the left front pocket of his jeans, pulling out two wrinkled blue ticket stubs. He handed them to the detective. Then he continued. "Hunter talked to a couple of kids he knew but I'm not sure of their names. I said hi to a few parents. Josh Daniels or Davids or something like that. And Katy Adler's parents were there. I can't remember their names but Katy goes to school with Hunter. We talked for a few minutes between the first two periods."

"Anyone else?"

"Yes, we saw my nephew there with two of his buddies. Gage. Gage Lennox. Didn't really talk much. Gage and Hunter aren't exactly best friends, but he saw us. We nodded and said hi in passing."

Detective Holmes raised his eyebrow but when Grey didn't add to the story, he decided to forego that line of questioning. He likely had enough to prove that Grey didn't kill his wife. Of course, they would still look into his financials, talk to neighbors, and try to see what kind of relationship Grey and Jody had. Just because Grey had an alibi, it didn't mean he didn't pay someone else to break into his house and kill her while he was gone. But that was all Holmes needed for right now. After all his years with the force, he was damn good at reading people, and his instinct was telling him that Grey Terrel was not a killer. "Any problem with my asking Hunter a few questions now? You can sit in if you like."

"No problem. He's going to tell you the same thing I did. We have nothing to hide. Please, just find out who did this." Not for the first time, Holmes saw a tear slide down Grey's cheek.

8 BETH

Beth awakened to the shrill ring of her cell phone. It was almost 4:00 in the morning. Who could be calling at this hour, she wondered. Jerry was lying in bed next to her, only slightly disturbed by the sudden break in silence. Both kids were home, safely tucked into their own beds. She slid the green button and groggily said, "Hello."

"Beth, I'm sorry to wake you. It's Grey. Beth? I have some bad news. Really bad. You need to wake up Jerry."

Beth, hearing the despair in Grey's voice, was instantly awake. She sat up and clicked on the light next to the bed. She reached over and gave Jerry a few quick shoves. "Jerry, wake up."

Jerry turned on his side. "What is it?"

"Sit up. It's Grey. Something's happened." As Jerry sat up and wiped the sleep out of his eyes, Beth put her cell phone on speaker. "Go ahead, Grey. You've got us both, and you're scaring the bejesus out of me. Is it Jody? Hunter? What's wrong?"

"Beth. I am so sorry to tell you this. It's Jody. She's gone. She's gone, Beth." With those words, Grey could no longer contain the misery he had been fighting to keep inside. He barely held it together when he found his wife's body, and when the police questioned him, and when he and Hunter were escorted to a hotel for the night because their house was wrapped in yellow crime scene tape. But he had now reached his limit and the tears poured out of him like lava from a volcano. Hunter was in the shower and couldn't hear him and Grey could not control his pain any longer. "Beth, Jerry, she was murdered."

The words were garbled as another rush of tears poured out of Grey; this time accompanied by a long, sorrowful moan. Beth gasped. The room started to spin and turn black around her. She reached out and grabbed Jerry's arm to steady herself. As she did, the cell phone slid from her hand and dropped to the blue quilted comforter on the bed. Grey's sobs could be heard coming from the cell phone.

Jerry reached over and retrieved Beth's phone. In a loud, stern voice he said, "Grey. Grey, please, get ahold of yourself and tell us what happened. Grey!"

Hearing his name, Grey was able to bring his sobs under control and explain to Beth and Jerry the events of the evening. He wanted to tell them what happened before Hunter finished his shower. He needed Beth to relay the information to the rest of the family. He didn't want to go over the details again and again in front of Hunter. Hunter was being strong, but a 16-year-old boy can only take so much.

A few minutes later, with a promise to call both Samantha and Delaney, and to make sure Paul was notified, Jerry clicked off the cell phone. Grey said he would talk to them in the morning once he talked to the police again. He knew there were arrangements to be made, but he couldn't think about that now. Right now, he couldn't deal with anything more than getting through the night. It would take all he had to take care of Hunter and survive the darkness until morning.

Beth sat in bed, not moving, barely breathing. Jody was dead. Murdered. How could that be? Who would kill Jody? She wanted to yell, to scream. She felt a sense of rage building up inside of her, but she couldn't move. She could only sit there, staring at the phone in Jerry's hand. Jody. Thoughts of her sister kept playing in her mind. Never once did she think half-sister.

Jerry reached over and put his arm around his wife. He pulled her close and held her, knowing that there were no words that could make her feel better. That would come in time, but not tonight. Not tomorrow. Not for a very long time.

They sat there for what seemed like an eternity, but may have been only a matter of minutes. Time is irrelevant in the midst of a crisis. Their silence was interrupted by a gentle knock at their bedroom door.

"Mom, Dad, what happened? I heard your phone go off, and voices. Something's wrong. I can tell."

Beth blinked, Gage's voice bringing her back from her despair and into reality. "Come here, Baby.

Come sit on the bed. We have some sad news to tell you."

Gage crossed the room slowly, not knowing what to expect, but knowing it was going to be bad. He only took a step or two before he sensed Grace enter the room behind him. As he walked across the floor to sit next to their mother, Grace's footsteps carried her to their dad's open arms. Once both of them settled on the bed, with a soft voice, Beth told them about the phone call she had just had with their Uncle Grey. She didn't go into great detail, only that Aunt Jody was dead. It was apparent to the police that she had been killed while Uncle Grey and Hunter were at the hockey game. She would get more information later once the family learned more.

Gage was stunned. He sat motionless and listened to his twin sister as she quietly sobbed on their dad's shoulder. Gage didn't cry. He didn't move. He just stared at the blue quilt on his parents' bed, focusing on the intricate floral design in front of him, as if nothing else in the world mattered. He could feel his mother's eyes staring at him, drilling into him, begging to know if he was okay. Finally, without turning his head toward her, he spoke. "Uncle Grey was at the game tonight with Hunter. I saw them. It must have happened while they were there. They were laughing and having fun. They didn't even know what was happening."

A chill ran down Beth's spine as she listened to her son's words, not so much what he said, but the monotone way in which he said it. No emotion, just fact.

He was processing the horror of what happened and he was hurting. He showed none of this, but she knew. She felt it.

Beth reached her arm slightly forward and gently stroked Gage's hand. He didn't react. She thought about her son's words. He was feeling sad for Grey and Hunter. She wasn't surprised. Gage was such a gentle soul. She fully understood why he felt the way he did. Grey was always kind to Gage. He was a good uncle. But Hunter, that was another story.

Even though Hunter and Gage were cousins, they were not close. This was obvious at most every family function. Hunter and Gage were both juniors at Cayne High School. While Hunter was usually in advanced, college-level classes and Gage was more focused on a career path, the school was small and sometimes their classes overlapped. On these occasions, Hunter always had better grades than Gage. Beth wasn't bothered by this, after all, Hunter wasn't nearly as popular as Gage, so he had plenty of time to study. Heck, even Grace was more popular than Hunter, which explained why her grades were better than Gage's, too. Beth was sure if Gage sat home every night and studied like Hunter did then he, too, would be a straight A student. But that wasn't Gage. Gage was tall and handsome and popular. He had lots of friends and a very active social life. He didn't need to focus on only schoolwork every single night. He wanted to make the most out of his high school years. If Hunter chose to be a nerd, well, perhaps chose wasn't the right word, Beth simpered to herself, but if Hunter was a know-it-all nerd, that was fine. He didn't have to be such a braggart. With his short stature and rather plain looks, he was probably forced into that role. But whatever, if he wanted to study every night, so be it. Gage was going to live his life. At least Jody wouldn't be around anymore to go on and on about how smart Hunter was and how accomplished Hunter was. It was like she had to take over every family gathering with speeches outlining every achievement and reciting every award that Hunter ever received. Of course, Beth knew she did this because she was so jealous of Gage's good looks and popularity, but still, it got old. She sure wouldn't miss that at the next family holiday.

"Mom, are you okay? Are you, are you smiling?"

Beth jerked her head up and turned toward her daughter, not actually seeing her for a second or two as she was lost in her memories. Then she pulled herself from her thoughts and smiled at Grace. "I was just thinking about Jody, about some of the happy times we've shared. I guess that made me smile. This is all so surreal. I can't believe she's gone. Grace, are you doing alright?"

Grace lifted her tear-stained face off her father's shoulder and pushed her hair away from her eyes. She felt a small tug of relief when her mother finally asked how she was; up until then her only concern had been for Gage. As usual. "I'll be fine, Mom. This isn't going to be easy, though, is it?"

"No, Sweetie. It's not."

Gage, not turning his head, his voice remaining soft and low, asked, "Do they have any idea who did it? Do they have any suspects?"

Jerry replied, "No, not yet. But they've barely had time to start investigating. There was a detective at the house who talked with Uncle Grey and Hunter. They started to collect evidence. We don't know any more than that right now. I'm sure we'll learn more later, but for now, that's all we have."

"Do you two want to go back to bed and get some sleep? Do you think you'll be able to, or should we all go to the kitchen and have an early breakfast? I can make blueberry muffins and cocoa. You know, comfort food. We can do whatever you want. Gage, Honey, what do you prefer? Grace?"

Jerry hugged his daughter tightly while waiting for his children to decide what to do next. Gage continued to sit motionless on the bed.

9 SAMANTHA

Samantha hung up the telephone. She had planned to drive to Daddy's to tell him about Jody, but when she got up, Derek and Raegan were still sleeping and she didn't want to wake them. She also wanted to be home to tell them about Jody. Samantha hated that she called Daddy instead of seeing him in person with the horrible news, but she needed to make sure he knew before he figured it out from the morning report on television. He hadn't taken it well, but Adeline was with him so he wasn't alone. Samantha wasn't crazy about Adeline, Daddy's girlfriend, but at least she would take good care of him until Samantha could get out to see him later.

Samantha made her way down the stairs into the kitchen. The house was dark. She only turned a small light on over the cooktop. No need to wake anyone else up yet. As quietly as possible, she made her first cup of coffee. She didn't even bother to bring it to the table to drink it. She stood at the kitchen sink and pulled her worn robe tightly around her, clutching the warm mug in her hand. Barely giving it time to cool, she drank it while staring into the backyard. It was usually a pretty backyard. In the spring it would be full of brightly colored shrubs and flowers, all surrounded by an eight-foot-high stockade fence. Right now, however, all Samantha could see was dead grass and intermittent mounds of leftover snow and ice that refused to melt. Looking at it made her cold. She didn't sip her coffee, she gulped it. Then she pulled another pod out of the glass cannister and brewed a second cup. It may have even been a third. She wasn't sure. She wasn't sure about anything right now. Nothing about this day felt real, not since Beth had called to tell her about Jody.

She got the call around 5:00 that morning. She had been awakened from a sound sleep by the loud, annoying ringtone of her cell phone. At first, she had trouble making out what Beth was telling her because Beth's words were coming out in muddled sounds and disjointed syllables. It wasn't until she was fully awake and aware that she realized Beth was crying and her words sounded broken because of her sobbing. Finally, Samantha was able to piece it together. Jody was dead. Murdered. Grey had come home from a hockey game with Hunter and found her. There were no suspects.

As she pieced together what Beth was saying, Samantha went cold inside. She actually felt a frigid sliver of air travel to the depths of her soul. She guessed it was sadness, a sorrow even deeper than she had felt when her own mother had died in a tragic car accident just a few months ago. She had heard people say a chill ran through them when they received tragic news, but this was no chill. This was ice, subzero, a deepfreeze that was so intense, it felt like all life had ceased to exist.

Samantha tried to understand her feelings. She loved Jody, and now Jody was gone. Jody was more than gone, she was dead and Samantha was lost. She didn't have very many people she was close to in this world. She barely spoke to her husband. Her daughters loved her but she imagined they must be tired of her constant crying. Delaney didn't give her the time of day. Beth tried to be nice to her. Beth tried to be nice to everybody, but it was clear she was more interested in baking muffins for the PTA, or finding another ceramic Mickey Mouse for her ridiculously large collection, than she was with spending time with her sister. That left Jody. Jody didn't call often, but when she did, it was sincere. And now Jody was gone and the pain in Samantha's heart was unbearable. There were no words to explain the way she was feeling.

Samantha noticed the first streaks of light were starting to fill the sky and she knew Derek and Raegan would be getting up soon. She had to force this numbness that was inside of her to dissipate so she could move. It was time to wake Derek and tell him what happened.

He hadn't been sleeping in the bed next to her when she got the phone call from Beth. He should have been, but he wasn't. Instead, he had fallen asleep on the couch in the living room. He probably laid down to watch television when he got home from work and fell asleep. She didn't mind. This was just one more sign of the current state of their marriage. Anyway, when he came to bed, he often woke her up with his loud snoring.

She clicked on the kitchen light and made her way past the table and down the short hall to the living room. Derek must have woken up at some point during the night; the television was off and he was covered with a brown fleece blanket that was stored in the ottoman in the corner of the room. She pushed the blanket to one side and sat on the couch next to him, watching his chest rise and fall with deep, even breaths. How easy it is for him to sleep, she thought. No matter what he does, it is always so easy for him.

"Derek, wake up. Something has happened."

Derek woke from his deep sleep easily. He didn't yawn or rub his eyes or appear the slightest bit confused. He propped himself up on one elbow and asked, "What's wrong? Are the girls okay?"

"The girls are fine. It's my sister, Jody." Samantha thought she had cried enough upstairs when Beth had first called her, but now, trying to tell Derek what happened, she couldn't control the tears from again rolling down her cheeks. She started to shake as she looked at her husband. Through her sobs she cried, "Grey called and it's Jody. She's dead."

With this news Derek bolted upright, swinging his long legs around Samantha and lowering his feet to the floor, pulling the fleece blanket with him. "Jody's dead? My God. What happened?" He stared intently into Samantha's eyes. His eyebrows were arched, causing several wrinkles in his usually smooth forehead. His lips were pursed tightly together. Samantha noticed his jaw was clenched and protruding slightly toward her as he anxiously waited for her to respond.

"She was murdered. Grey came home and found her in his office. She was covered in blood."

In a clumsy attempt to console his wife, Derek grabbed Samantha by her upper arms with both of his hands. He squeezed her tightly. "Who killed her?"

"Derek, stop, you're hurting me," Samantha mumbled as she pushed his hands away. The look on her face was a cross between shock that Derek tried to console her, and repulsiveness.

Derek released his grip, only managing to mutter, "I'm sorry."

For the next half hour, Samantha and Derek sat mostly in silence, sipping coffee and staring at their cell phones, until Raegan came into the kitchen. Then, together they told her about her Aunt Jody. It was the most difficult discussion they ever had.

Raegan, ignoring Derek completely, walked over to Samantha and put her arms around her. "Are you okay, Mom? Is there anything I can do?"

Samantha put her head on Raegan's shoulder and started to cry. As Raegan stroked her mother's hair, Samantha whispered softly, "What am I going to do without Jody?" They stayed this way for several minutes until Samantha broke free. Using the sleeve of her robe, she wiped the tears from her eyes and off her cheeks and gave Raegan a tight squeeze, showing her appreciation of her youngest daughter. "I'm sorry for that. It's just such a shock. How are you holding up?"

Raegan took a step back and looked at her mother, her own eyes glistening with tears. "I just can't believe this is real. Everyone loved Aunt Jody."

After several more minutes, Samantha said they needed to call Chelsie. Chelsie advised she was going to come right home. It would take her a few hours to get her things together and make the drive, but she would be home as soon as possible. She promised to be careful on the highway and told Samantha how sorry she was and that she loved her.

Later, as Samantha was pouring her fourth, or maybe fifth cup of coffee, she was shocked to see Derek come down the stairs fully dressed and ready for work, especially after his exaggerated emotional reaction to Jody's death just hours earlier. "I have to go in," he explained. "There are a few things I need to take care of. I'll be back as soon as I can get things done. Try to understand, Samantha. Please."

She said she would try, but in her heart, she knew she wouldn't. Her sister had just been murdered and like always, he was putting work ahead of her. This time she felt the cold chill run down her spine.

10 HOLMES

Ronan Holmes had ruled both Grey and Hunter Terrel out as the killers of Jody Terrel. Not only did they both have solid alibis that he felt certain would check out, his gut instinct told him they were innocent. While he didn't rely solely on instinct, with thirty years in law enforcement, he did give it a great deal of respect. Of course, that meant he currently had exactly zero suspects in this case, and that was a number he did not like. Not one bit.

His preliminary investigation did not give him any leads, but that didn't worry him. The husband may not have known of anyone who wanted to see his wife dead, but often times husbands didn't know everything going on in their wives' lives. He was sure there would be secrets that would be revealing themselves in no time. Plus, Jody Terrel was from a large family. He had yet to meet a family with that many siblings where everyone got along. Of course, it could have been a random murder. If so, that could prove to be a bit more difficult, but Ronan didn't think that would be the case. The house was too neat, too tidy. No one had searched through closets or drawers. Nothing appeared to be missing, so it didn't look like a robbery. A perp looking for drugs would have messed the house up. At the very least, the medicine cabinet would have been rifled through. A stranger would have broken a window, pushed their way in, scuffed a floor or damaged something somewhere. There would have been a telltale sign. The Terrel house showed none of these things. It looked like Jody Terrel had opened the door for whoever killed her. No, this wasn't going to be random. This was going to be someone she knew. He could feel it in his bones and that feeling had never let him down in the past.

Ronan's past included a long line of law enforcement officers that extended back to the old country. Both his grandfather and his father had been police officers in Belfast, Ireland, as had his favorite uncle, Uncle Fergus. The Holmes family lived on the Catholic nationalist side of the peace walls of Belfast, or at least they had since the 1970s when the walls were built. Both Uncle Fergus and Shane, Ronan's father, started their careers as police officers in the 1960s, when the conflict between the Catholic nationalists and the Irish republicans became heated. The Catholics wanted Northern Ireland to join a united Ireland, while the Protestants wanted to remain part of the United Kingdom. The numbers on both sides were almost equal and the violence between the two sides was increasing.

While the peace walls were supposed to segregate

the two sides, they did little to decrease the violence. Ronan remembered seldom being allowed to play in his backyard as a young boy because their house abutted the walls and there was always a risk of a pipe bomb being thrown over from the other side. The pipe bombs were never thrown the other way because the houses on the Protestant side were much further away from the walls than on the Catholic side. The day that stood out most in Ronan's mind was the day his Uncle Fergus was killed.

Uncle Fergus was the epitome of a big ole Irishman. He was tall and a bit on the heavy side with curly red hair and a red moustache that twirled under his prominent nose. He had bright green eyes, ruddy cheeks and an infectious smile. Uncle Fergus was a police officer on the Catholic side of the walls, but he would cheerfully respond to any call at any location. He was there to help people in need and he didn't care what side of the gates he was on. Everyone who knew him loved him, Catholic and Protestant alike. That alone made him an enigma in a world filled with so much hatred.

In the early morning of a chilly September day, a call came out for a woman in need. Ronan couldn't remember exactly what the call was for, or perhaps he never knew. After all, he was just a small boy at the time. Uncle Fergus was sitting at his favorite diner enjoying a full Irish breakfast when the call came in. With a quick wink to Maeve, who understood that meant to hold his plate until he came back, he jumped up and headed to his squad car parked just around the corner. He ran to his car with one thought on his mind, there was a woman who needed him. He pulled open the driver's door and probably never heard the explosion, never saw the blinding light that engulfed him, and never felt the shrapnel as it flew at three thousand feet per second into his chest, his heart, and his lungs. Hopefully, he never knew that his body was blown into pieces that covered almost a full city block. Obviously, he could never recover. Neither could Ronan's mum, who was Fergus' baby sister. Before Christmas of that very same year, Ronan and his parents had left their home, left Belfast, and moved to the United States to start a new life in Boston. Shane Holmes still worked as a police officer, much to the dismay of Molly, his wife. He said he had to, if for no other reason than to honor Fergus. Years later when Ronan was an adult and had to choose a career, Molly was again dismayed when he, too, chose law enforcement.

Ronan's days as a police officer in Boston were many years ago. He worked the beat, moved up in the department, made detective, corporal, sergeant, lieutenant and finally, captain. Then he decided he had enough. He took an early twenty-year retirement and moved to Maine. Once there he found he was far too bored to sit around or fish all day, so he joined the police force, this time as a detective. He wasn't as busy as he had been in Boston, but to his surprise, there was enough serious crime to keep his mind active and his skills sharp. Now he had the murder of Jody Terrel to solve, and solve it he would.

Ronan pulled out his notepad. Some of the younger detectives used their cell phones, or even a tablet, for their note taking, but he clung to a small pad of paper. On it he had jotted down the names of Jody

Terrel's father and her siblings, three sisters who all lived in the area. The three sisters were all married. He wanted to interview each one of them as well as their spouses. His interest was also piqued by a comment Grey had made about one of the sister's children, Gage. Apparently, Gage didn't get along with Hunter, Jody and Grey's son. He would want to check into that.

Ronan's partner, Wes Campbell, was running financials on the Terrel family to see if there were any serious concerns with their debt, and to look for any sudden payments. He was also checking for life insurance policies that may have been on Jody and if he found any, who were the beneficiaries. Additionally, Wes would check telephone records, credit card statements, and everything else that was available to him without a warrant. Ronan didn't think he would find anything and he didn't suspect Grey, but it had to be done. In the meantime, Ronan was going to make a pot of tea and find a couple of donuts to munch on. Preferably jelly donuts, as they were his favorite. Then he would start visiting Jody's sisters and their husbands while waiting for crime scene reports.

11 DELANEY

Delaney loved her sister. She understood her actions may not make that fact obvious to a casual observer, but she truly did. There were things she had to do and her being torn apart inside about Jody didn't change the need to get them done. It was because of Jody's death that the urgency to do these things existed.

She was well aware that no one understood why she needed to be out running errands this morning, just hours after Beth had called to tell her that Jody was dead. She could see the shock on Jack's face when she came downstairs in search of her car keys. He was sure she would stay home comforting their two children.

"I have things I have to get done this morning," she explained. "Things that just can't wait."

"Like what?" Jack tilted his head to the side as he stared at her, drying his hands on a dishtowel. The creases in his forehead indicated he was troubled and did not understand her decision to leave the house. "And what about the kids? They need you right now."

This was exactly the line of questioning Delaney did not want to face. She was hoping to come down the stairs, purse in hand, and run out before Jack could give her the third degree. But then she realized she didn't have her keys. Damn, where had she left them? "I know, Jack, and I won't be long. Wyatt is on his computer and Roxie is sitting in her bed reading. They're fine. I told them to call me if they need me. I won't be long. I promise."

"I don't understand what is so damn important that you have to run out the day after your sister was killed." Jack mumbled those words as much to himself as to Delaney, shaking his head in what very well could have been disgust.

Delaney, suddenly remembering that her keys were still in her car in the garage, wanted to ignore him and leave while she had the chance. Guilt wouldn't allow her to do that. Instead, she put on her coat and turned toward him. "For right this minute, I'm doing okay and the kids are fine. I just have a few work things that can't wait. I shouldn't be more than an hour or two, and you can call me if you need me. I don't like leaving, but the world can't stop just because, well, you know." Delaney peered into Jack's eyes, innocuous hazel in color, but surrounded with long, heavy lashes that gave them a perpetually sensual look. She smiled slightly. "I need to get away, just for a while. To work through this. I have to do something normal, something routine. I'm sorry. I just need a little time. I mean, God, Jack, it's Jody. She's gone."

"I know, Babe, I know. I'm sorry I didn't understand that you needed a little time alone. We'll be fine. You do what you need to do. I'll be here with the kids, but don't be gone long. We need you here with us." Jack put his hands on either side of Delaney's face and raised her head so she was again staring directly into his eyes. Gently, his thumbs grazed her cheeks. "We'll get through this, together," he said. "I promise."

With that, Delaney hugged her husband, zipped her coat, and ventured out into the cold Maine air. Seeing the love on Jack's face, and feeling the same for him in return, only made her feel guilty for the lies she had just told him. She didn't need normalcy. She didn't need to run work errands. She didn't even need time to herself to work through Jody's death—that would come later. What she needed right now was to talk to her lawyer.

****

"Delaney, please, come in. Have a seat. I'm so sorry to hear about your sister. I saw something about it on the local news, but I didn't realize who it was until you called me this morning. I'm glad I had an opening in my schedule."

"Thank you for squeezing me in, Tom. I wasn't sure what to do or who to talk to."

"I'm glad you called. Now what's this all about?"

Tom Wilcox was a tall, stocky man of about sixty with blue eyes, dewy white skin and a full head of wavy white hair. He was dressed in a three-piece, navy-blue suit, and even though that look had gone out of style years ago, he still managed to appear quite fashionable. He didn't sit behind his desk, but instead took the chair in front of it, next to Delaney. He crossed one long leg over the other and leaned forward, yellow legal pad resting on his knee. His black Montblanc pen was poised and ready to take notes as soon as she began talking. He smiled at her, eyes peering over his silver-framed glasses, and waited patiently for her to begin.

"Tom, I know how this is going to sound. I know I shouldn't be here, with Jody only being dead a few hours, but you know how I am. I worry and I don't know what else to do. I can talk to you, right? We have that whole attorney/client privilege thing and you can't repeat what I say?"

"Yes, that's correct. What you say to me is confidential."

Delaney exhaled and leaned back in her chair. She started by telling him about the DNA testing and how Beth had called her. Beth said she knew either she or Jody was not Paul's daughter, but she didn't know which one of them. She admitted to Tom that she, Delaney, did know. Her previous medical training had made it easy to figure out based on things like Jody's eye color. Plus, just by looking at them it would be an easy call, with Jody's olive skin and dark hair and eyes. Honestly, Delaney said she was surprised no one had already figured it out. She knew it was only a matter of time before the DNA testing would link family names and everyone would know that Paul was not Jody's father.

Tom nodded patiently, but he was beginning to understand what Delaney was alluding to. Since Jody was not Paul's daughter, she would likely not be entitled to a share of his inheritance. His will would indicate that it was to go to his children. That meant there would have been a good chance Jody would have wanted half of her mother's inheritance. Up until now, Delaney was to receive all of their mother's inheritance. Suddenly, Tom did not like where this conversation was heading. Still, he didn't respond other than to nod, encouraging Delaney to continue.

"Anyway," Delaney said, "the night Beth called to tell me about Jody, I was on my way home. I wanted to have dinner with Jack and the kids, but I pulled over to talk to her and by the time we hung up, I knew it was too late. I had missed dinner, so I didn't go right home. I'm sure the police are going to question me about where I was that night. Jack watches a lot of *Law and Order* on television and they always question the close family members." She laughed, but it was a nervous laughter, the kind that never reached her eyes. "What I want to know is, if they decide to try and figure out where I was that night by checking where my cell phone pinged, can they tell my exact location, or just close to it?"

Tom was startled by this question, but other than a slight clenching of the pen in his hand and a sudden upward jerk of his head, the surprise he felt would be unnoticeable to an onlooker. "Should I be curious about why you are asking?"

Delaney again released a nervous chuckle as she fidgeted with the hem of her sweater. "Of course you should be curious, but what I need you to do is just answer the question. So, let's say I was at Target when my phone pinged. Would the police know I was at Target, or could I have been at the restaurant across the street, or the grocery store on the next block? How accurate is this cell phone pinging?"

Tom shifted in his chair, uncrossed his legs and sat straight up before replying. "This is not my area of expertise, but I believe the accuracy of cell phone pinging will vary depending on the number of towers in that specific location. One tower, perhaps, will be as accurate as within one-third to one-half mile. Cell tower triangulation is probably accurate to within a three-quarter square mile area. I imagine the location of the tower or towers, however, could make a difference."

"Interesting, so they are not all that precise."

"The technology would be more useful in determining general location than an exact location. Probably more useful in a rural setting than in a city setting." Tom wanted to question her about her motive for asking him this, but since he had not been hired as her defense attorney, he kept his curiosity in check and remained silent.

Delaney sat across from him a few minutes longer, making no attempt to ask further questions. She seemed to be pondering his responses. Finally, the hint of a smile crossed her face and she reached to the floor to pick up her purse. She stood and smoothed both her sweater and her pants. "Tom, thank you so much for seeing me on such short notice. I would like to ask that we wrap up the paperwork on the inheritance as quickly as possible. I know it may be awkward, reaching out to Samantha and Beth for signatures with everything going on, but perhaps we could still try to move forward with that before, well, let's just keep pushing to get it done."

Tom liked Delaney. He always admired her straight-forward, no-nonsense attitude. She was smart, open, a straight-shooter. But today he felt like he was seeing a different side of her and it was making him a little uncomfortable. Not that he hadn't dealt with all kinds of people in his line of work, or that he even minded. It was just a surprise.

Delaney had slipped her jacket back on and now she stood before him, her hand extended to Tom for their final goodbye. "Just bill me as always, Tom. I do wish we could have seen each other today under better circumstances. Give your wife my regards."

Tom grasped Delaney's hand and shook it warmly. Although she hadn't asked, he did feel obligated to give her one more piece of information before she left. "Delaney, cell phone pinging isn't all that accurate, but you should know that the average American citizen is picked up by security cameras on average as much as seventy-five to eighty times per day."

12 THE VISITOR

I didn't think I would be able to sleep after last night. I mean, I never killed anyone before. I never killed anything, well, other than a bug, but honestly, does a bug really count? Let's face it, by the time a human is five, chances are they had probably killed a bug. They might have done it on purpose, or maybe by accident, but either way, whether they ripped off the wings of a fly for fun, or stepped on an unsuspecting ant by walking down the sidewalk, the bug is dead.

When I turned to look at the clock next to the bed, I was surprised to see it was morning. I had slept all night. Light had crept in around the edge of the roman shades and I heard the sounds of my family from within the house. I stretched slowly, but then the memories of last night flooded into my mind. "Oh, shit, what have I done?" I mumbled this thought out loud before I could get control of myself. Thank God I was alone in my room.

My mind was racing. I killed Jody. How could I

have done that? I mean, I love Jody. She's my family. How the fuck could I have killed her?

I wanted to cry as I lay there. My mind kept playing scenes of Jody slumped over in her chair, the blood draining from the giant gash in her neck. If I closed my eyes, I could see the red puddle below her lifeless body getting bigger and bigger. I wanted to turn my mind off, to make the images stop, but they wouldn't. I wished I could bury myself under my covers and forget about last night, but there was no escaping what I had done.

I didn't want to get out of bed, but lying there was worse. Images of last night kept going through my head. I had never planned to kill Jody. I was only going to tell her why it was so important that she keep everything a secret. I wanted her to understand that it would be too hurtful if she told. How was I supposed to know that she didn't have a clue? She should have known.

I needed to sit up. I felt nauseated. I pulled my knees to my chest and rocked back-and-forth. The shock of what I had done was suffocating me. I was having trouble breathing. I killed Jody. But honestly, she didn't give me any other choice. I tried to reason with her. I tried to explain things to her, but she kept saying "No." She made me do it. I didn't want to, but I had to. It was her fault, and I wasn't going to sit here and let myself feel guilty about it. I only went over there to talk to her and she threatened me. Not only me, but the person I loved most in life. Then she said she was going to open her big mouth and tell everyone. Who the fuck did she think she was? She never was any good at minding her own business. Really, it was more her fault than mine that she died. She was acting so selfish, ranting about her money, like that was what was important. No, I didn't plan to kill her last night, and I'm sorry that she's dead. But it's not like she gave me a choice.

I fluffed my pillow behind me and lingered in bed a little longer. I was still surprised that Jody was home alone last night. I didn't plan it that way, it just happened. As it turned out, that was probably a good thing. Jody wouldn't have wanted Grey or Hunter to hear our conversation. I mean, Hunter wouldn't have listened, but Grey might have. He always had his nose all up in Jody's business. But they were both gone so they never knew what Jody and I said to each other. They never even knew I was there.

Also, I'm glad I had parked on the street and not in Jody's driveway. Her garage is in front and sticks out further than the rest of the house. If she had looked out the window, she wouldn't have been able to see my car. If she had been on the telephone, she wouldn't have been able to tell anyone who was visiting her. Now I didn't have to worry that someone knew it was me.

It was also helpful that Jody and Grey live in a quiet, zero-crime neighborhood. I remember Jody and Grey had talked about getting a Ring camera, but they decided not to because they said they didn't need it. No one in their neighborhood had one. I don't think I will get caught.

I felt slightly reassured so reluctantly, I pushed the comforter away and stood on the hardwood floor, feeling the cold against the soles of my bare feet. I pulled on navy-blue sweatpants and a matching sweatshirt. Then I thought about my clothes from last night. When I had returned home, I had thrown them in the washer and turned the machine on, setting it to heavy duty. When the load was done, I remembered to turn the washing machine's setting back to regular wash so there would be nothing unusual about it. I often did laundry when I got home. My shoes had been a bit more concerning, but fortunately, I watched a lot of *Forensic Files* and knew that killers were often caught by matching the prints of their shoes to prints at the crime scene. Before leaving Jody's house, I checked to make sure there were no bloody prints around the body. So cliché, I thought. Even an amateur like me knew better than to get caught that way. There were no prints in the house. At the doorway, I had again assured there wasn't so much as one bloody print on the floor. Then I simply took off my shoes and carried them to the car. Once I got home, I popped them into the washing machine with the rest of my clothes. Luckily, Converse is washable. Just think, I had almost worn winter boots. Now that could have been a problem.

Before I left my room, I opened my closet door and peered into the back to make sure everything was exactly as I had left it. Of course it was. Wrapped in an old flannel shirt and stuffed into a canvas bag tucked in back of a plastic bin filled with miscellaneous items was a medieval dagger. It had been thoroughly washed in hydrogen peroxide and bleach. I heard that hydrogen peroxide is a great way to remove blood, and bleach will degrade DNA, just in case the hydrogen peroxide didn't do its job. I was trying to be careful. Later, I'll need to dispose of the dagger.

Briefly, a feeling of regret fluttered through my mind when I thought about discarding the weapon. I knew I needed to dispose of it, and I longed to put it someplace where I would never have to see it again. But a cold realization came over me and I knew I couldn't do that. I couldn't get rid of it. I had to keep the dagger. Hiding it made more sense. After all, maybe Jody didn't know the secret until I told her, but I'm pretty sure there is someone else who does.

13 HOLMES

Most days, Ronan didn't pay much attention to what he was wearing, but today was different. He spent a few extra minutes selecting his outfit, not that it would make a noticeable difference. The suit he wore to the funeral would be the same suit he wore to work. Either way, he wasn't going to fit in; he was going to look like a cop. Maybe it was his short hair. Maybe it was the hardened glare of his green eyes. He didn't know. He just knew that when the family, friends and mourners of the deceased passed by him, they would know he wasn't one of them.

He smoothed his black suit as best he could and assured his gun, a GLOCK 22, wasn't visible under his jacket. He shoved his wallet in his pocket, grabbed his cell phone, and headed out the door. He wanted to be early to Jody Terrel's funeral.

Ronan parked his car discretely on a side road next to the small chapel where Jody's family had not yet started to gather. Good. He wanted to be inside before anyone arrived. There would be an officer positioned outside in an unmarked vehicle to take pictures of the mourners. Wes Campbell, his partner, would be seated near the back of the church observing the people as they entered. Ronan chose to go upstairs to the mezzanine. Since there was no choir utilizing the balcony, he would be alone and free to observe everyone unobstructed. He would not take photos; he did not want to call attention to himself. He wanted to watch the people as they paid their respects to Jody's family. He was confident that Jody knew her murderer and it made perfect sense that one of those in attendance was that person. From up here, he could watch for any unusual behavior, any oddity that struck him as suspicious. The slightest vibe or hunch or simple gut feeling he could get from someone might give him a starting point to finding Jody Terrel's killer.

He settled into the choir seat in the far-right corner of the balcony and silenced his cell phone just as the first mourners entered the church. It wasn't just one or two people trickling in like he expected, but a group of ten entering together. He immediately recognized Grey and Hunter who both appeared pale and shell-shocked. Neither of them was handling Jody's death well. Ronan had already removed them from his suspect list. In his mind, it was clear they did not kill Jody, plus both of their alibis had checked out, making it impossible for them to be in two places at the same time.

Along with Grey and Hunter a striking couple, both tall and thin. The man had dark hair and a neatly trimmed beard and moustache. His arm was flung protectively around the back of the woman. She was wearing a black dress that managed to give off an expensive vibe, despite its simplicity. There were two stylishly dressed children trailing behind them, a boy and a girl. Ronan recognized this group as Jody's youngest sister, Delaney, and her family.

Also in the crowd of early arrivers was a small blond woman, her husband, and their son and daughter. That would be another sister, Beth, and her family. Beth was rummaging through her handbag looking for something. As Ronan watched, she discreetly removed a pill from a brown bottle and tossed it in her mouth, swallowing it without any type of drink. Impressive, Ronan thought. Then he switched his focus to Beth's son, Gage. He knew that Gage and Hunter did not get along very well. He did note that wherever Gage went, his mother followed. Grace stayed closer to her father. Ronan pulled his notepad out of his pocket and thumbed through the pages. Jerry. Beth's husband is Jerry. Grace stayed closer to Jerry and Beth clearly hovered around Gage.

By now several other people had entered the church. Ronan scanned through another fifteen or twenty people of all ages. He didn't recognize anyone in particular. No one stood out to him. Finally, just coming through the door, he spotted the last sister. This would be Samantha. Her thin frame was slightly hunched forward and her eyes were cast downward as she navigated the main aisle of the church. She was flanked by her two daughters; one held her hand while the other had her arm firmly around her waist, supporting her while she walked. Samantha's husband, Derek, followed closely behind the three of them. Samantha had a severe look on her face that Ronan attributed to anguish. Her daughters looked sad, protective as they comforted their mother. Ronan watched them for a few minutes and noted that they did not join the others but instead sat on the opposite side of the church. That was odd, he thought to himself.

Then his attention was drawn to an elderly man and a well-dressed woman who appeared to be several years his junior as they approached Samantha and her family. He leaned in and kissed Samantha on the cheek. Then he shook hands with Derek and gave both girls a hearty hug. That must be Paul, Ronan surmised. Jody, Beth, and Samantha's father.

Ronan quickly lost interest in Samantha and her family, instead focusing not on Paul, but on his companion. Clearly she played a large role in Paul's life, yet until now Ronan wasn't aware of her existence. The deep frown on his face indicated he was not happy that his investigation had not made him aware of her presence.

The woman looked to be in her mid-fifties, although it was hard to know from this distance. She had short, platinum blond hair, neatly styled in waves around her face. She was dressed in an elegant black pantsuit with beige trim. Her interaction with Samantha's family seemed polite, but not exceptionally warm. He watched to see how she did with the other family members. Ronan was hoping Paul and his companion, who was now clinging to his arm as they neared the front of the church, would go to each sister, but instead they went directly to the front pew. They both hugged Hunter. Then Paul sat down, blocking the woman from doing more than reaching around him to give Grey a pat of condolence. It did appear they knew her well and liked her. Ronan jotted a note to find out her identity and how she fit into the family.

As the service began, Ronan continued his vigilance from his perch high up in the church. His focus was on the three sisters, although the father's companion did consume a fair amount of his attention. All of the behavior exhibited by these women was what would be expected by family members at a funeral. At one time or another, each of the sisters cried. Delaney's eyes often filled with tears, while Beth openly wept. Samantha tried to put on a stoic front, but there were times during the service that Ronan could see her wiping tears from her eyes. It was sweet the way her youngest daughter would put her arm around her shoulder and try to comfort Samantha when she was clearly overcome by grief. Both Beth and Delaney were consoled by their respective husbands. Paul's companion didn't cry, but did divide her attention between Paul, Hunter and Grey. Ronan noted that her hand never left Paul's during the entire service.

Sobs and moans could be heard throughout the service. Ronan spent a few minutes watching each of the sisters' husbands. He was a bit surprised that Samantha's husband, Derek, cried. Ronan did not expect him to be the emotional type. Jerry clearly appeared upset. Delaney's husband, Jack, seemed indifferent.

Ronan also watched each of the sisters' children. Samantha's oldest daughter cried more than her youngest daughter. The younger one looked upset and remained focused on her mother. Beth's son, Gage, was fidgeting, and her daughter, Grace, was quiet. At some point during the service, Grace had eased her hand into her father's. Lastly, he watched Delaney's two children. For the most part, they sat perfectly still, perfectly well-behaved. Almost too perfectly, Ronan thought. Attractive, well dressed, well-behaved—Ronan wondered if perfection was a requirement in that household. He might want to interview that family sooner rather than later.

Ronan glanced around at the other mourners attending the service. There must have been a hundred people scattered among the pews below him. Many of the people he recognized from around town. After all, Cayne was not a very large place. It was interesting how people tended to sit in groups. One section had several teachers from the high school. These were probably co-workers of Grey. Ronan was confident that the fifth row from the back were the people from the gym Jody attended. It was nice that they came, Ronan thought. Several rows up from them was a group of high school kids. That did pique Ronan's interest; he was under the impression that Hunter didn't have many friends, so why

were there ten or twelve high schoolers here? And from
the look of them, they were not the nerdy type. A couple
of them looked like they could fit into the jock category.
Ronan scribbled a few more notes down on his pad.

The service continued, but Ronan had lost
interest. He felt he had all the information he was going
to get from his attendance. Then he noticed Wes give a
subtle point to his cell phone. Ronan nodded and pulled
his out of his jacket pocket. He saw he had several
incoming messages, including finalized test results from
the crime scene. Ronan opened the attached document
with anticipation, but was disappointed with the results.
There were no unusual fingerprints found on the
doorknobs, doors, chairs, walls, or anyplace else that the
killer might have touched. There were no footprints, no
shoeprints. Only family hairs were found in the office.
There were some fibers found, but nothing that could be
determined to be that of the killer. There was a small
trace of blood found in the front foyer that may have
been on the killer's shoe, but not enough for any kind of
print. The blood type matched Jody's. There were also a
few black wool fibers near the front heating vent, but
nothing with DNA. They could have been from a family
member and they could have been there for a long time.
Nothing of use. Ronan sighed and continued reading.
There were no cameras, doorbell or otherwise, in the
neighborhood. None of the neighbors are reporting
having seen anything suspicious.

Discouraged, Ronan clicked out of that report.
Not one useful thing there. It was too soon to have an

official autopsy report, although he had spoken earlier to the coroner. "Not much mystery with this murder," Ken Tashiro had told him. "Jody Terrel died of having her neck sliced open, exsanguination. She was cut left to right, indicating a right-handed killer. No hesitation wounds, no signs of struggle. She never saw it coming." Ken continued to advise that the weapon used was incredibly lethal. He emphasized that the left jugular vein was completely severed and the left carotid artery was opened. Jody never had a chance. When pressured by Ronan about the size of the killer, Ken responded, "I really can't give you more. Jody was seated, back to the killer. They came on hard and fast with an unusual weapon. They easily overpowered her, but since she was seated, and because she didn't expect it, they didn't have to be a lot bigger or a lot stronger than her. You want more on their size, get me the weapon." Ronan shook his head, unhappy that he didn't have more to go on. Ken gazed up at him. "I can tell you this. She didn't suffer. Death was quick. Probably within seconds. Of course, none of this is official. The official report won't come out for weeks. But it won't change. I'm sure of it."

By the time Ronan stopped reviewing the reports on his cell phone and stopped thinking about his conversation with Dr. Tashiro, the coroner, the service had ended and people were walking toward either Grey and Hunter or the back of the church. Some were offering condolences, others were leaving. There would be no gravesite service at this time. It was March and this was Maine. The ground was still frozen. The body would be held in a special vault until late spring and then the family and friends would all be called together for another service to lower the casket into the ground. Just the thought of it made Ronan shudder.

Ronan stayed in the mezzanine until the church was empty, looking at his list of people to interview. Who should he visit first? Samantha, the sister that kept her distance from the others? Beth, who had the son who didn't get along with Hunter? Or Delaney, the cold, perfect little sister, er, make that half-sister. Or should he skip the three sisters and start with the father's companion? What role did she play in all of this? He closed his notepad and headed toward the stairs. First things first, he thought. He wanted to talk to Wes about what he had learned from his research into the families' financial situations.

14 BETH

Beth carried the tray into the living room and gently placed it on the coffee table. Not only did it contain the three steaming mugs of coffee she had promised, but also a plate of homemade apple-cinnamon squares. "Please, help yourself, Detective Holmes." Beth smiled as she sat in one of the two oversized chairs directly across from the couch where Ronan was seated. Jerry sat next to her in the other chair.

Ronan reached for one of the mugs, ignoring the cream and sugar and instead opting to drink his black. He couldn't resist not one, but three of the little square pastries. They tasted as delicious as they looked and he didn't hesitate to share that assessment with Beth. Once he finished eating, he sipped the coffee and set the mug on the table. Then he turned his attention to the patiently waiting Beth and Jerry. "This shouldn't take too long. I just have a few routine questions for you. You understand, you never know what bit of information someone might provide that could be useful in a case like this one."

"Of course, Detective. We're happy to help in any way we can," Beth replied, still beaming from the compliments he had paid her.

"Good. Let's start with the basics. Beth, where were you the night Jody was killed?"

"Well, let me see. I had made cookies that day for the bake sale. I was going to bring them to the school myself, but I didn't need to. Grace volunteered to take them for me. She wanted my car for drama club so she said she would drop them off." Turning to Jerry she added, "That was the night you worked late so I hadn't bothered to cook dinner." She paused long enough to sip her coffee, then smiled at the detective. "Gage didn't need my car. He was going to the hockey game with some friends. He didn't want dinner, either. They were going out for pizza first. Since no one wanted to eat and I was alone, I just called it an early night. I was home by myself."

"Did you talk to anyone? Have any visitors? Did you make any calls?"

"No, no visitors. I called my sister, Delaney, and we chatted for a bit. Not too long, but no one else. As I recall, I took a long, hot bath. Not something I get to do very often, with all the cooking and cleaning and baking I have to do." Beth sighed. She tried to make it sound like work, but Ronan got the distinct impression that she loved every minute of taking care of her family. "After that, I just went to bed."

"Did you go right to sleep, or did you watch

some television?"

"I'm not much of a television person. Those silly talk shows don't interest me. Neither do shows with violence. No, I would have read one of my books for a while before I went to sleep. I do like to read."

Ronan raised his eyebrows as he reached for his coffee. "Any recommendations? I'm always looking for a good book."

"I doubt if you would enjoy the kind of books I like. I'm into the mushy, romantic-type stories. You look more like the 'whodunit' type."

Ronan nodded his head as he chatted a bit longer with Beth. He asked her a few meaningless questions, mostly to keep her talking about things she could easily answer. Then he surprised her by asking, "how would you describe your relationship with Jody? Were there any problems?" He watched closely for her reaction; he wasn't disappointed. Her hands, which had been loosely folded on her lap, suddenly tensed and became tightly locked together. She inhaled sharply. She paused before responding, only for a second or two, but long enough for Ronan to understand she was uncertain with how she should respond.

"I loved Jody. I mean, we had our moments, as all sisters do. We still called and visited each other. Why, it was only a couple of weeks ago that we went shopping together. But that doesn't mean we didn't have our differences."

"What were some of those differences?"

Beth again clenched her hands together, wishing

she could have served wine instead of coffee. Realizing what she was doing, she relaxed, but after only a moment, she started to twist her wedding band with the fingers of her right hand. Around and around the wedding band went, circling her left ring finger. "Well, for instance, she cooked all her food with a lot of spices and I don't like spicey food. We didn't agree on that at all."

Ronan sat quietly. That was not the disagreement that she found troubling. He waited for her to keep talking.

"She was always after me to go to the gym with her. I would tell her I didn't want to, and with running the PTA, my book club, volunteering at the pet shelter, who has the time? But she kept pushing me. Why couldn't she just accept that I wasn't interested in going to the gym?"

Again, Ronan waited. Beth was just finding things to talk about, this was not what was on her mind. There was something else. What was it? He remained silent; his eyes focused on her. He could sense her discomfort.

"I guess I didn't like the way she was always bragging about Hunter. Just because he did better in school than Gage, she didn't have to go on and on about it. Every family party, every get-together, that's all we heard. Hunter this and Hunter that. Christ, it was like the kid walked on water."

Bingo, Ronan thought to himself. He remained quiet while Beth continued. It was like the floodgates

109

had been opened. Now that she started talking about what was really on her mind, she couldn't stop. Ronan could see her husband trying to catch her eye, trying to get her to stop talking, but Ronan stared directly into her eyes. He did not want her to be distracted by Jerry. He would rather she keep sharing her every thought.

"Of course Hunter does better in school. It's not like he does anything else. The kid doesn't have any friends. He never goes anyplace, except maybe to the school library. You never see him at school functions. And don't get me started on school sports. I'm pretty sure Jody protected him so much that he's afraid of everything. Well, I guess he plays soccer, but it's soccer. That's not a real sport. Not like what my Gage plays. Gage lettered in football. And he plays baseball and I'd bet he could beat most anyone in a game of tennis. He is a natural athlete. And he has so many friends. Gage isn't the one sitting home every Friday night. He doesn't have time to study, Detective Holmes. That's why his grades aren't as good as Hunter's. Because he actually has a life."

Suddenly Beth realized that she had been talking nonstop. A deep crimson spread across her face and she put her hand over her mouth. "I am so sorry. I guess I went on a bit there. I tend to get overprotective about Gage. I do wish his grades were better. You can tell it's an area that concerns me."

Ronan smiled and summoned the most soothing voice he could muster. "Not to worry, Beth. Good parents are always protective of their children." Beth smiled weakly in return, not noticing Jerry's cold stare.

As soon as Ronan had finished his interrogation of Beth, she immediately excused herself and went into the kitchen. Out of the corner of his eye he could see her grab a small bottle from her purse that had been lying on the kitchen counter. He turned to Jerry and began asking him questions. As with Beth, his first question was, "Can you tell me where you were the night Jody was killed?"

Jerry did not hesitate with his response. "Sure. I was at work. I own a small garage over on Third Street. Business has been good lately and I had a couple of repairs I had to get done. I stayed late to complete them. I can give you the names of the customers if you want."

Ronan chose to neither accept nor deny that request at this time. He had no doubt Jerry could provide those names. He seemed very prepared for his questions. "How late were you there?"

"I would say until about 10:15. Maybe as late as 10:30. I'm not exactly sure. I own the place so I don't punch a timeclock."

"Were you alone or was someone else with you?"

Jerry squirmed slightly in his chair. "I was alone. If I could afford to have someone else there, I would have been home." The sarcasm in Jerry's voice was unmistakable.

"What time did you get home?"

"It's about a fifteen-minute drive, so I'd guess around 10:30, 10:45. Again, I'm not one hundred percent sure of what time I left. There wasn't any traffic."

"Did you come right home?"

"Yes."

"Did anyone come to see you while you were working?"

With this, Jerry hesitated. The delay was brief, barely noticeable, but Ronan, a seasoned cop, picked up on it. "No one came to see me. I was alone all night."

"What about the people who wanted their cars fixed? Didn't they come and pick them up?"

"No, not until the next morning. But early. One came right at opening. Eight o'clock. The other there sometime before nine."

As with Beth, Ronan asked several generic questions of Jerry that he didn't care about the answers to. They were mostly just busy work questions to keep him talking. Then, instead of asking Jerry about his relationship with Jody because he felt confident Jerry would reply that it was good, he asked Jerry how he felt about the Hunter and Gage situation.

"Honestly, I'm not as bothered by it as Beth is. Jody liked to run her mouth about a lot of things. That's just how she was. If one of those things was about how great her kid was, so what. He is a great kid. It took her and Grey years to have Hunter, and they never managed to have another. He was her whole life, so what's the big deal? I let it go in one ear and out the other."

Indicating that the interrogation was complete, Ronan stood and snapped his notebook closed. He shook hands with Jerry and then turned to Beth. "Thank you so much for your hospitality. The coffee and dessert, best I've ever had. I think I have everything I need from the both of you."

Beth beamed at the detective as both she and Jerry stood, expecting to walk Detective Holmes to the door. Ronan started to take a step in that direction, but just before he did, he hesitated, a smile still plastered on his face, and said, "Would you mind if I ran upstairs and had a word with Grace and Gage before I left? It will only take a minute. Just a few i's to dot, a few t's to cross. Unless you have concerns, of course. You two can wait down here. I won't be long."

Jerry, still looking relieved that he was no longer being questioned, and Beth, cheerful that the interview went so well and that Detective Holmes was very complimentary of both her mothering and her baking, nodded in agreement.

Ronan practically sprang up the stairs and knocked on the second door on the right, which Beth said was Gage's room. He had no need to talk to Grace. He had already verified that she was at the high school the night of the murder. She dropped off cookies and was with other members of the drama club. Several students, plus the drama teacher, were able to verify this. He only included her to make his desire to talk with the children sound casual. What Ronan really wanted was to talk to Gage before Beth and Jerry changed their minds.

15 HOLMES

Ronan could tell that Gage was surprised when he was the one that walked into his room after Gage had yelled 'enter' in response to his knock. He was probably expecting a parent, or maybe his sister.

"Hi, Gage. I'm Detective Holmes. Your mom and dad said it was okay if I came up and asked you a few questions about the night your Aunt Jody was killed."

Gage pulled his headset off and laid it on the desk next to his keyboard. He paused the game on his computer, stood up and pushed the swivel chair toward Ronan, motioning for him to be seated. Then he sat on the bed. He didn't appear nervous, just confused. "Am I a suspect?"

Ronan wanted to congratulate Gage; he was the only family member who thought to ask that question. Instead he replied, "No, these are just routine questions. Often times people don't realize they may know something that is helpful to an investigation. I'm talking to everyone who had a close relationship with your aunt."

Any tension Gage may have been concealing now eased out of his shoulders as he ran his hand through his brown hair, pushing the thick waves away from his eyes. "Ask away."

Ronan started with the usual questions about where Gage was the night of the murder. When Gage responded that he and two friends started at a pizza place before the game, Ronan took a few minutes to get the names, addresses and telephone numbers of both friends. Then he sent a text to his partner, Wes, and provided him with this information. It was a tactic the two partners often used when interrogating a witness. So far, Ronan didn't need Wes to do anything with this information, but depending on how the interview progressed, he may need to send Wes another text. He would either have Wes immediately contact the two additional witnesses to corroborate information provided by Gage, or pretend to. Which of these actions he utilized remained to be seen.

"After you finished your pizza and went to the game, did you see anyone you knew?" Ronan asked Gage this as he flipped through his notepad, hoping Gage would confirm that he did see Grey and Hunter there.

"I saw a few friends." He listed several of his high school buddies and then added, "I think that's it. I think those are all the friends I saw that night."

"Anyone else?"

"Mr. Baxter was there. My English teacher. And

Coach Longley. And I did see Uncle Grey and Hunter. We didn't talk, just a quick hello. I think that's it."

"And did you remain at the game until it was done?" At this, Ronan was surprised to see Gage hesitate. He sat straight up on the bed and crossed his arms over his chest. That was not a reaction Ronan was expecting. Usually, when someone crossed their arms, it was a defensive stance, like they were hiding something. "Gage, did you stay at the game all night?"

Gage stared up and to the left, almost like he was looking at his ceiling. After a few seconds, he answered. "I think so. I don't remember leaving."

The boy was lying. Ronan was sure of it. Hell, a rookie uniformed officer would be sure of it. Time to deploy action 'fake text' to Wes. He didn't think he would need to interrupt Wes with a real one; the boy was going to break at the mere thought that his story was being confirmed. "Hold on a minute, Gage," Ronan said as he pulled out his cell phone, acting like he was responding to an incoming message. "My partner is trying to contact one of your friends to confirm your alibi for the night of the murder. I sent him Matt's telephone number when you gave it to me but I may have sent the wrong number. Can you give it to me again?"

"Your partner is calling Matt right now?" Gage asked as he rubbed his hands up and down his arms while he crossed and uncrossed his feet.

"Yes, he is just going to give him a call. No need to drive all the way over there to see him when he only has to ask him about the one night." Ronan smiled at Gage as he let this lie roll off his tongue. The boy was getting ready to tell him the truth.

"I guess I might have left the game for a little while," Gage said. "I went outside for a few minutes."

"Who did you leave with?"

"No one. I went outside alone."

"Alone? In the cold?"

"I wasn't out there long. I just needed some air?"

Ronan looked up from his phone. Why was Gage asking him his reason for going outside? He was trying to see if his reasoning was plausible. Again, Ronan knew he wasn't being truthful. He continued his questioning. "What did you do outside?"

"Nothing. Just walked around."

"Did you see anyone that you knew while you were out there?"

Gage looked down, his feet tapping rapidly. "No."

Damn, Ronan thought to himself. He's still not being upfront with me. I guess I will have to ask Wes to talk to the other two boys Gage was with after all. "Gage, it's important that you be honest with me. It seems a bit odd that you left your two friends at a hockey game that you were excited to attend to go outside and walk around alone. Is that the story you want to stick to?"

Gage looked Ronan in the eye. "Yes," he said, his voice only slightly more than a whisper.

At that moment, Jerry walked into the room. "I

think that's probably enough questioning for today, Detective Holmes. I'm sure you won't mind talking to Grace another time. The children have had enough to deal with since their aunt was murdered. You understand."

Reluctantly, Ronan got up from the chair to leave the bedroom. He turned back to give Gage his most intimidating stare before exiting. Gage glanced up for a second, long enough to meet Ronan's eyes, but he quickly looked away and adamantly refused to meet Ronan's gaze a second time.

After his father ushered the detective out of his room and closed the bedroom door, Gage continued to sit on his bed. His mind kept replaying the night of the hockey game and the real reason why he went outside; the reason he could not share with the detective. Gage knew that the detective was well aware he was being lied to, but how could he tell him the truth? It was Gage's secret, a secret he was not ready to share, especially not with Detective Holmes.

16 SAMANTHA

Samantha hadn't liked meeting with Detective Holmes earlier today. She hadn't liked it one bit. She felt like he could see through them, like in addition to hearing their words, he could hear their thoughts. It made her uncomfortable to be so exposed.

It started off easy enough. He came to the house early in the afternoon. He had already interviewed Grey and Beth. She didn't know if he had been to see Delaney yet. She hadn't talked to Delaney since the funeral and even then, it wasn't more than a few polite words.

The detective had called to see if they would be home around 1:00 to answer a few routine questions. He wanted to speak with all four of them, Samantha, Derek, Raegan and Chelsie. Not a problem, she had responded, and she meant it. They were anxious to help find Jody's killer. But then he showed up with his in-depth questions and intense demeaner and that look that went right through you, almost like he could see all the way into your soul. It was unnerving. She didn't like it and she was sorry she ever said he could come into their home.

"Thank you for seeing me." Ronan quickly looked at his notepad. "Mr. Derek Anderson. Mrs. Sam Anderson."

"It's not Sam. It's Samantha. My name is Mrs. Samantha Anderson."

Ronan looked up from his pad, surprised at the sharpness in Samantha's tone. "My apologies, Mrs. Anderson." He followed her and Derek into the kitchen. "This shouldn't take too long. Just a few routine questions to help us solve the murder of your sister."

"Of course. Nothing is more important to us than finding Jody's killer. Please, sit down."

Ronan slipped out of his gray woolen coat and sat at the end of the large oak table in the kitchen. He turned his attention to Samantha. Without consulting his notepad, he looked directly into her eyes. Deciding to forego any small talk, he immediately asked, "Let's start with the night of the murder. Can you tell me where you were that night?"

Samantha thought she was prepared for his questions. She had anticipated this would be the first thing he asked. Still, she was annoyed at how he rudely shortened her name and this caused her mind to momentarily go blank. She hesitated before responding. She folded and unfolded her hands on her lap. Finally, she said in a curt tone, "I was home. As usual, Derek was at the office. Chelsie was at school and Raegan was out. I was home alone all night. That's not unusual for a mother of teenage girls."

Ronan, clearly feeling her defensiveness, didn't smile and didn't break his stare. "I'm sure. What did you do while you were home alone?"

"I watched television for a while, and played on my phone a bit. You know, checked email, Facebook, that sort of thing. Then I worked on a quilt I've been making for at least an hour or two. After that I took a shower and went to bed. Nothing unusual."

"Did you talk to anyone on the telephone? Did anyone come to visit you?"

"No visitors. I didn't talk to anyone. My phone rang. Beth called, but I didn't answer it. I didn't feel like talking, so I just let it ring."

"Why is that?"

Samantha tried to outstare the detective. It was none of his business, why she didn't feel like talking to Beth. Her personal life was just that, personal. She shifted her position in her chair and finally let her eyes drop to her hands, once again folded on her lap. Slowly she looked back at him, his eyes still piercing into hers. She shrugged her shoulders. "I don't know. I just didn't feel like talking. I was tired."

Ronan stared at her a little longer but did not speak. Samantha, too, remained silent. Then he turned his attention to Derek and asked the same question he had initially asked of Samantha.

Derek sat stiffly in the oak chair, his arms folded across his chest in front of him. He bit his upper lip, then his lower, while Ronan watched him, patiently waiting for an answer. Finally, Derek responded. "I was at my office working late. We are in the middle of a rather large project and we're on a deadline." Derek winced, realizing his poor choice of words. "Timeline. We're on a tight timeline with this project."

"Was anyone working with you or were you alone?"

"I was alone."

"Is there any way to confirm you were in the building? Cameras? Doorman? Do you sign in or out?"

Derek shook his head. "No. At my level, I don't exactly punch a timecard. There are cameras in the rear of the building, but not in the front. It is well-lit and on a busy street."

"And no one saw you in the building? You didn't see someone else catching up on work? A co-worker? A cleaning person? Anyone who can confirm you were there?" Ronan stared at Derek. He didn't so much as blink. He was onto something. He wasn't sure what, but he knew Derek had some detail he was hiding.

Derek shifted in the chair. His arms were not just folded, but clenched tightly across his chest. He tried to look anywhere except at Ronan, but no matter where he focused his eyes, he could feel the detective's intense stare directed at him. Finally, with a weak voice he said, "Wait, I did see someone. When I first got there, one of the secretaries was at her desk. I passed by her. She may remember seeing me."

Ronan didn't smile, but he did have a moment of satisfaction. He was onto something. "Her name, please."

Derek looked at his hands, still clenched together. "Krystal. Krystal Maynard."

Samantha didn't say a word but when Derek said the name Krystal, Ronan was surprised to see her suddenly sit straight up in her chair and look at Derek with what could only be described as a death stare. Her eyes were narrowed, unblinking. Her forehead was creased and her mouth was pursed into a straight, tight line. Ronan could almost feel the cold radiating off of her. He glanced at both Chelsie and Raegan and saw that they, too, were staring at their mother, surprised looks on both of their faces. Ronan made a mental note to dig deeper into this Krystal Maynard. Why would the mere mention of her name bring such a strong reaction from Samantha Anderson? He had a feeling there was more going than met the eye. He wondered if it somehow tied into the Jody Terrel murder.

Ronan followed his interrogation of Derek with a quick questioning of Chelsie and then Raegan. Chelsie had been a hundred miles away at school the night of the murder. Raegan said she had softball practice followed by time spent at the library. Neither had any problems with their Aunt Jody and they did not know of anyone who would have any reason to kill her.

Ronan wrapped up the interviews and headed out to his car. He started the engine and while the car warmed up, he pulled out his cell phone and signed into his Facebook page. He didn't use his real name, law enforcement personnel seldom bothered with social media. Instead, he signed into a fake account he had created with the sole purpose of being able to look up people who did like to share their lives on social media.

After less than three minutes online, he managed to find a Facebook account on one Krystal Maynard who lived in Cayne. Krystal was 38-years-old. She was a petite blond with blue eyes and from the look of her profile picture, she liked to drink Allagash White while sitting on a lawn chair wearing a bikini. She was single and more than a little attractive. Ronan knew it was incredibly judgmental of him, but he could imagine that she was exactly the kind of woman a forty-something wife and mother of two would not want her husband to be working with at the office late into the night. Especially when that husband got very nervous just mentioning that he may have said hello to her when he passed by her desk. Especially when he passed by that desk all alone, at night, when he was working late.

17 HOLMES

Adeline Lizotte was the longtime girlfriend of Paul Peralta, father to Samantha, Beth and Jody. When Ronan had called her to set up an interview, she was agreeable and suggested he come right over. He plugged her address into his GPS and here he was, driving in one of the nicest neighborhoods in town.

Adeline's house was much larger than Ronan had expected. The two-story colonial sat far off the street on a well-manicured lot. Crisp, white paint, black shutters and a bright red door gave the house a quintessential New England look. Ronan pulled into the circular front drive and parked. He barely had time to ring the doorbell before Adeline opened the right side of the double-door entrance and welcomed him into her home. "Please, Detective Holmes, do come in."

Adeline led him to the rear of the house where a fire was burning in the brick fireplace in the hearth room, open to the kitchen. "I have coffee poured for us. I believe you take yours black?"

"Yes, thank you," Ronan said as he sat on the cream-colored couch directly across from Adeline. She was a neat, trim woman and Ronan could see why Paul Peralta, the sisters' father, was attracted to her. She had pretty blue eyes and her platinum blond hair was arranged in soft waves around her face. There were fine lines in her skin, but still, she looked much younger than her sixty-three years of age. She carried herself with a certain elegance that suggested she came from a privileged class of family, or royalty, he thought to himself.

Ronan was happy that Adeline had agreed to see him so quickly after Jody's funeral. He had been curious to learn more about her and her relationship to Jody's family, especially after he dug a bit into her background.

At Adeline's insistence, he reached for one of the mini-tarts delicately arranged on a silver tray on the table in front of him and popped it into his mouth. Then he sipped his coffee.

"You have questions about Jody's murder?"

Ronan appreciated that Adeline did not waste any time. His reason for being there was obvious. "What can you tell me about Jody's family? Do they get along?"

"Surely, Detective, you can't think a family with that many sisters, that close in age, never has any issues?"

Ronan chuckled but shook his head. "No, can't say I've ever thought about it. Why don't you tell me more about the sisters."

"Certainly." Adeline sipped her coffee and ran her finger around the top of her mug. Then she looked up at Ronan. "Where to begin," she muttered under her breath. "First, Detective, let me say that individually, they are lovely girls. They are all good women who are kind and loving and would give you the shirts off their backs. It's only when they get together that they can bring out the worst in each other."

Ronan remained quiet, appearing to focus on his tart while he waited for her to continue.

"As you can imagine, I'm not as close to Delaney as I am to the older girls. She's not Paul's daughter and while they like each other well enough, she doesn't come to visit like the others do. I don't know her and her family very well. I mostly only see her at family functions. She seems nice enough. Jack is always polite, offers us a drink, makes sure we are comfortable, that sort of thing. The children are well behaved. Delaney will chat with us. She is intelligent, she can speak on most any topic. She's a bit opinionated, but generally I agree with her. We do quite well together. Yes, I like Delaney, but as I said, I don't spend a great deal of time with her. Neither does Paul."

Ronan nodded. Delaney was the youngest of the sisters and was not Paul's daughter. Her father, David Todd, had been killed along with the girls' mother, Caroline, several months ago in a car crash. Delaney had been close to her own father, and while she got along well with Paul, she never considered him more than the father of her three sisters. Nothing Adeline said was a surprise to Ronan.

"Then there was Jody. Now, she was a cute little

thing and Paul adored her. She was quite the athlete when she was little. Did you know that, Detective? Why, she could run races against boys twice her size--and win! Paul was so proud of her. She was always so active. Up until the day she died, she could be found at the gym, or playing softball or pickleball, or just out walking or running. A bit of a health nut, that one." Adeline's eyes took on a faraway look as she sat in the high-backed chair across from the sofa, remembering Jody, a smile pasted on her face. The fondness she felt for Paul's youngest daughter was obvious. There's not a day that goes by that Paul doesn't grieve for her, Detective. Not one single day."

Ronan lowered his eyes, acutely aware that the family was still feeling the pain from the loss of Jody. He gulped his coffee to regain his composure and then asked, "What about Beth and Samantha? How do you feel about those two?"

"I'm probably closest to Beth. It would be hard not to be. She is such a gentle soul. She comes over often and she's always bringing cookies or pie or something freshly baked. She is so considerate. She will call to see if we need anything. She asks how we are. She remembers to ask about my family, something the others seldom do. A few weeks back when Paul had a touch of the flu, Beth was here every day with homemade soup and magazines, and running to the pharmacy. She's a saint, that one."

"A saint, you say."

"Well, mostly. She's very sweet and always so

considerate of us. But she's not without her own issues. I hate to speak ill of her because, like I said, she treats Paul and I like royalty, but she could be a tad bit nicer to that daughter of hers."

"Grace? How so?"

"Well, it's not that she isn't a good mother. She is. She does everything a good mother should do. She just does so much more of it for her son." Adeline stopped talking and let that information sink in. Then she was quiet. It was obvious she didn't like speaking poorly of Beth. Ronan decided not to ask any follow-up questions. He didn't consider Beth a suspect in the murder of Jody.

"And Samantha?"

"Ah, Samantha. Now that one is a little trickier to explain. She has always been, how shall I say this? Let's call her difficult. If you say something is black, she'll say it's white. It doesn't matter who you are--Paul, me, one of the sisters, she just has to disagree. There is seldom a conversation that doesn't end up in a tiff."

"I'm not sure I understand. She likes to argue with everyone?"

"I wouldn't say she likes to argue; she just has to push people. I don't know if it's because she's unhappy, or if she's testing them, or if she just thrives on discord. All I know is that everyone feels like they are walking on eggshells with her."

"Did she get along with Jody?"

"I know where you're going with that line of questioning, Detective, and you can stop right now. Just because she can be difficult doesn't mean she would hurt anyone. Especially her sisters. She would never do that, not in a million years. She is one hundred percent dedicated to this family. She loves her sisters, even if her own unhappiness makes it difficult for her to show it. If you haven't ruled her out, you need to. There is no way she would hurt Jody. You can bet your life on that."

Ronan added a few notes to his ever-present notebook. He finished his tart, drank more coffee, and then changed his line of questioning. "Mrs. Lizotte, I'd like to ask you about your family. I did a bit of checking and it looks like you've been married, let's see, four times?" Ronan raised an eyebrow but Adeline remained quiet. Apparently, she was going to wait for an actual question before responding. "That seems a bit unusual."

"Does it?"

Ronan was not impressed. During most interrogations, this would cause the person on the other side of the table to launch into an explanation of why there were so many marriages. They would justify each marriage, explain each divorce, talk about each time they were widowed. Adeline merely sat there. Clearly, he would have to ask her specific questions if he wanted to get her talking. "Your first husband was only 27-years-old and he died in a boating accident. Is that correct?"

"Yes."

Shit. She still wasn't going to offer anything extra. "Were there any unusual circumstances? Any investigations?"

"No. Neither."

Ronan tried another angle, although he already knew the answer. "Did you receive any insurance or any other financial benefit from his death?"

"I received twenty-five thousand dollars from an insurance policy. But Detective, you already know that. Shall we move on?"

"Tell me about your second husband."

"There isn't much to tell. We married. Three years later, we divorced. Next."

"Okay, third husband?"

"Martin Lizotte. We married and had two children. That's why I retained his name. We stayed together for fifteen years, although the last five were mostly for the children. Then we divorced. I did receive child support until they were both through college. I assume you want to know about my financial gain."

This time Ronan was surprised. He didn't like being caught off-guard, but until this moment, he didn't realize that Adeline even had children. "Please, tell me about your children."

Adeline smiled. "Got you, didn't I, Detective? I have two. My son, Stephen, is a rear admiral in the Navy. He hopes to be a vice admiral soon. My daughter, Ciere, is an orthodontist. She lives in Ocean Beach, California. They are both married with families of their own. We are all on good terms."

Ronan took his time filling his pad with the names and occupations of Adeline's children. He would have to verify this information to make sure Adeline was being truthful. When he looked up, Adeline was watching him, waiting patiently for him to continue with his questions. There was a trace of a smirk on her face. She was enjoying herself. He referred to his notepad and asked, "Your fourth husband, Conrad Westerguard, I believe you are widowed from him?"

"Yes, that's correct. He was a bit older than me. I came home and found him dead on the couch. He suffered a massive heart attack. He did have a history of heart disease, Detective. And yes, I did inherit a substantial sum of money. His children were not happy that the money came to me and not them, but since they hadn't talked to him in over ten years, it seemed fitting. Also, in case you're wondering, there was nothing suspicious about his death."

Ronan finished his coffee and stood to stretch. He glanced around the room. He noted that the room was well decorated, the furnishings were expensive. He picked up his coffee cup and empty plate and carried them both into the adjoining kitchen. He was surrounded by high-end appliances, gleaming marble countertops and a well-stocked China cabinet. He turned back to Adeline and again raised his eyebrow. He knew she would read what was on his mind. She didn't disappoint.

"Detective, in your research of me, did you happen to notice my mother's last name?" Ronan nodded in the affirmative. "Doesn't that name sound familiar to you, like, perhaps you've heard it before? Especially in relation to a common beverage that you have purchased at the local grocery store?" Again, Ronan nodded, a little bit faster as he was beginning to understand what Adeline was saying to him. "Yes, Detective, I am from the same family as that beverage. So you see, I do not need money from life insurance policies of husbands, past or future. I have enough in the way of trust funds that I could buy and sell the lot of them if I chose to do so. And my children certainly do not need to worry about money, either. They are both quite successful on their own, but they, too, have rather large trust funds to fall back on if they should ever feel the need. So you see, I have no reason to harm anyone in Paul's family. I don't need Paul's money. As a matter of fact, Paul has proposed to me, and if the time should ever come where I do decide to take him up on his offer, you can bet that any prenup that will be in place would be to protect my assets, not his."

Ronan stared at Adeline, unable to speak. Damn, how could he not have known this? Why had he not looked a little deeper into her history instead of just brushing her aside as not important to his investigation? It's not that he thought she was any more important than she was an hour ago, she wasn't a suspect, but damn, he didn't like feeling like such an incompetent fool. Not knowing what else to say, he reached for his coat and turned toward the door. Before leaving, he stopped and thanked Adeline for her time. She stood close to him, resting her hand on the doorknob of the open door and said, "No problem at all, Detective Holmes. Please feel free to contact me again if you have any further questions. And when you're in the grocery store buying a particular brand of soda, please do think of me."

Satisfied with the answers he received from Adeline, while annoyed that she had clearly been toying with him throughout the entire interrogation, Ronan walked into the chilly morning air.

18 THE VISITOR

Life wasn't exactly back to routine, but almost. People were trying to do whatever it was they were doing before the murder, whether that meant work or school or staying home and doing nothing. Sure, there was the funeral, with everyone crying and carrying on, but it was ridiculous. People who barely knew Jody were acting like they had just lost their best friend. Seriously, they didn't even know her. They only knew the image she projected. They didn't see the side of her that could be hurtful, the side that focused too much on money, on material things. How many of the mourners knew that she would hurt her own family just to get what she wanted? Did they know how selfish she could be? And if they did, would they still be sitting in the church with their blotchy red faces and their big, crocodile tears pouring down their cheeks?

They were all such phonies, acting like they cared. They hardly even knew Jody. All I could figure is that they were looking for attention.

Look how sad I am.

No, I'm sadder than you.

Their manufactured cries replayed in my mind. Did they upset me because I believed they didn't know the real Jody, or because they did, and I killed her anyway?

But none of that mattered anymore. The funeral was over and people were trying to return to normal. Mostly things had settled down, other than that cop was still hanging around. Detective Holmes. I'm not fond of him. I tried to tell myself it was because he had a stupid name and that he was a total embarrassment to the real Detective Holmes. The real Sherlock Holmes would roll over in his grave at the thought of him investigating a murder case. Well, he would roll over in his grave if he wasn't a fictional character. But I knew that wasn't the issue. My problem with him was that he scared me. He kept digging and asking questions and he never let up. I was afraid that sooner or later he would find some of the answers he was looking for. But usually I didn't let myself think about him. I did what I had to do, and like I said, people have been returning to normal.

Part of returning to normal seemed to include forgetting about Jody. That was okay. I didn't mind if people erased her from their memory. I understood it. They needed to move on so they could get past their grief. It was reasonable. Plus, it was probably safer for me if they did forget. I didn't want to get caught. I was careful, but there always the chance I missed something. It wasn't like I had a lot of experience with killing people. I wanted to put all of this behind me. I did what I had to do and now it was time to leave it in the past.

Before I did, though, I closed my eyes and let one last thought flow through my mind. What I did was right. I saved the person I loved most in this world from experiencing a lot of pain. Jody was going to cause so much hurt, so much suffering, and I could not allow that. The shadow of a smile came across my lips as my thoughts continued. I was actually quite proud of myself for stepping into the role of protector. I'm sure I did the right thing. Killing Jody may seem cruel to some people, but inside, I know it was necessary to protect the one I love. There was no one else who could do it. There was only me. I am the savior.

19 DELANEY

Delaney knew the detective hadn't believed her. Not that his face showed any expression, not even his emerald green eyes gave a hint as to what was going on in what Delaney perceived to be his sharp, intuitive mind. But something in his manner gave him away. Or maybe it was because his manner never changed. He never relaxed. He never seemed satisfied with her responses. He just kept staring at her, willing her to tell the truth. But how could she? She was in enough trouble as it was. What would Jack say if he had known what she had really done that night?

"Mom!" Roxie's voice startled Delaney and brought her back to the present. She looked at her 11-year-old daughter standing before her. Roxie's arms were folded over her chest, her foot anxiously tapping on the floor. "Why are you just holding my waffles? You need to let me eat them so I won't be late for school."

Delaney looked at the two waffles she had pulled from the toaster, now cool in her hand. "Silly me," she said, trying to laugh it off. "I'll rewarm these for you. Go sit down. It will just take a second."

She dropped the waffles back in the toaster, watching as Roxie took her seat at the table. She shouldn't delay her daughter; Roxie was always the last one to eat breakfast, the last one to change out of her pajamas, the last one to be ready for school. Luckily, today she was already dressed.

The toaster popped and before she was caught holding the waffles and not moving again, she brought them to Roxie, adding butter and syrup before putting the plate on the table. "Now eat quickly, Sweetie, we don't want to be late." Delaney could actually feel her daughter's eyeroll as she went upstairs to check on Wyatt.

Wyatt was dressed and ready to be dropped off at Cayne's middle school where he was in the eighth grade. Delaney smiled. "Leaving in ten minutes," she said as she turned and went down the hall to her own room.

Delaney took a quick look in the mirror and flattened down a few stray hairs that had escaped the loose bun at the back of her head. Then she selected a necklace from her oversized jewelry box and clipped it around her neck. She chose a silver heart completely outlined in sparkling diamonds. Jack bought it for her one Valentine's Day a few years back. He liked to buy her jewelry. He was good at it. She thought about Jack and how different things had been when they first got married.

He had been working as a plumber back then, almost sixteen years ago. He worked for a small company making an hourly wage. He was good at what he did, his finish work was the best around. Not only could he plumb anything, but he had also been licensed to do electrical work. He had a solid understanding of all facets of the construction business.

Delaney had been working as a nurse and making decent money. They were doing well financially, but then they learned there was a baby on the way. Once Wyatt was born, Delaney found she couldn't maintain a demanding nursing schedule and care for a new infant. She gave her notice at the hospital and they dropped to a one-income family. Money was tight and Jack was always on call trying to earn enough to make ends meet.

After years of barely getting by, Delaney started pushing Jack to open his own construction company. Why should he make all that money for his boss when he had both the talent and the skill to start his own business? Jack resisted because he enjoyed the job he was doing, but Delaney didn't let up. Three years later, when Roxie arrived, Jack realized that they couldn't go on the way they were. He was gone all the time and Delaney never got a break from the children. He began working with both city and state officials to set up his own business, and soon Jack Mac Construction was up and running. It didn't take long before Jack had more business than he could handle. He started hiring additional workers and subbing other trades. Soon he found himself in more of a management role than a hands-on role. Delaney knew Jack missed getting his hands dirty, but the money he was earning gave him the ability to work decent hours and spend more time with her and the kids. He seemed satisfied with knowing his family was benefiting from his expanding company.

Jack's company continued to grow over the years. It now stretched from Cayne to Lewiston, Portland, and even as far north as Bangor. Soon he was building not only new houses, but entire developments. Once Roxie was old enough to attend preschool, Delaney decided she was ready to return to work. Instead of going back to nursing, she got her real estate license and entered the work world with Jack. He built houses; she sold them. They were a successful team and the money started rolling in. She enjoyed selling houses, but she discovered she enjoyed designing them, too. She liked picking out the paint and floors and tile. She was good at coordinating the colors and shopping for the best deals to make each house warm and inviting. Soon she was working more hours than Jack was, all the while insisting it was because they needed the money to secure their future. After all, they did have two children to put through college someday.

While she was scheduling appointments at night, Jack was home making dinner for the kids. Delaney would laugh, saying that was good since he was the better cook, but she knew Jack never understood why she chose to be gone so much. When he worked those long hours, it was out of necessity. She was doing it out of choice. She tried to convince herself otherwise, but deep down, she knew that he didn't care about the big house, the expensive furniture and the fancy clothes. He would be happy with the basics. But she wouldn't be. She wanted all of those things, and she was willing to give up time with the family to work for them. What was the big deal? At least, that's how she felt until lately. Until things started to go wrong. Suddenly she was making mistakes at work, and these mistakes were leading to other problems. And now she was in big trouble and she didn't know what to do. She pretended everything was alright, but it wasn't. She could feel everything closing in and she was scared. What would happen if Jack found out about the mess she was in? Would he stay by her side or would he leave? And their children, what would happen to them? It would only be a matter of time before that Detective Holmes figured it out. Fuck. She needed that will to be finalized, and fast.

20 HUNTER

Hunter missed his mom. She was one of the few people who understood him. She didn't care that he wasn't good looking, or that he wasn't a big high school sports star. He didn't have to be popular or have lots of friends. So what if he didn't get invited to all the high school parties or if he was a geek. She loved him for who he was, a short, smart, nerdy, 16-year-old, who missed his mother every minute of every day.

He pulled his scarf tighter around his neck in an attempt to keep himself warm against the brisk wind. It was late March, but still the temperature dipped below freezing. It had taken some doing to get his dad to let him walk home from school after math club. At first, his father had insisted on giving him a ride. It was only after Hunter agreed to go straight home, stay on the roads and not take the shortcut through the park, and switch coats with his father so he would be 'plenty warm,' that he was finally allowed to make the twenty-minute walk by himself. Hunter understood it was difficult for his father, but he needed some time alone. His dad had done nothing but hover these past few weeks and it was too much. He needed time to himself. He wanted to think about his mom. He needed to remember the good times. The happy times. Not the murder. It seemed that whenever he closed his eyes, all he could see was the way she was slumped over the chair in the office, her hair hanging down, blood pooling on the floor. He didn't want to think of her that way. He wanted to remember her happy, smiling, alive.

He nuzzled his mouth further into his scarf and tucked his gloved hands into his pockets. He crossed Maple Street and headed down Sycamore. It wasn't late but the street was empty. The frigid air and stale snow made everything seem baron. The night was quiet and clear. He looked up. Stars were shining in the black sky and for just a moment he wondered if one of those stars could be his mother watching over him. Then he felt the tears well up in his eyes. Of course his mother wasn't a star. A star was nothing more than a luminous ball of gas held together by gravity.

He continued walking, his head low, watching his feet as he moved forward one step at a time. He didn't hurry. He liked the peacefulness that surrounded him. Every time his mind tried to picture his mother slouched in that damn chair in the office, he forced a different memory to replace it. A happy memory, like the time when he was eight and he wanted to be in the talent show at school.

All the kids in Hunter's class were going to be in the Cayne Elementary Talent Show and Hunter didn't want to be left out. The problem was, he couldn't sing or dance and he had no special skill to perform. Some of the other students were doing gymnastics. A few were playing musical instruments. Three of the girls got together to perform a cheer routine. Hunter didn't have anything. Upset, sure he wouldn't be able to be in the show, he looked at his mother and cried. "What am I supposed to do? Recite science facts?"

Jody smiled. "That's exactly what you can do, but with a twist."

Jody proceeded to help him put together an entire act where Hunter would provide interesting facts about science by using humor. For example, he gave the definition of gravity. Then he would follow it with a silly joke. "Last night I was reading the best book ever about gravity. I couldn't put it down." His comedy sketch was a hit and not one other kid had anything like it.

Just thinking about his performance made Hunter laugh out loud as he walked alone down the dark street. Once he was laughing, the good memories poured into his mind. He could see his mother in the kitchen making his favorite meal. She was a fantastic cook. No restaurant food for her family. She made everything from scratch. In the summer she would use vegetables from the huge garden she had in the backyard. How many times she would yell, "Hunter, run outside and see if there is a big, green pepper to pick." Or, "Check the garden for some tomatoes and cucumbers please." And how he loved the desserts she would whip up. Apple pie or brownies or his favorite, chocolate cheesecake. He wondered if he would ever be able to eat chocolate cheesecake again.

Then he thought about the dance parties they used to have in the living room. Sometimes his dad would join in and the three of them would leap around in their pajamas to the tunes of Billy Joel or The Beach Boys. How they would laugh on those nights. He remembered decorating Christmas trees and racing down the stairs early in the morning to find his Easter basket and blowing out candles on his birthday cake every year. Every single Mother's Day his dad would let him pick out a bouquet of flowers to bring to his mother. He never imagined he would be bringing a bouquet to her grave.

He quickly pushed that thought from his mind. Instead, he focused on more recent times when he and his parents would watch scary movies together. The music would get tense and his mom would grab a pillow and cover her eyes. Then Hunter would yell and she would scream and his dad would laugh.

As he walked, head down and lost in his memories, Hunter could almost hear the roar of his father's deep laugh in the distance. He could feel his teeth starting to ache from the cold as he smiled beneath his scarf. Then he noticed the roar getting louder. That's odd, he thought. Why would my dad's laugh get louder? Suddenly he realized that the sound he was hearing wasn't a laugh at all. It was a roar. The roar of an engine. And it was getting louder. Too loud. It didn't fit in with this quiet neighborhood street.

The smile left his face and he turned to see two headlights closing in far too quickly in back of him. The car was coming directly toward him. Instead of slowing down, it appeared to be speeding up. He could hear the engine revving like the driver was pushing harder on the gas pedal. For an instant, Hunter froze, finally understanding the adage, 'deer in the headlights.'

The car was almost upon him when Hunter finally sprang into action. He turned to run but the street was straight for at least another fifty feet. The car was too close. He would never make it to the intersection.

Without further thought, he jumped over the snowbank, slamming his face on the frozen surface of the sidewalk. He didn't take time to stand; he half crawled, half crab-walked up the nearest driveway. He did not stop until he was hiding between the car that was parked in that driveway and the garage. At the same time a light in the yard came on. Maybe the person inside the house heard the noise and turned the light on, maybe it was a motion detector. Hunter didn't know. Either way, he was thankful. The car that just tried to run him over didn't turn around and come back, it continued down the street into the blackness.

Shaking and too scared to move from his hiding place, Hunter reached into the chest pocket of his parka and pulled out his cell phone. "Dad! Dad, come pick me up! Please, hurry!"

21 BETH

It was too late to hang up, the phone was already ringing. I'm being silly, Beth thought as she debated on sticking a second gummy into her mouth. Delaney agreed it was a good idea, and we have to do something. This family needs to pull together. After what happened to Jody, and what could have happened to Hunter, something is terribly wrong. We need to support each other. To talk, to reunite. To remember that we are a family. The phone stopped ringing and she heard Samantha's voice. "Hello."

"Samantha, hi. It's me. Beth."

As usual, Samantha's tone was cool, but her words were friendly enough. "Hello. How are you doing?"

"I'm okay. As good as can be with everything that has been happening. How are you holding up?"

"I'm fine."

Beth wished Samantha would have stopped there, but she didn't. Instead, her voice hardened and she added, "Derek and Raegan are busy, as always. I'm anxious for Chelsie to be home for the summer. Raegan has been helping me around the house as much as possible. Things are back to normal, at least as normal as can be expected. There, are we all caught up? Can we hang up now?"

Typical Samantha, Beth thought. She always has to come across so negative. Beth briefly wondered why Samantha was like that, but she always came to the same conclusion. Samantha was unhappy with her life, and instead of doing something about it, she took it out on others. What she needed to do was dump her sleazebag of a husband. What she did was cry and complain to her poor, impressionable daughters. But this was not the time to think about Samantha's issues. Instead, she ignored Samantha's sarcasm and replied, "Oh, let's not hang up yet. We're trying to get back to normal, too. Jerry is busy at the garage. Gage is playing baseball. Grace changed her mind about acting in the school play this year and decided to work behind the scenes instead. I think she's struggling but trying to stay busy. That's why I called. I think we need to get the family together. It would be good for everyone."

"Seriously? A family party? You think that would be a good thing?" Samantha sighed loudly into the phone. After a minute she said, "What do you have in mind?"

Again, Beth ignored the irritation in Samantha's voice. She expected it. "Next Friday night, a potluck supper at Delaney's. She has more room. What do you think? Can you, Derek and the girls make it?"

"If it's at Delaney's, why didn't she call to invite me herself? Is she too good to call me or do you just like doing all her dirty work?"

"She didn't call because I'm the one who thought of it. It's my party. I'm only having it at her house because she has so much more room than I do. Don't turn this into something it's not. Now, can you come?"

After a few seconds of silence, followed by another loud sigh, Samantha responded. "I'll have to check with Derek. I'm not the kind of wife that speaks for her husband without talking to him first, but most likely, sure, we will be there. What time?"

Beth rolled her eyes but managed to keep any hint of sarcasm out of her voice. Samantha spoke for everyone, Derek included. She was just being difficult because Delaney didn't call her. "How about 6:00?"

"That sounds fine. Friday at six. We'll plan on being there, unless Derek has other plans. I'll bring a taco casserole. That work?"

"I was hoping you would volunteer to bring that. Sounds perfect. See you then!"

The two sisters said their goodbyes and disconnected from their cell phones. Beth stared at hers, shaking her head in disbelief before finally laying it down on the counter. Lord forgive her, but nine times out of ten she hated calling Samantha. Still, it went much smoother than anticipated, she thought. She then added the dish that Samantha said she would bring to the yellow pad of paper she had been writing on.

She knew Samantha would bring enough taco salad to serve twice as many people as were attending. That, plus the bean salad from Grey, along with the pizza and wings that Delaney agreed to supply, should be enough food. Beth had volunteered to provide all the drinks and desserts; maybe even an appetizer or two. There would likely be more; people always showed up carrying random food items that they hadn't told her about. Daddy and Adeline would bring something, although she didn't ask them to. She felt they should be exempt from her task list. Even if they didn't, there would be more than enough to feed everyone. One less thing to worry about.

Normally she would plan games and maybe door prizes for a party, but she decided that wouldn't be wise this time. This was the first family gathering since the funeral and she didn't think it should be too festive. It was more important to give everyone an opportunity to talk and reconnect and maybe let each other know how they have been dealing with the loss of Jody. Then there was the whole Hunter thing. Beth still couldn't believe it. Someone actually tried to run Hunter over with their car! Who would do such a thing? It was obvious, at least to her, that whoever killed Jody was now trying to kill Hunter. Who had it out for the Terrel family? She had talked to Grey about it but he didn't have a clue who hated his family that much. He seemed to be in a perpetual state of shock, and from what she gathered, he didn't let Hunter out of his site now. That was another reason she wanted to have this family get-together. It

151

might give Grey and Hunter a chance to relax, at least for an evening.

It was bad enough losing Jody, but knowing that the murderer was out there and still after members of her family was almost too much to bear. She wondered if this would be discussed next Friday night. If everyone got together and talked about it, would they be able to figure out who killed Jody? Or who might be after Hunter? Individually they didn't know, but as a family, could they piece it together?

So far Detective Holmes didn't have the answer, at least he hadn't arrested anyone yet. Beth was getting more uncomfortable with this every day. She was afraid to let Gage and Grace go anywhere. After all, if someone was after Hunter, who's to say they wouldn't be after her children, too? She tried to talk to Jerry, but he told her to leave it up to Detective Holmes. If anyone was going to figure it out, he would. He also insisted that no one was after them; it was something to do with Grey's family, and only Grey's family. Beth was not comforted by this. How did Jerry know?

She tried to talk to Delaney about the murder and attempted murder. Delaney wasn't much help, either. While she couldn't deny that Jody had been murdered, Delaney fell short of believing someone attempted to kill Hunter. She was more of the attitude that a car slid on an icy street and Hunter's imagination played tricks on him. She insisted that, under the circumstances, she didn't blame him. After all, he was walking home alone at night, and his mother had just been murdered. Of course his mind would jump to that conclusion. She didn't actually believe someone made an attempt on his life. "We have all been a little jumpy, a little paranoid, these days," Delaney had said to her.

The attitudes of both Jerry and Delaney did nothing but annoy Beth. She thought they were both being far too lackadaisical about the danger they could all be in. She tried to explain her fears to them, but they disregarded her concerns. Still, both Gage and Grace had strict curfews. Neither of them was allowed to be out alone and she had to know where they were every minute of every day. Grace didn't seem to mind, but Gage was not as willing to participate with her rules. It was only when she threatened to put a tracker on his cell phone that he became more cooperative about his whereabouts.

22 DELANEY

The whole idea of a family party was stupid, but Delaney didn't have the heart to say that to Beth. Beth was trying to bring everyone together. Instead, Delaney offered to have the party at her house. It was much more suited to entertaining than Beth's house. She had a bigger kitchen, a game room that would give the kids someplace to go to escape the adults, and if it wasn't too cold, a gorgeous deck with a gas firepit and a view of the distant mountains. Yes, her house was much better than Beth's small Cape Cod.

Delaney had a lot of things that were different from her sisters, and it wasn't just that she and Jack were more financially successful than Samantha, Beth or Jody. There was something deeper than that, something that kept her from being as close to her sisters as they were to each other. When it came to the three of them, she gravitated mostly to Beth, but overall, there was a distance there that she was never able to overcome. She often wondered if that was because she was a half-sister, or if it was because of the way they were raised. Nature or nurture, she wondered. Probably a bit of both.

She knew early on she never quite fit in. Take their names, for example. Samantha Violet, Beth Magnolia, and Jody Dahlia. All three of them had a pretty flower for their middle name. And what did Delaney have? Bay. Her middle name was Bay. Not a luscious flower, but a body of water. Or a leaf. Or a place where you park a truck. Even worse, her father chose it because when he was little, he had a horse with reddish-brown hair. When Delaney was born, she had a fuzzy patch of red hair that reminded him of his horse— a bay mare. Her sisters were all named after the most beautiful thing nature had to offer. She was named after a horse. Great way to start on the old self-esteem, name the tiny infant girl after a horse.

But that wasn't the only reason she felt differently. As she got older, she started to outgrow her sisters. She was taller than both Beth and Jody and she had the longest legs. They used to make fun of her for it. They called her 'spider-legs' because she was so tall and gangly. They thought they were being funny. In reality, they were just adding to her poor self-esteem, making her believe that tall and lanky was a bad thing.

Her sisters all had standard hair colors. Beth was a natural blond. Samantha and Jody both had chestnut brown hair, except when Jody dyed hers to match Beth's. No one ever tried to match Delaney's strawberry blond hair. Beth and Samantha had hazel eyes. Jody had beautiful chocolatey-brown eyes. Delaney's were green.

The other three were popular in school and had many friends. Delaney was a loner. While Delaney had better grades and was more successful academically than the others, that was of little consolation to a teenage girl who longed to have a date for the dance on a Friday night like her sisters always did.

Yes, Delaney felt at odds with her sisters as far back as she could remember. That difference was ever-present with Samantha and Jody, but with Beth, not as much. Somehow, they managed to bridge the gap and find a way to get closer. To be more like real sisters. You might even say friends. So, when Beth said she wanted to have a party to try and unite the family in the wake of tragedy, Delaney felt she had no choice but to say yes. Then, to show her seal of approval, she offered up her house. Of course, there was an ulterior motive. Having the party at her house would also give her a place to escape. It would be so much easier to sneak away to her bedroom for a break when she had enough of Samantha's whining or Grey's crying or everyone's incessant complaining.

It's not that Delaney didn't love her family. She did. She had lots of fond memories of all of them. She just didn't get along with them as well as she wanted. Especially her sisters. As much as she hated to admit it, she was never that close to Jody or Samantha. That's not to say there were never any good times. There were a few. She closed her eyes and forced her mind to drift back to her childhood, sorting through different times, different events, until she remembered a particular summer day when all she wanted was ice-cream.

It must have been July, or maybe August, and it was hot. All Delaney could think about was how badly she wanted to go to the little drug store on Pine Street and have an ice-cream sundae. Chocolate ice-cream, a banana, whipped topping, jimmies (or if you grew up someplace other than Maine, sprinkles), and a cherry. She was trying not to cry when her mother was too busy to take her, but then her big sister, Samantha, said she would bring her. She held Delaney by the hand and walked her several blocks until they got to the little drug store that had an old-fashioned bar where one could order light lunches and ice-cream treats. She let Delaney order exactly the kind of ice-cream sundae she wanted. They talked about school and all the fun that summer brought and how they wished their mother would let them have a puppy. Typical stuff for a 6-year-old and a young teenager. When they were done, Samantha dipped Delaney's napkin in her water glass and used it to wipe the chocolate off Delaney's smiling face. Then Samantha paid the check, held Delaney's hand, and walked her back home. It was a wonderful afternoon that still stood out as a highlight in Delaney's mind.

Unfortunately, those types of moments with Samantha were far-and-few between, and as they got older, they were almost nonexistent. They were replaced with arguments and tense moments over their differences in lifestyles and raising children and other life choices. Delaney was sure that most of Samantha's bitchiness was a result of her unhappiness. After all, Samantha and Derek had a pretty bad marriage.

157

Everyone knew that Derek couldn't keep it in his pants, and Samantha just sat home and let it happen. And if that wasn't bad enough, he was a terrible father to those poor daughters of his. He never bothered with either one of them. He was always too busy with work, or at least that was the story he told them. Honestly, why Samantha didn't dump that loser husband of hers, Delaney couldn't understand. Still, that was no reason to treat everyone else the way she did. Delaney may understand why Samantha was so bitchy, but that didn't mean she wanted to be around it.

It was different with Jody. They were closer in age and had more interaction; they just didn't share many interests. Jody was an athlete, while Delaney basically had two left feet. Jody played soccer and softball and in between the two, she cheered for the boy's hockey team. Delaney, on the other hand, tripped walking up the stairs. What Delaney did do well was understand all of her subjects in school. She was a straight A student, taking mostly advanced level courses. She loved to read and write and never needed to study for a test. Still, when she and Jody were together, Delaney only saw the things that Jody could do and she could not, never the other way around. Because of these differences, and probably a multitude of other things that both sisters were too young to understand, the two never became as close as they might have under other circumstances.

Once the news broke about Jody being a half-sister, Delaney saw her as a threat. Jody was already cuter and more fun than she was. Now, Delaney realized, Jody would likely be coming after half of their mother's inheritance that she alone was supposed to receive. It was hard enough for Jody to sign off on that inheritance when she thought she would be receiving millions when Paul, her father, died. Once Jody realized that could be taken away from her, surely she would insist on sharing in her mother's money.

The way it was right now, before that DNA test result came out, the three whole sisters had agreed that Delaney could keep all the money from their mother, a sum of around five hundred thousand dollars. It was enough money to pay off the real estate mistakes that Delaney had made, as well as some other money that Delaney didn't want to think about. That additional debt could remain her little secret. Jack would never know. But once Jody realized she was not Paul's daughter, everything would change. She would understand that she would no longer be entitled to Paul's inheritance, which was significantly more than what their mother had left behind. Paul's money would be split between only Samantha and Beth. Since Jody would be out of Paul's will, certainly she would be filing for half of their mother's money right away, much faster than Delaney could get the final paperwork completed with her lawyer. Then Delaney would not have enough money to pay off her massive debt and still tell Jack that they had received a nice sum of money from her mother's inheritance. Jack would find out about her secret. Then what would he do? Sell their home? Divorce her? Take the kids and leave her? No, she couldn't risk any of that. She couldn't let Jody have that money. She needed to push the finalization of the will through before Jody could get her hands on it. She felt bad, but honestly, they weren't all that close to begin with. And she was sure, given the same circumstances, Jody would not have hesitated to do the same thing to her.

23 HOLMES

Ronan had been busy since the funeral. He was able to rule a few people out as suspects, and so far, he only had a short list of potentials. No one person was jumping out as Jody's killer and this troubled him. Usually, by now his instinct had kicked in and he knew who did it. It was only a matter of proving his suspicion. This time he still wasn't sure. He stared at his pad and chewed on the end of his pencil. Frustration was gnawing at his insides.

After the funeral, his short list included only four people. First was Samantha, because of her lack of ability to get along with the other sisters. There was an aloofness about her. He sensed she had secrets, although he was completely unaware as to what they could be. There were some internal things going on within her own family. It didn't take much to know that some, if not all of those things, were tied to her relationship with Derek.

Then there was Beth. She came across as the sweetest of the sisters. She was the kindhearted, cookie-making, gentle soul who was the head of the PTA and volunteered at the local rescue shelter. On paper, she looked like a saint, but the one thing that stood out with her was her overbearing, almost abnormal mothering of Gage. If this characteristic covered both of her children, he wouldn't be suspicious. Because she so obviously favored her son, he felt like it was obsessive, perhaps even compulsive. Once words like obsessive and compulsive came to mind, he wanted to know more about what was happening in a person's head.

There was also something about Gage that bothered him. He wasn't sure what it was; he had to find a way to spend more time with the boy. Preferably without his parents.

Ronan's instinct, or simply the facts of the case, also told him that he needed to further verify Delaney's alibi for the night of Jody's murder. She was able to account for her evening, but there were gaps.

Ronan leaned back in his chair and closed his eyes, clasping his hands together over his stomach. Why would someone try to kill Hunter, he asked himself for the one-hundredth time. With Jody, there was potential for financial gain for a couple of different people, but that gain did not exist with Hunter. What motive did anyone have for killing him? Ronan went over it in his mind again and again, but he always came back to only two possibilities.

First, could Hunter and Gage have had some kind of argument? Ronan knew there was bad blood between the two. Was it bad enough that Gage would try to run him over? Or Beth? That seemed like a reach, but Beth was obsessively protective of Gage.

The other possibility, which was probably the more likely of the two, was that no one tried to kill Hunter. Hunter mistook a car that slid on an ice patch as an intentional threat on his life. After all, the boy just experienced the gruesome murder of his mother and he knew the killer was still out there. It would be an easy mistake to make. No one would blame Hunter for jumping to that conclusion. Ronan would not share that theory with the family, but it was the one that made the most sense.

Opening his eyes, Ronan again picked up his notepad and pencil, ticking off each of the people he needed to check into. He still needed to check with Wes to see what everyone's financial records looked like. Wes was also putting together phone records on a few of the suspects, just to make sure they were where they said they were on the night of the murder. In the meantime, Ronan would pay Samantha Anderson a visit.

24 SAMANTHA

The truth was staring her in the face. She knew it. She could feel it with every fiber of her being. It was just like the first time, and the time after that, and the time after that. Only this time she wasn't going to pretend everything was alright. She refused to be a doormat again. Her nights of crying herself to sleep were over. This time she was going to do something about it. But what?

It was late as she sat in the kitchen, alone. Chelsie was at school and Raegan was upstairs on her phone, or playing some morbid computer game about zombies or dragons or evil overlords. Samantha's fingers circled her mug of tea, gently tapping the side of her cup. Her eyes were open but not focused on anything in front of her. She was remembering the first time Derek had an affair. Of course, she couldn't prove it. She never followed him or confronted him or did any of the things she should have done back then, but she knew. A wife always knows.

It must have been seventeen years ago. They were still at the house on Primrose Avenue when she first became suspicious. No, not suspicious. She was sure he was cheating on her. It wasn't anything specific. She didn't find ticket stubs in his pocket or lipstick on his collar. That would have been too cliché. He wasn't running into the other room to take secret telephone calls. There wasn't an increase in business trips or extra charges on the credit cards. He just seemed different, detached. It was a subtle difference. At first, she thought it was her imagination, but slowly, as other little things crept in and they added up, she knew.

He stopped talking to her as much. He never wanted to do anything; no matter what she suggested, he said he was tired. He worked longer hours. Finally, when Derek again refused her advances toward him in the bedroom, she found the nerve to confront him with her suspicion.

He was lying on his back next to her, eyes open, staring at the ceiling. The only light was coming from the lamp next to the bed. Samantha had clicked it back on after he gently pushed her aside telling her he was tired. The light cast an eerie yellow glow across his face, making his skin take on a deathlike pallor. She stared at him, but said nothing. She was sure he could feel the intensity of her eyes. He didn't blink. He didn't move. His chest barely rose and fell with his breath. He was waiting for her to speak.

When she did, her voice was soft. "Derek, look at me."

His head turned. He gazed directly into her eyes. A slight bead of sweat formed above his lip but he said nothing.

"Derek, I have to know. Have you found someone else?"

He turned toward her. His gaze never faltered. He didn't

look away as he shook his head ever so slightly. "No."

Samantha waited for him to say more, but he remained silent. Her question had been answered, but she knew it was a lie. Her heart went cold inside. How could he lie so easily?

Turning on her side, she clicked off the light and lay unmoving for hours. Eventually she heard the steady sound of his breathing indicating he was asleep. When he got up in the morning, she didn't move, feigning sleep, but she hadn't slept a wink all night. He was cheating on her. She was sure.

He went to work and she continued with her routine, but the pain in her heart was overwhelming. She found it difficult to function, crying even more than her toddler daughter did. Then there was a knock on her door and she found herself pouring her entire heartache out to a dear friend. They clung to each other. It gave her the strength to get through the darkest time of her life.

Samantha was at a crossroads and she decided enough was enough. Lying in bed next to Derek, she leaned in close and kissed him, not giving him a chance to come up with any of his pathetic excuses. She decided if she was going to lose him, it wouldn't be without a fight. At first, he was reluctant, but she pushed into him closer, harder, and it wasn't long before he responded. They made love for the first time in months, and when they fell asleep, it was with her head tucked into the soft spot between his chest and his shoulder. His arms wrapped around her and she felt safe, happy in a way that she hadn't been for a very long time.

She had won him back; she was sure of it. He started paying attention to her again. He was around the house more often. He played with Chelsie in the evening and joined in family conversations. He was home from work shortly after five most *nights. And six weeks later when Samantha told him she was expecting, he agreed to go house hunting with her. After all, with an expanding family, they would need a bigger home. Everything seemed perfect.*

Over the years, Samantha had wondered what caused Derek to change. She knew he had grown away from her and even Chelsie, and suddenly he was back. On the darkest days, she figured there had been another woman, and when the woman left him, he came back to her. She was nothing more than a consolation prize. When those thoughts occurred, Samantha found the strength to force them into a deep corner of her mind where they would stay buried and she wouldn't have to think about them. Instead she would focus on how Derek behaved after that night, after he found out she was pregnant. There was a time when he was home more, he was more attentive, he had helped her to pick out a new house for their growing family. Did it matter that she saw a distance in his eyes that she had never noticed before? That had probably been just her imagination. She needed to learn to stop worrying and let herself be happy.

But here she was, sitting in her cheery white and yellow kitchen with daisy print wallpaper, and the same feeling that she had all those years ago was back in her heart. The same feeling that had haunted her so many times during her marriage was preying on her again. Only this time was going to be different. This time she wasn't the naïve young mother she was the first time, or even the forgiving, middle-aged wife she had grown into. This time she was going to find out exactly what was going on with her husband. She was fed up with playing the role of the fool. She had played it all too well over the years, and she was done. Damn it, she was nobody's fool. She spent so many years wondering and second-guessing herself because she never looked into what he was up to. She wasn't going to spend the next twenty years doing the same thing. This time she was going to find out. Starting right now.

She slipped off her robe and tossed it on the bed in her room. She changed into black yoga pants and a gray sweater. Then she pulled on boots and grabbed a coat from the hall closet. Leaving her tea on the table, she called up to Raegan, who probably didn't hear her over the rumble of a battle she was fighting on her computer. "Be right back. Need to run to the store." Then she started up the Toyota that was parked on her side of the garage and backed out, making sure the door closed behind her. She didn't head toward the grocery store. Instead she drove to her husband's office to see if his car was in the parking lot since he was working late. Again.

25 BETH

Beth was tired and ready to go to bed. She rinsed her wine glass in the sink, turned off the kitchen light and joined Jerry in his office. Gage and Grace had been upstairs sleeping for hours, but Jerry continued sorting through ubiquitous stacks of paperwork and she didn't want to leave him alone. Even though his tax deadline had been extended, she knew he didn't want to put off getting the documents together so he could drop them off with the accountant. Next year he was hoping to have everything computerized, but that was next year. That hope was of no use to them right now.

She glanced at the clock and noted it was just after midnight. He had been at this for over four hours straight, not counting the previous nights he sat at this same desk doing the same tedious sorting. Finally, she thought with a sigh of relief, he paper-clipped the last stack of invoices together and added them to the rather large pile of random documents he had accumulated. He was done. Thank the Lord, she thought to herself.

Tomorrow, he would drop it off at his accountant's office and pay some exorbitant tax bill that they couldn't afford, but at least it would be done.

Beth watched as Jerry stood up and stretched. He seemed to enjoy the sensation after having sat in the same position for the last four hours. She knew that Jerry was not a desk kind of guy; he preferred more of a moving around, hands on lifestyle.

"You ready to head upstairs?" she asked.

"You bet. I'm exhausted." He smiled at her as he walked around the desk toward the door. Just as he reached to turn the overhead light off, he felt his cell phone vibrate deep in his jeans pocket. "You go on up, Beth. I want to check one more thing. I'll be right there."

Beth, already part way up the stairs and too tired to wonder what he had to look into, continued to their room. "I'll leave the light on for you," she called over her shoulder.

Jerry went back into the office and pulled his cell phone out of his pocket. Who would be calling me at this hour, he thought. He glanced at the screen and saw Delaney's name flash across in dull blue letters. Shit, he thought, this can't be good.

He quietly pushed the office door closed and as softly as possible so as not to disturb Beth, he practically whispered into his phone, "Hello."

"Jerry, it's me. Delaney. Is this a bad time?"

"It's midnight. What do you think? Do you have the money?"

"No. Not yet. But I'm working on it. You know

I'm good for it."

"Delaney, I told you, I can't keep putting him off. He wants his money and he wants it now."

"I know, Jerry. And I should have had it by now. I talked to my lawyer and everything should have been finalized. But then Jody, and the whole DNA thing, it slowed down the entire process."

"Shit, Delaney. That was weeks ago. You said you were taking care of it."

"I know, and I am, but it takes time."

"You don't have any more time."

"I need more. I mean, what the fuck do you want me to do, Jerry? I don't have the money right now. I said I would get it and I will, but it's going to be at least another week. Maybe two."

"What about Jack? Can't you get it from him?"

"Jack doesn't know. I can't tell him. He'll be furious."

"Furious is better than dead."

Delaney remained silent and several minutes passed. Her breathing could be heard on the phone but she didn't speak. Finally, her voice cracked as she said, "What about your family savings account? Do you think you could pull money out of that without Beth noticing? You know I would pay you back."

"You want me to lie to Beth?"

"You wouldn't be lying. You would just not tell her that I borrowed a little money. That's all."

"A little money? I don't consider six digits to be a little money, Delaney. And if it's so easy to lie about it, go to Jack. I'm done covering for you."

"Jerry, please."

"No, don't Jerry me. We're done. I'm not lying for you anymore. Get the money, and get it now. Do you understand? He won't keep waiting, and I'm not covering for you again." Jerry hit the red end button on his phone. The mellow feeling that had started to come over him when he had finished the tax paperwork was now gone. He could feel anxiety well up inside of him, swearing under his breath as he began pacing the floor.

What was he going to do? His bookie wanted his money and Delaney didn't have it. He was caught in the middle. It wasn't his fault she was desperate, but until tonight he didn't realize how desperate. His bookie wasn't kidding about wanting his money and he was willing to go to any length to get it. He didn't care that Delaney said she was good for it. He was going to teach her a lesson. Delaney knew this and still, she would not go to Jack. She was willing to take the risk. Jerry was worried. What else was she willing to do?

26 GAGE

Gage sat in the dark car in the driveway wondering why the downstairs lights were still on this late. It was after midnight. His parents were usually asleep by ten or eleven at the latest. When he had snuck out of the house several hours ago, they were both in the office fully engrossed in the company taxes. He had told them he was going to do some homework and then he would go to sleep. Instead, he quietly slipped out the front door. They were both so wrapped up in their lives, they never even heard the door close behind him. Now, sitting in the cold car, he would have to wait until whoever was up went to bed before he attempted to sneak back into the house. He managed to be gone all evening; he didn't want to get caught now.

He felt bad lying to his parents, but he had to get away. He couldn't take the constant surveillance by his mother. She wouldn't leave him alone. Where are you going, Gage? Who are you going to be with tonight? What are you doing? When will you be home? God, she was driving him crazy. He understood she was worried because of what happened to Aunt Jody and Hunter, but shit, she couldn't keep watch over him twenty-four hours a day. She wasn't even as strict with Grace as she was with him. It was insane.

When he first left, he drove around by himself. It felt so good to be alone, no one watching his every move. He expected his cell phone to go off with his mother yelling for him to return home immediately, but it didn't. She didn't know he was gone. Relief washed over him and he felt free for the first time in weeks.

Feeling rebellious, he headed to Burger King. He wasn't hungry, but eating a greasy whopper and fries just sounded right. Not wanting the car to pick up a fast-food smell, he went inside and placed his order. There were a few other people inside; four high-school kids at one booth, a middle-aged couple sharing another, two different men eating alone at the other side of the restaurant, and a few employees behind the counter. No one was paying any attention to him and no one looked too threatening. God, he couldn't believe that's what he was thinking. His mother must be getting to him.

He picked up his tray and sat at a booth in the far corner of the restaurant where he could observe anyone who came in or out. He practically inhaled his food, grease dripping down his chin from the oversized burger. He grabbed a napkin from the tray and wiped it off, then stuffed the last few French fries into his mouth. Everything tasted delicious. It was only a little after nine, way too early to go home.

Brushing the salt from his fingers on his pants, he hesitated only a moment before he picked up his cell phone and sent a text that consisted of only one word.

hey

Almost immediately, he could see three little dots appear.

hey to u. whats up

at bk eating a whopper. u s/b here. lol

Gage stared at his phone but no more text messages appeared. He picked up his tray and brought it to the trash can, dumping the contents and putting it on the rack. He then pushed through the glass door and headed back to his car, disappointed that the conversation was short. Just as he settled inside, his phone began to vibrate. Shit, he thought to himself, his mother realized he was gone. He wasn't sure if he was more upset that he was going to be in trouble or that he would have to go home now. He wasn't ready to be back in that house, which had begun to feel more like a prison than a home. He pulled his phone out of his jeans pocket and said hello.

"Hey, it's me. Seemed kind of silly to keep texting when we could talk."

Relief flooded through Gage's mind and a smile played on his lips. "I guess that's why I'm the good looking one in this relationship. You've got the brains."

Snickering could be heard over the phone. "I can't believe your mother let you out alone. How the hell did you manage that?"

"Easy. She doesn't know."

"Seriously? You snuck out?"

"I had to. I couldn't take it anymore."

"So, if I told you I was on my way to meet you, would that be okay? Since you're already sneaking around."

"Are you? I mean, that would be great. I'd love to see you."

"Ya, I'm heading now. But instead of BK, why don't we meet in the parking lot behind the football field? It should be empty this late. And a little more private."

"Sure, I'll go there now."

"By the way, did you ever tell the police that you were with me the night that your aunt was killed? Remember, they wanted to know why you left the hockey game and you said you told them you went outside, but you didn't tell them where you went?"

"No, I didn't think it was any of their business. They haven't asked again, so I think our secret is safe."

"You know that your dorky cousin knows about us, right?"

"What are you talking about?"

"You know, your cousin. The one with glasses that goes to our school. The one you make fun of. He was at the hockey game."

"Hunter?"

"Ya, Hunter."

"What makes you think he knows about us?"

"For one thing, he saw us that night in the parking lot. He was only out there for a minute, but he saw us. Trust me, he knows."

"Shit."

"Don't worry, Gage. If he was going to say something, he would have said it by now."

Gage pulled into the furthest space of the school's parking lot by the football field. Good timing, he thought, as another vehicle's headlights came down the access road to the same parking lot. He could feel the excitement rise as the blue Ford Ranger got closer. He hated being this anxious, but he couldn't wait to open the passenger door, jump in, and wrap his arms around the driver. With his mother's constant surveillance, there had not been many opportunities to do this.

The truck parked and Gage could hear the distinct sound of the front doors being unlocked. He smiled as he reached for the door handle and pulled it open, raising himself into the cab of the truck. It was warm inside, in harsh contrast to the cold night air. Without hesitation, he reached over and pulled the driver close to him. The two were quickly wrapped in an intense hug and a long, passionate kiss.

"Tyler," Gage sighed, "I've missed you so much."

27 GRACE

Grace was pissed. She couldn't believe what she was seeing as she stood at her bedroom window looking out over the street. Gage was sneaking out of the house. At least, she assumed he was sneaking by the way he was walking down the front stairs practically on his tiptoes. She watched as he slowly pulled the car handle up as if trying not to let it click. Then he slid into the driver's seat and gently pulled the door closed, careful not to slam it. He didn't even turn the headlights on until he was halfway down the block. Unbelievable. The golden boy snuck out of the house. She didn't think he ever did anything wrong.

She wondered what her mother would say if she told her what she just saw. How would she be able to spin that, Grace thought, to make Gage still come out looking like the perfect son? But she wouldn't tell on him. It wasn't his fault that their mother favored him over her. He knew it and he didn't like it, either. He was sick to death of his mother constantly hovering over him. Grace knew he wished she would just leave him alone.

Grace let the curtain drop when she could no longer see the brake lights of their mother's car. She wondered where Gage was heading. She was tempted to call him but didn't want to risk their mother hearing her. She wouldn't do anything that would cause Gage to get caught. He deserved a night of freedom. Honestly, it wasn't anger that she was feeling. If anything, she was jealous. Once again, he comes out ahead. He gets a night of freedom while she's stuck at home.

She sat back on her bed and kicked her slippers off, the cool air forcing her to tuck her cold feet under the covers on her bed. The warmth brought by her heavy yellow comforter felt good and helped her to relax. She leaned back and closed her eyes. Why does her mother like Gage so much more than she likes me, she wondered. I never get in trouble, I help more around the house, I do better in school, and still, it's always Gage this and Gage that. Why? Why does her mother always prefer Gage?

The first time she clearly remembered noticing this preference was on a sunny day in July. Grace and Gage couldn't have been more than five or six years old. The family had gone to the beach —Beth, Jerry, Grace and Gage. Beth liked to dress the children alike because they were twins; that day they wore red and blue bathing suits with white stars.

The two had been playing together building a large sandcastle not too far from where the waves broke along the shoreline. They used an assortment of pails and plastic toys to structure the different towers. Jerry was dozing on a quilt while Beth was reading a book not more than fifteen feet away.

So engrossed were the twins in perfecting their castle that they never noticed the large wave forming just behind them. Without warning, the Atlantic crashed all around them, dragging both twins and their castle out to sea. Luckily, Grace had managed to get one high-pitched shriek out before the water plunged over their heads.

Upon hearing her daughter's scream, Beth glanced up from her book and immediately realized what had happened, causing her to let out a scream of her own. She jumped so quickly to her feet that her chair fell on its side and sand kicked on the quilt where Jerry was fast asleep.

Without hesitation, Beth plunged into the icy water, ignoring the numbness that immediately threatened to cramp her muscles. She forced her legs to move forward, water past her ankles, her knees, her thighs. By the time she was up to her waist and water was rushing back and forth, she was able to reach her children. She stretched and grabbed for Gage, pulling him to her. He was cold and shivering. She wrapped her arms around him tightly, relief flowing through her freezing body. As she started to make her way to the shore, she noticed Jerry fling himself past her, diving headfirst into the water until he had Grace in his arms. The current had been pulling her further out to sea. Beth could hear her sobs as Jerry rescued her from the cold water.

The entire incident only took minutes. Beth and Gage made it back to shore first, soon joined by Jerry and Grace. The two parents wrapped their shivering children in towels that were warm from lying in the sun. They hugged them tightly, each parent thanking God that they were okay. Grace was crying. Gage was *complaining that the castle was gone. Jerry remained quiet, replaying what had just happened in his mind. He wondered if Grace would remember this day, praying she would forget. Ten years later, she remembered every detail, like it was yesterday.*

Grace never blamed Gage for their mother's behavior. It wasn't his fault she acted like that. They talked about it once in a while, or at least they used to. Gage didn't understand it any more than Grace did. He didn't like it and he wished their mother would stop. He didn't try to deny it. That would have been worse. At least he had the decency not to lie to her by pretending it wasn't true when it was so obvious that their mother preferred him. They both realized that their father tried to make up for Beth's unfairness. He went out of his way to make Grace feel loved and cared for. And she did. She knew how special she was to her father. But that could only help so much.

Instead, Grace had spent years trying to be the perfect daughter to win her mother's love. So far, nothing had worked. It seemed that no matter what she did, even if she did it better than Gage, their mother would always prefer him over her. Was it truly that Gage was so much better than she was, or was it something about her mother? Did Beth simply prefer boys over girls?

Grace picked at an errant thread on her quilt and wondered if it would make a difference if her mother knew about Gage's little secret. Would she love her as much as she loved Gage then?

28 THE VISITOR

One thing was certain, I was not going to make so many mistakes again. My commitment was solid, even though I shook when I thought about how bad everything almost went the other night. How the fuck could I have been so stupid? I had almost run over Hunter! Not Grey, but Hunter! I mean, that would have been awful. I never would have forgiven myself if I had killed Hunter, and for no reason. No reason at all.

I thought I had planned everything out so well. I knew Grey's schedule. He was the one who always walked home. Hunter went to math club and Grey left him the car and walked home. He did this every single week. Grey said he liked to walk; he said it cleared his head. Plus, it gave Hunter some driving time because he had only gotten his license six months ago. So why the fuck was Hunter the one walking that night? And why was Hunter wearing Grey's ugly royal blue coat? Hunter's coat wasn't blue, it was black. Was Hunter trying to look like Grey? I was so relieved that Hunter managed to dodge the car I was driving, and not just because it wasn't Hunter I was trying to kill.

Honestly, looking back I realize that it was not a well thought out plan. Even if it had been Grey like it was supposed to be, there was a good chance he would not have died, but only been injured. His brain could have remained intact and he could have seen me! Then he would have told everyone who was driving. Even worse, he would still have had the chance to follow through on Jody's plan and tell everyone what should remain a secret.

Later that night, even after I knew everything was going to be alright, I couldn't stop shaking. Hunter was fine, but I kept thinking about what I almost did. It made me sick to my stomach. I knew I had to be more careful. I never wanted to hurt Hunter, but I also didn't want to get caught.

I don't think there would have been a problem with the car. It was stolen so it couldn't be traced back to me by the registration, and there wouldn't be fingerprints since I wore gloves. I wore dark, nondescript clothing and a black watch cap to cover my hair to avoid DNA evidence being left behind. I had also checked the parking lot of the apartment building where I took the car for cameras, but I didn't see any on the building or the poles surrounding it. There were no fences there, and not many lights. It wasn't a well-to-do part of town where people would worry about theft of their snooty vehicles. There sure as shit were no Land Rovers or BMWs parked there. Lord knows the one I stole wasn't an expensive vehicle, just an old black Ford. Nothing about it stood out.

I remember thinking if there had been cameras, they could be used to help determine my height, but probably not my weight because I wore an oversize ski parka. I even thought to put a piece of black tape over the brand name to make it more difficult to identify where the jacket came from. I saw that trick on television. It made it harder for the police to know what kind of stores I shopped at.

Of course, none of that mattered now since Hunter had reacted so fast and I missed him completely. Luckily, he was so shaken up that he wasn't able to identify the make or model of the vehicle. For a kid that was supposed to be so fucking smart, he didn't think too well on his feet. I remember putting my hand over my mouth and chuckling over my pun—on his feet. Even then I knew that wasn't funny. I shouldn't have laughed when it popped into my head. I think my nerves were fried. Sometimes when I get nervous, or scared, I laugh. But I wouldn't have been laughing if I had hurt Hunter.

After I missed hitting him, I didn't know what to do so I drove back to the apartments from where I took the car. I parked it back in the same space and hoped that the owner would never even know it had been missing. I had been shaking when I stuck the keys behind the visor where I found them, closed the door, and walked away into the night.

By the time I got back to my own car, I had experienced a mix of emotions. I was so thankful that I hadn't accidently killed Hunter. God, that would have been awful. But I was disappointed that Grey was still alive. He would still be able to tell the secret and cause pain to the one person I am trying to protect.

One thing was for sure, though, I had already formulated a new plan, and I was sure the new plan would not fail. The new plan was so much better than the silly hit-and-run. I had done my homework and I was confident with the decisions I had made. This plan was much smarter than the car escapade. This time, I would be successful in my attempt to kill Grey.

I felt bad, although not as bad as I had when I killed Jody. I mean, it wasn't that I didn't like Grey, I did. But he knew, so he remained a problem. I didn't have a choice. I had to protect the person I love. Wasn't that the right thing to do?

This time, I put a lot of thought into how Grey should die. This was not a spur of the moment plan. I decided my weapon of choice would be poison. Poison was a much cleaner, tidier method of murder than either knives or vehicles, although it definitely required more finesse. I would have to make sure that Grey was the only one to die. I wouldn't want anyone else to accidently ingest the tainted food that was meant for Grey. I mean, this was my family I was talking about. I loved them and I didn't want anyone else to get hurt. It would be hard enough to hurt Grey, but in his case, it was necessary.

I was worried about how I would react when I watched Grey ingest the poison. I kept thinking about how, when I get nervous, I laugh. It's not that I think things are funny, it's just the way I react to stressful situations. It's how I release tension. I'm afraid that when Grey starts to feel the effects of the poison and falls to the floor, I'll burst out laughing instead of displaying the proper emotion. Even though I'll be the cause of him dying, I'll still be horrified. I only hope I can control this laughter, this totally inappropriate response. It's almost like a nervous tick that happens at completely the wrong time. I really don't want to call attention to myself.

Fortunately, there will still be time to practice. I've already spent lots of time in front of the bathroom mirror making sure my facial expressions are appropriate: terror when I realize what is happening, sadness when I understand how serious it is, horror when I comprehend that the killer must be a family member. And the one I rehearsed the most? Confusion for when that detective starts asking questions. I knew I would have to be good with my facial expressions, so I have practiced them a lot. What is it they say? Practice makes perfect.

I tried so hard to think of everything this time. I was cautious when I did my research on poison. I was clever enough not to use my own computer for this. When that cop starts checking search engines, I won't have a problem letting him check mine. It will be clean. My research was done under an anonymous name at a branch of the library in a neighboring town. Again, I'm so thankful that I watch a lot of *Forensic Files* on television.

I have learned so much about poison. Belladonna would have been an awesome one to use. It would only take a single leaf of that highly toxic plant to kill someone, but since that was more popular in the Middle Ages than it is now, I didn't have a clue where to get it.

Hemlock was another poisonous plant that grew in the area, but I didn't know exactly how to use it. Was it cut and mixed with food? Was the root needed? Did it need to be boiled? I didn't know and I couldn't figure it out. After all, I'm not Socrates.

Arsenic was a good choice, but nowadays, I thought it might be too easily detected and treated. There were no guarantees with that one.

The one I found most interesting was strychnine. Strychnine causes paralysis which leads to respiratory failure. That's how it kills. Best of all, my research indicated there was no known antidote. Interestingly enough, strychnine used to be the active ingredient in rat poison. It wasn't anymore, it was replaced with safer toxins. But fortunately, I knew of an old shed where old cupboards contain old boxes of old chemicals, including old containers of rat poison. Lucky for me, I've always been the inquisitive type. Whoever said curiosity kills the cat, should have just said, curiosity kills...

29 JACK

Jack was glad to see Detective Holmes leave. He didn't like the way Detective Holmes could see right through him, like he was translucent and all of his inner thoughts were fully exposed. It's not that he had any secrets. When Holmes asked him about his alibi the night of Jody's murder, he told the truth. He was home with his children. He made them supper, checked their homework and put them to bed. He had an equally substantial alibi for the night someone tried to run Hunter over with their car. Anyway, he didn't drive a sedan. He had a big, four-wheel-drive truck. Hunter would have easily recognized the difference. No, he wasn't trying to hide anything about his whereabouts from the detective. He was more concerned about his wife.

The night of Jody's murder, Delaney had called to say she was on her way home. Then, not too long after, she called to say there had been a change of plans and she was going to be late. She made up some reason he hadn't paid attention to; he had been annoyed that she was working late again. But now he wished he had been more focused. He wished he had known exactly where she said she was going that night. What he really wished was that she had skipped work and come straight home. She was working far too much lately. The kids needed to spend more time with her. Hell, so did he.

He pushed out of the chair behind his desk and walked around the small office, feeling restless ever since Detective Holmes left fifteen minutes ago. He had to get some fresh air. He grabbed his coat from a hook on the back of the door and walked down the short hall and through the lobby, not acknowledging anyone as he headed to the front door. He felt a couple of people stare at him as he walked by but he didn't care. Let them gossip. He had to get out of there.

Once outside he didn't have any place to go, so he headed toward the black Ford truck parked along the building's perimeter. He got inside and started the engine, pulling out of the parking lot like he had an actual destination in mind. It wasn't until he was several blocks away that he started to calm down.

He kept playing the night of the murder over in his mind. Just where had Delaney been that night? She had started to come home around 6:00, called and said her plans changed, and didn't make it home until after 10:00. She had told him she was working, but she was so agitated when she got in, he hadn't asked her anything about the project. Usually when she worked late, she came in cheerful, sometimes even exhilarated. Why hadn't he questioned her more that night?

As he turned left on Broad Street, he chastised himself. What the hell was he saying? Did he think that Delaney killed her sister? Why? For what purpose? And if she had, would she have come back home wearing the same outfit she left the house in without a drop of blood on her? From what he had heard, the crime scene had been a gory mess. Jody's neck had been slit and there was blood everywhere. No, he was being ridiculous. Delaney was not the kind of person who could murder her sister. He had to get these crazy thoughts out of his head.

That was why he was so uncomfortable around Detective Holmes. Not because he did anything wrong, but because of Delaney. In his heart, he knew that his wife could not have murdered her sister. But he did know she was keeping something from him, and he didn't know what that something was. He was sure that Holmes knew it, too. That guy had a sixth sense about him. He could tell when people weren't being completely honest, and he knew Jack was hiding something. Holmes was the kind of detective that wasn't going to stop until he figured out what it was. Jack was sure of that.

Jack drove around the streets of Cayne aimlessly, trying to decide what to do. No matter which road he took, or which way his mind traveled, he always came back to the same thing. He had to talk to Delaney. There was more on his mind than Detective Holmes. He had some pretty major concerns of his own that he had been carrying around. He didn't want to add more to

Delaney's burdens, especially so soon after Jody's murder, but he couldn't keep going on the way he was feeling. He had to talk to her. Maybe if he was one hundred percent honest with her, she would do the same with him.

He wanted to tell her that he loved her. He loved the kids. He was proud of the life they had made, but he wasn't happy. He hadn't been happy for years. He never wanted to run some big building and design company. He didn't care about making millions of dollars and living in a big, fancy house. He didn't want a lake house they never used or a membership at a golf club. He didn't even like golf. He had no interest in designer clothes or fancy cars. If he was honest with himself, he didn't even care about having big bank accounts. None of those things mattered, not if it meant having to sit behind a desk sixty hours a week while his wife worked another sixty. He didn't want his kids to spend more time with nannies than they did with their parents. He hated being a boss and pushing papers all day. He missed building things with his own two hands. God, how he missed that feeling of satisfaction when he was able to solve a problem that no one else could fix, even if it was something as simple as a leaky pipe. He longed for those days. He would give up the company, the money, all of it, just to have time with his wife and kids again. He longed to be the simple man he felt he was destined to be.

The more he thought about it, the more his mind was made up. He would tell Delaney what he wanted, what would make him happy. They could sell Jack Mac Construction. They would surely make a huge profit on the business. After all, it had started with nothing and was now a multimillion-dollar company. Then he would go back to work as a plumber, working regular hours for regular pay. She could continue to design if she wanted, or sell real-estate, but not both. She would have to choose one or the other so she could be home every night with him and the kids. She could even go back to nursing. They would have the proceeds from the sale of the company to fall back on. She wouldn't have to work such long hours. Hell, they could sell their oversized house and buy a nice colonial in a family neighborhood. Did they really need six thousand square feet with a view? They could give up all the extras. He didn't care about them anyway. They could go back to a simple life. A life that offered them more time together. They could be a family again.

Just thinking about this plan made Jack happy. He could feel hope pour into every part of his body. The gray cloud he had been living under was breaking away and the warm sunshine was starting to burn through the darkness. Rays of hope were making him smile. All the pressures of maintaining their wealthy lifestyle were going to vanish. They were going to be comfortable, but not rich. Instead, they were going to be happy.

He needed to talk to Delaney right away, tonight. Jack decided he was going to have her meet him in a restaurant so she would be forced to sit quietly and listen to his plan. He wanted her to stare into his eyes as he talked about their future. He needed her to see the sparkle, the fire that he was sure would emanate from his eyes. He imagined himself holding her hand and recapturing the love he knew was simmering just beneath their busy lives. He moved his thumb toward the button on his steering wheel to call her, but just as he did, the voice in his overhead console announced an incoming call. The call was from Delaney Mackensie.

Jack smiled. It must be fate, he thought as he hit the button that had a diagram of a little telephone and said, "Delaney. I was just getting ready to call you. What's up?"

"Jack," her voice was low, troubled. "Can we meet? We have to talk."

30 SAMANTHA

Traffic was light. Samantha figured most people had enough sense to stay home on a night when the precipitation was undecisive between cold rain or actual ice. She drove slowly, careful not to let the car slide on the slick, wet roads. She traveled north toward Derek's office, unsure what she hoped to find once she arrived. If his car was there, alone in the parking lot, he wasn't lying to her. If the car wasn't there, then his excuse about working late was a cover story and he was probably having an affair. Was that really what she wanted to discover? She would know the truth, but did she want to know? Wouldn't pretending everything was alright be better? She honestly wasn't sure how to answer that question.

She flicked her blinker on and turned right. What would she do if Derek was cheating on her? She couldn't ignore it again. Not this time. She cringed when she thought of him touching another woman, and lately she thought of it often. She couldn't continue driving herself crazy thinking about Derek holding someone else, loving her when he should be home. It was too much. She didn't want to cry every night. She was tired of the hurt, the pain, the constant ache in her heart. She shook her head, trying to rid it of those images. No, she wasn't going to live like that any longer. She had made up her mind.

She merged onto Main Street and slowed to a crawl. His office was coming up and she wondered what she should do. If she pulled into the parking lot and he was working alone, he might see her car. She had no excuse for being there. She didn't want to anger him if he was doing nothing wrong. Why didn't she think to bring him some food or coffee or something? Then she would look like a good wife instead of a suspicious one. Of course, if his car wasn't there it wouldn't make a bit of difference. Unfortunately, she wouldn't know until she pulled in, and then it would be too late.

She finally decided to drive by the first time and see if there were lights on in the building. That might give her some indication of what was going on. She could always circle back for a closer look. Hopefully, he wouldn't be peering out a window and notice her car. It wasn't likely. She drove a black Camry and there must be hundreds of them on the road. Plus, it was dark and rainy. His mind wouldn't automatically jump to thinking it was her car, even if he did see it go by.

As she approached the building, she slowed the Camry to well below the speed limit. Main Street had four lanes in this section; she stayed in the far left even though his office was on the right. There were no cars anywhere around to impede her view.

Derek's building was two stories high and almost all glass in front. His office was on the second floor. He was quite proud of having a corner office, the largest in the entire building. He had a reserved parking space just below where his office sat. He only had to walk a few feet to the side door which led directly upstairs, leaving the spaces in the front available for visitors. Most other employees parked in the garage in the back.

Samantha approached his office and noticed one lone car parked near the front door. It was a small car, but easy to spot because it was bright yellow. She wasn't sure what the model was, but it appeared to be new and quite sporty. Looking up at the building, she could see there were a couple of lights on upstairs, including one in her husband's office. As she edged past, she craned her neck and saw Derek's SUV in its usual spot, first space on the side. So he is working, she thought.

She continued past the building, feeling a wave of relief pass over her. She was barely aware of the gnawing feeling in her stomach that something wasn't quite right. She made it as far as the corner of Main and Lisbon Streets before it hit her. The yellow car. Derek said he was working alone, but clearly that wasn't true. Someone else was working with him, and then she remembered. The yellow car belonged to his secretary, Krystal. He was working late with Krystal, the petite blond that seemed far too interested in him at the Christmas party just a few short months ago.

No, she thought, that car could belong to anybody, but she knew that wasn't the case. She knew it was Krystal's. She remembered Derek coming home and talking about it. He actually told her how hot his secretary's new car was. He even used that word. Hot. Like he was a teenager or something. She didn't like it then and she liked it a whole lot less now.

She abruptly turned into a parking lot on the other side of the street and pulled back out in the opposite direction. Luckily, there was no traffic either way on the cold, black night. She again drove by her husband's office, this time not concerned about him looking out the window and seeing her car. She tried to peer in the windows, but she could only see that the lights were on. The offices were too high and the rain was heavy enough to block the view. Damn, she thought. She debated pulling into the parking lot and trying to run up the stairs to catch them in the act, but that was a ridiculous notion. The front door would be locked and she would have to be buzzed in. They would first see her and simply lie and tell her they were working on a project together. She also thought about waiting in the shadows until they came out, but what would that prove? They would most likely each go to their own vehicles and drive home. The only thing that would show would be that she is out driving around alone at night like a crazy person. No, her best bet would be to go home and not tell Derek that she was aware of anything. She needed time to think. To plan. She had to be smart about this.

She continued past the building, her mind racing,

while trying to ignore the sick feeling in her stomach. One minute she was angry as hell, the next minute she was fighting off tears. Feeling lost, she headed home.

By the time she hit the button to raise the garage door, it was raining harder. A chill had settled in her and she was anxious to get back inside the warm house. She wanted to get into her pajamas and wrap herself in her fleece robe before Derek got home. She might even heat up a fresh cup of tea to help calm her nerves while she thought about what her next move should be.

These were her thoughts as she pulled up the long driveway and into the garage. She never once looked up to see her youngest daughter staring out her bedroom window, her face filled with concern as she wondered where her mother had gone so late on a cold, rainy night.

31 HOLMES

Ronan sat alone in the living room, his stockinged feet propped up on the worn leather stool that he had owned since college. On the tray table next to him was his ever-present notepad along with several sheets of yellow lined paper. The paper was filled with his small, precise handwriting. He took another bite from the sandwich on his lap and chased it with several long swigs of Guinness, or as he liked to think of it, a little taste of home. The paper closest to him had a list of every family member related to Jody Terrel. Initially, each and every one of them was a suspect in Jody's murder. As his investigation continued, he removed those family members that he was absolutely sure could not be Jody's killer.

He had crossed off several names already; Delaney's two children, for obvious reasons, and Chelsie, the oldest daughter of Samantha. He was able to verify that Chelsie was several hours away at college on the night Jody was murdered. Grace's name was also scratched off. Her drama club teacher and several

199

students verified she was at school until after 10:00 on the night of the murder. Ronan was also able to confirm that both Grey and Hunter were in attendance at the high school hockey game and neither had time to leave the game, cross town, murder Jody, clean up after themselves, and return to the same parking spot without anyone realizing they were gone. Plus, there was no reason that Ronan could find for either of them to want her dead. Grey and Jody had a solid marriage. She was a good mother and she did not have any life insurance. Both Grey and Hunter's names were crossed off Ronan's list.

That still left far too many possibilities. In his mind, he actually had a much shorter list. There were only a few people that he was truly suspicious of, but on paper, the number of suspects was long. No one got their name removed from this longer list until he was absolutely certain they could not be the killer.

As he reviewed the ten remaining names, he sighed and picked up the black pen lying on the table. It was time to shorten the list to nine. Ronan had met with Jack Mackensie earlier this week and noticed Jack signing a few documents for a secretary that was in his office as the detective entered. Jack was left-handed. Jack had already been low on the suspect list. His alibi about being home with his children the night of the murder did check out. That, and the fact that Dr. Tashiro, the coroner, had stated the killer was right-handed, let Jack off the hook. Ronan scratched through Jack's name, bringing his list of possibilities down to nine: Samantha,

Derek, Raegan, Beth, Jerry, Gage, Delaney, Paul and Adeline. He wanted to cross through a few more. Some of these family members had no motive. He started to move the pen toward the paper, but then he stopped. He had a method, his own modus operandi, and he was not going to break tradition now. He would scratch off names when he had absolute proof they should be removed, and not one iota before.

He finished his sandwich and wiped the excess mayo from his long, thick fingers. The extra swigs of beer felt cool and refreshing on his throat. Then he shifted in his chair, tossed the wrinkled sandwich wrapper aside, and studied the documents in front of him. He was excited that he had a new lead to explore. He had recently learned that Jody was not Paul's daughter. It seemed that the sisters had been playing around with some DNA testing, a place called GeneScreen, and they had learned that Jody was a half-sister. While this may not have changed their feelings toward her, it definitely could have an impact on the inheritance of the three oldest sisters. Ronan was well aware that Paul Peralta was a very wealthy man, and usually wealth was inherited by blood relatives. Looks like it was time to pay the bereaved father a visit.

32 BETH

This has been the worst day of my life, Beth thought to herself. She practically collapsed into the pink, velvety chair next to her bed, fighting back the tears. She and Jerry just had their biggest fight ever. Gage and Grace were both angry with her. Samantha totally betrayed her. Jody was gone, and Delaney wasn't answering her phone. What was next? Topper, the family dog, was going to run away? She tried to laugh at the thought of the big German Shepard packing a little bag and leaving home, but she couldn't force a smile on her lips. Instead, she tucked her legs underneath her and wrapped her arms around them. She lowered her chin to her knees. Her tears fell. How had everything gone so wrong?

That morning started like every other Saturday. She got up and made a big, hearty breakfast for her family. Everyone seemed fine as they ate their pancakes with fresh berries. She even made special vegan pancakes for Grace. Then the kids started talking about their plans for the day. Gage said he was going to hang out with friends. All Beth did was ask where he was going and with what friends. That wasn't such an unusual thing to ask. Any good mother would want to know. But instead of answering her, Gage blew up. He rose so fast from the table that he knocked his chair to the floor. Beth looked up at him, startled. "Gage, Honey, what's wrong? Did I upset you, Baby?"

"Baby? Seriously, Mom, did you just call me Baby? I'm not a baby. I'm sixteen. I'm twice your size. When are you going to stop treating me like I'm still a baby? Another two years and I won't even be living here. What are you going to do then, Mom? Are you going to move away with me so you can still treat me like I'm your baby?"

Beth was shocked. She gently placed her fork on her plate and pushed the plate with only half of her breakfast eaten away from her. Then she raised her eyes to Gage and said, "I don't understand. I was just wondering what you were doing today. I didn't mean anything. It's just that I love you and I worry about you."

"I know that, Mom. I get it. Everyone gets it. I get it. Dad gets it. Grace gets it. My friends get it. Hell, the people down the street get it. But it has to stop. It's too much! You have got to give me some space. Just leave me alone!" Gage kicked his chair out of the way and slammed out of the kitchen. He didn't try to hide his anger as he banged his way up the stairs and pushed his bedroom door shut with so much force it rattled the pictures on the wall. Beth, Jerry and Grace sat at the table staring at each other, none of them knowing what to say.

Beth slowly stood, taking her plate and cup with her. Once she deposited them in the sink, she turned to Jerry and Grace. Her voice was low. "Either of you two have anything to say?" Grace kept her eyes down, focused on her pancakes like they were the most interesting thing in the world. Jerry pushed his around on his plate before he finally dropped his fork and looked at Beth.

"He's not wrong."

"What do you mean, he's not wrong? I shouldn't ask what his plans are? He's a teenager, not an adult. It's my right, no, my responsibility, as his mother."

"You just take it too far, Beth. Where Gage is concerned, you take it too far."

"What's that supposed to mean?"

Jerry looked at her with a mix of skepticism and surprise. "Don't make me say it aloud, Beth. You know what I mean."

"No, Jerry. I don't. Say what you mean. Explain it to me." Beth was angry now. She had walked back to the table and stood over him, hands on her hips, foot tapping on the shiny tile floor. Her stare was relentless as she waited for him to answer, but he remained motionless.

It was Grace who broke the silence. "You favor Gage, Mom. Dad doesn't want to say it in front of me, but it doesn't matter. We all know it. You love Gage more than you love me. You want to know where he is and what he is doing all the time, but you never ask me.

You don't care what I'm doing. It's always been that way. That's what Dad is thinking, but he doesn't want to hurt my feelings by saying it." Grace turned her head to face her father, tears in her eyes. She was angry, but her face softened as she met eyes with him. "It's okay, Dad. I know. I've always known."

Beth choked back a gasp and put her small hand over her mouth. "Grace, no, I don't."

"You do, Mom. Whether you mean to or not. You do."

As the two Lennox women stared at each other, Jerry continued playing with the food on his plate. None of the three of them knew what to do now that this awful truth was exposed. It was only when Beth's cell phone rang and she pulled it out of her pocket to see who was calling that Grace took advantage of the moment to run out of the room. A minute later, her door could be heard slamming shut, just like Gage's had only moments earlier.

Beth stalled, unsure if she should talk to Jerry, go after Grace, or answer her phone. Jerry, sensing her hesitation, shook his head in disgust. "Don't worry about your daughter, Beth. Why should you start now?" He pushed past her and headed up the same staircase where both of their children had just made their dramatic exits. Beth could hear him calling softly to Grace as he reached the hall at the top of the stairs. Then her attention returned to the still ringing phone in her hand. It was Samantha.

"Hello."

"Is this a good time to talk? I know you wanted to talk about the DNA test you and Jody took and I figured we might as well get it over with."

Beth glanced at the stairs. She knew she should go up there and work things out with Jerry and the kids, but Samantha always made things so difficult. If she didn't talk to her now, who knew when she would get another chance. "Sure, now's good."

"What, exactly, did you want to talk about?"

"Did you talk to Jody before she, well, you know. Or did Delaney tell you? Do you know the results of our DNA tests?"

"Why don't you just tell me, Beth, instead of beating around the bush? It will be easier."

"Okay. Sure." Beth took a deep breath and twirled a lock of hair around her finger. Then she blurted out, "Jody and I got our results back on the same day. We are half-sisters. We have different fathers."

There, it was out. She said the words out loud. Then she waited for Samantha to respond. It seemed like several minutes had passed but it was probably only a few seconds. Finally, Samantha said, "So now you know."

"What do you mean, so now I know? Are you saying you already knew? You aren't surprised by this?"

"Honestly, no. I knew."

"How? How did you know?"

"I heard Mom on the phone a long time ago, like twenty or twenty-five years ago, talking to Nana. I heard her talking about it. Mom saw me and yelled at me for snooping. She was some mad, that's for sure." Samantha laughed as she remembered. "Before that day, I don't think I had ever seen her that angry."

"You think this is funny? Jody and I were devastated. We found out that we were half-sisters. That one of us wasn't Paul's daughter. And you think it's funny?"

Samantha cleared her throat and took on a serious tone. "No, it's not funny. I shouldn't have laughed. It must have been a difficult thing for you to find out."

"Why didn't you tell us?"

"Why? I mean, what good would it do? It's not like it was going to change anything. Plus, I did promise Mom I wouldn't tell. I can keep a promise, you know."

"I guess. But it's hard to understand how you could have known all these years and not told us that one of us had a different father."

"Honestly, I didn't think that much about it. It didn't matter to me. I didn't really think it would matter to you."

"Well, it does. We deserve to know who our father is. We don't even know which one of us isn't Paul's. Jody died not knowing. Even now, I don't know if Paul is my real father or if he was Jody's real father."

"That's easy. I can help you with that. Paul is your father by blood. Jody was only his daughter by love."

33 HOLMES

Ronan knocked on the heavy oak door and was invited in by Paul Peralta. Paul wore a grim expression as he stood in the impressive entryway of his large, two-story home that was located on several acres just a short drive from town. A fourteen-foot ceiling, oak-paneled walls and marble floor surrounded the two men. To the far left, a grand staircase circled to the second floor. The elegant foyer was in sharp contrast to the worn sweatshirt and blue jeans that Paul wore as he led the detective through the double doors on the right of the foyer.

Here they entered a large but comfortable combination office and library. A fire was burning in the gray stone fireplace on the far wall of the room. Two plump leather chairs were placed at an angle directly in front of it. Paul sat in the closest of these chairs and indicated to Ronan that he should take the other. A small wooden table between them contained a glass decanter and two lead-crystal glasses. Without saying a word, Paul splashed a bit of amber liquid into each of the glasses and replaced the decanter to its spot on the table. He picked up his glass and waited for Ronan to retrieve his, which he did without hesitation. Only then did Paul look at Ronan. "Detective Holmes," he said, "do you know who murdered my little girl?"

Ronan was taken aback when he peered into the older man's eyes. They were gray and surrounded by heavy lines and drooped lids, but mostly, they were filled with sorrow. The pain this man was feeling emanated from him with his every movement. Ronan felt chilled as he thought about the conversation he was getting ready to have. He took a swig of the whiskey, grateful for the fluid warming his insides. "No. Not yet. But we are getting closer."

"What does that mean? Do you have a suspect?"

Ronan didn't want to lie, but he knew the answers he could provide would only cause Paul more pain. Still, he was sure that Paul wouldn't tolerate any bullshit. He decided to play it straight. "It wasn't a stranger that killed Jody. We're sure. It was someone she knew. She let them into her house that night."

He could see Paul tense, but he didn't say a word as he absorbed this information. He continued to stare into the fire before asking, "You're sure?" Paul asked, but it was more because he needed to say something, to respond. He already knew the answer.

Ronan nodded his head. "Yes, we're sure. There were no signs of a break-in. Nothing was stolen. There was no indication that whoever entered the house that night even rummaged through anything. No signs of a struggle. No fingerprints. It appears that Jody opened the door and let the person in, went to the office, sat down and worked on her checkbook. Whoever it was grabbed a knife from the weapons display and snuck up in back of her. It was quick. Jody had no time to respond."

"So at least she didn't feel any pain. Is that what you're trying to tell me? I should take comfort in that?"

Ronan brought his glass up to his lips but stopped short of taking a drink. He looked at the man sitting next to him. "I can't tell you to find comfort in any of this. I've worked too many cases to believe words like that will help."

Paul raised his head slightly. He stayed in that position for a few minutes. Then he sighed and leaned back in his chair. He downed the remainder of his drink and poured another. Ronan waved off a refill. Then Paul turned his stare toward Ronan, his gaze steady. "Who are your suspects? Someone I don't know? Grey? Tony?"

Ronan started to respond, but the realization of what Paul just said struck him. Tony. Who was Tony? He swirled his drink and collected his thoughts. He was usually a step ahead of the people he was interrogating, not the other way around. "Not likely a stranger. Also, not Grey. He has an alibi for the night of the murder, and honestly, he doesn't have a motive. At least not one that we could find. He and Jody had a solid marriage. They were financially stable. There wasn't any life insurance for him to collect. Tell me about Tony."

Paul raised an eyebrow. "You don't know about

210

Tony, do you? You're wondering who he is, but you don't want to come right out and ask."

Ronan remained still, curious where this conversation was heading.

Paul turned his head and focused his gray eyes directly on Ronan, something he hadn't done since Ronan entered the house. Ronan ran his finger under his collar to loosen his shirt. He didn't care for the prickling sensation he felt under the intensity of Paul's stare. He briefly wondered if this is how the people he questioned felt when he did to them what Paul was currently forcing him to experience.

"That's okay, Detective. You don't have to answer me. We both already know what the answer is." A sly smile crossed Paul's face. It was quick, but it did not go unnoticed by Ronan. "Tony is Jody's biological father."

Not very much in this world startled Ronan Holmes, but those words coming out of Paul's mouth caused him to jerk forward, almost spilling his drink down the front of his pants. Paul knew that he was not Jody's father? Did one of the sisters just tell him or had he always known? Luckily, Ronan recovered quickly. He steadied his hand, downed the remainder of his drink, and set the empty glass on the table. He met Paul's gaze. "How long have you known?"

"Jody would have turned forty-three this coming September, so I reckon I've known about forty-three years. Caroline, that's the girls' mother, was good at a lot of things, but keeping secrets from me wasn't one of them."

"And did Tony know?"

"He knew alright. Didn't give a shit, but he knew."

"So why do you think he might be the one who killed her?"

"I don't really, but I can't think of anyone else who would want to hurt her. She was a lovely girl. Good wife. Good mother. The only one who knew her and didn't love her was Tony. Biggest fool I ever met."

Paul fell quiet, his gray eyes glistening in the firelight. Ronan honored his silence, but finally broke it by saying, "Why don't you tell me about it? What happened all those years ago?"

"Pick your glass back up for a refill. You'll have time for it to settle before you need to drive again." Ronan did as he was told and waited patiently for Paul to tell him the tale that began forty-three years ago.

"Caroline and I had been married about seven years. I was working as a forest ranger and Caroline was trying her best to be content as a stay-at-home mother. We had two little ones by then, Samantha was three and Beth was two. Those two were both as cute as they could be, but they wore Caroline down. Samantha was a terror. I never knew a 3-year-old could have such a temper, but that one sure did. She could argue and yell and throw the most God-awful tantrums you ever saw. Now the little one wasn't a fighter, she was a gentle soul, but she clung to Caroline like poison clings to ivy. There were days she wrapped her arms around Caroline's leg and wouldn't let go. This made for tough times for a woman who was probably more suited for a career than being a housewife." Paul paused, swigged his drink, and leaned forward in his chair to poke at the fire. Then he settled back and continued.

"We were making the most of it. I was working long days, but coming home and helping as much as I could every night. Often times I would make supper so Caroline could get some much-needed rest. I would try to clean up around the house, or throw some laundry in, or even give the girls a bath. Those two were a handful. Then Caroline told me that she needed a little time to herself, away from the girls. After all, she was with them all day, all night. Sometimes she just needed a break. I understood that. To be honest, as much as I loved the little pumpkins, I was only home for a few hours and there was a smile on my face when it was their bedtime. So once a week she took a class at the local college. I don't remember exactly what it was. Creative writing or literature or something like that. It made her happy and that was all that mattered."

Ronan sat quietly in the big leather chair enjoying the warmth of the fire while Paul traveled into the past to share his story. Ronan's pad was on his lap, his pencil in hand, but so far, he hadn't written a single note. He was mesmerized by Paul's every word. He subtly nodded his head and Paul continued.

"This went on for a few weeks and soon Caroline seemed happier. She was more relaxed. After a couple of months, Caroline signed up for another class.

Then she was going twice a week. At first, I didn't think much of it. She was happy and the girls were thriving. What was helping out two nights a week to make my wife happy? She was even encouraging me to start hanging out a bit with my friends. It had been a long time since I spent a Friday night at the pub with the boys, and let me tell you, I didn't mind going down there when she suggested it."

Up until now, Paul's voice had been steady and monotonous, but suddenly Ronan noticed a change in his demeanor. His voice took on a sad, hollow tone. While one hand was still wrapped around the glass that held his partially finished drink, the fingers on his other hand were tapping the arm of the leather chair in rapid succession.

"I was so wrapped up in what was making me happy, I didn't see what was right in front of my face, what was making Caroline happy. It was about six months later that she came to me. She had been crying. She looked scared. It was late and the two little ones were down for the night. Usually this was our cue to collapse into bed, but she said we needed to talk. It was important. I could tell by the look on her face that it wasn't going to be good. I tried to brace myself for whatever she was going to say. My mind was racing. Was she sick? Was something wrong with one of the girls? I had no idea. Then she told me she was pregnant. She said she was about three months along." Paul paused long enough to drain his glass and fill it for a third time. "Fool that I was, I thought she was anxious because she figured I didn't want a third baby. I started off by being happy. I was overjoyed to be welcoming another little one into our home. Then she got right in my face and told me to think. To think long and hard about where our relationship was three months ago. It took a few minutes. I have to admit I wasn't too quick, but eventually it hit me. I hadn't touched her in a lot longer than that. That's when I knew the new life growing in her belly wasn't put there by me."

At that, Paul fell silent. Ronan waited patiently for him to begin, but minutes ticked by and Paul just sat there, staring at the fire. Ronan waited, unsure of what he should do. Paul was a big man, even now well into his sixties, but at this minute he looked smaller, somehow shrunken with the pain of this memory. Finally, Paul cleared his throat and adjusted himself in his chair. Then he continued.

"I'll skip the words that were said that night. Can't say I'm proud of most of them. My first thought was to tell Caroline to get out of the house and leave me and my girls alone. She didn't deserve to be my wife or their mother. But after I settled down, I started to understand things more from her side. I was gone so much, and while I thought I was helping, in all fairness, I was only home a few hours, a couple of nights a week. I was working six, seven days a week. I should have been there for her more than that. She was asking, I just wasn't listening. When I asked her who the father was, she didn't hesitate. She told me his name was Tony. Tony Cardello, an Italian man who sat next to her in her night class. They just started by talking and one thing led to another. Again, I won't go into the details. I'm sure you can figure them out. But she was only with him twice, and she figured it was the second time that made her pregnant. She told him about the baby, but he wanted nothing to do with her or the child. Now I ask you, what kind of man wants nothing to do with his own child?"

Ronan, sensing the question was rhetorical, remained quiet.

"Pretty soon Caroline began to show and people just assumed the baby was mine. We didn't correct them. The doctor said the baby would come around the end of October, but in late-September, Caroline went into labor. We weren't ready. We didn't have a crib set up or a name picked out or anything. I was still referring to the baby as Caroline's, not ours. Anyway, I drove her to the hospital and out popped this tiny little girl. She didn't weigh but five pounds. Tiniest little thing I ever saw. Sweet red face, dark eyes, and the hair on her--jet black, just about covering the top of her head. I had to admit it, what I felt for that baby girl was instant love. It didn't matter that she wasn't mine. I loved her just like I loved the other two. Later, when Caroline and I were sitting together, Caroline asked me what I thought we should name her. I told her I wanted to call her Jody after a favorite aunt of mine. Caroline said okay, just like that. Hell, I didn't get any say in the naming of the other two, but this time, she let me pick out the name. Since that moment, that baby girl was as much mine as Samantha and Beth. There is nobody who is going to tell me any different."

Ronan wiped his eyes as he took in everything Paul had just told him. He was fascinated with the man seated next to him, almost honored to be in his presence. At that moment, he was sure he could remove Paul from his list of suspects. That man loved Jody far too much to harm her, let alone kill her. Still, he had a job to do, so he did want to review Paul's alibi one more time for the night of the murder. Also, he still needed Paul to explain why he thought Tony, Jody's blood father, might be involved.

"Mr. Peralta..."

"Paul. Call me Paul."

"Okay, Paul. Why do you think Tony could be involved in Jody's murder? Has he been involved in her life?"

"No, even before Jody was born, Tony moved away. I think he was terrified that Caroline was going to ask him for money. He knew she wasn't working and that I was only a forest ranger. Good work, not great pay." Paul snickered and shook his head. "Stupid ass. Little did he know that I worked as a ranger by choice. I loved that job. It fulfilled me and kept me an honest man. Caroline and I didn't need the money. I had a family trust fund that took care of that."

"Do you know where he moved to?"

"I heard he went down south in Virginia. Somewhere in the Blue Ridge Mountains. He hightailed it out of Cayne so fast that he didn't have time to leave a forwarding address. For forty years I haven't seen or heard a word from him."

"And Jody?"

"Nah, we never told her the truth. Why should we? She was happy being my daughter. I was happy being her father. There was never a reason to tell her any differently."

"But Mr. Pe..., I mean, Paul, that still doesn't explain why you think he should be a suspect in her murder."

"I'm sure by now you know, Detective, that I am a wealthy man. Old family money and a few healthy investments of my own. When I die, the majority of my fortune will be split among my three daughters. And by three, I mean Samantha, Beth and Jody. I meant it when I said she is my daughter. Now, there are provisions for others, although I doubt they are aware of them. There's a tidy sum for Delaney. She's not my daughter, but she is their sister. I don't want to leave her out. And there's Adeline. She's been good to me for quite a few years now. I have some favorite charities, that sort of thing, but mostly I'm looking out for my girls."

"That seems logical. Please go on."

"What if Tony was hoping to cash in on that fortune and Jody rejected him? If she was out of the picture, her share would go to Hunter. I understand that there was also an attempt on Hunter's life."

"You know about that?"

"I'm old, Detective, not stupid. I'm aware of so much more than my girls seem to think." He looked at

Ronan with a smirk on his face. "If both Jody and Hunter were out of the picture, would Tony somehow be in line for the inheritance as a blood relative?"

"I wouldn't think so, but I guess it depends on the specifics of your will."

"I agree, I know it doesn't all fit together. I was thinking maybe there's an angle I'm not seeing. I only started wondering because I heard Tony was back in town recently. It could be nothing, but I thought it warranted your investigating."

"Yes, we will definitely look into it. Now, I hate to ask, but I understand you and Ms. Lizotte were out with some business acquaintances the night your daughter was killed?"

"Yes. I provided your partner, Detective Campbell, with their names, the restaurant where we had dinner, and receipts. I believe he was going to check with the wait staff. I would never hurt Jody, Detective. I would give my own life before I would hurt her."

Ronan looked not only into Paul's eyes, but through them into his soul. He believed every word Paul was saying to him. There was no way this man would ever hurt his daughter. Of course he would verify with Wes everything Paul was telling him, but as far as he was concerned, Paul was off the suspect list.

34 DELANEY

Delaney knew she had to come clean. What was that old line from that poem by Sir Walter Scott? 'O, what a tangled web we weave when first we practice to deceive!' *Marmion*? That's what she had done, gotten herself into one hell of a tangled web with her lies. That detective had already called her to say he was going to stop by so they could have a conversation. Jack knew she wasn't being upfront with him. It was all going to come crashing down. Better to head it off before that happened.

She wasn't sure who to come clean with first, Jack or Detective Holmes. She also wasn't sure which truth should be the priority, the money or where she was the night of Jody's murder. Both would eventually come out. She couldn't hide either one of them much longer. She had tried and failed. When Jack found out, she could lose her marriage. When Detective Holmes found out, she could go to prison. Shit, what should she do?

She thought about calling Tom, her lawyer. After

all, it would be safe to tell him everything. He would have to advise her about the best way to handle things and he couldn't rat her out to anyone. She had even picked up her cell phone to call him, but she never entered his number. Deep down she knew that wasn't the route she should follow. Instead, she reached out to the first person she should have called all along.

"Hey, it's me. Is now a good time to meet?"

Jack's voice went from rushed to almost cheerful when he realized why she was calling. "Yes, absolutely. How about an early lunch? Let's say The Harbor House in thirty minutes?"

"Perfect. I'll meet you there."

Delaney didn't feel the exhilaration that she could hear in Jack's voice, but she was relieved that she was finally going to tell him the truth. The lies she had been carrying around for the last several weeks were coming to an end. She knew what she was about to tell him could change her life. She could lose everything, but at least it would be over. There would be no more wondering what was going to happen. No more trying to cover what she had done. The truth would bring her peace.

She changed into navy blue pants and a crisp, white blouse that she topped with a burgundy sweater. She pulled on boots and grabbed her favorite Sea Bags purse. It would only take her ten minutes to drive to the restaurant, but she headed out the door. She wanted to arrive early enough to snag a table by the window. Plus, she knew Detective Holmes was going to arrive sometime today and she wanted to be out of the house before he could detain her for questioning. She owed it to Jack to tell him the truth first.

She sat near the rear of the restaurant by the large windows that overlooked the still-bare trees on the side of the mountains. Usually, the tables on the other side of the window would be lined with patrons eating on the outside deck, but the early April weather was still too cold to enjoy outside dining. That deck remained closed for the season, giving the table she had selected the illusion of privacy.

When Jack walked in, Delaney couldn't help but notice how handsome her husband truly was. He was tall with thick, dark hair and broad shoulders. He had an unintentional swagger to his walk, almost a bounce in his step, that indicated both confidence and boyish charm, neither of which he was aware. When he spotted her, his pace quickened and a smile came across his face, the dimples she knew existed were hidden by his neatly trimmed beard. She smiled up at him as he approached the table. He leaned over and planted a kiss on her cheek before sitting directly across from her.

He shrugged out of his jacket and reached across the table, enclosing both of her hands in his. "I'm glad you had time to meet me today. I have something very important to talk to you about. I'm not sure how it will make you feel, but I'm hoping you'll be open to it. It's something that can't wait."

Delaney was surprised. She was there to share some pretty significant news of her own. She had forgotten that he had previously requested time with her to talk about an issue that was important to him. Now what should she do? Talk or listen?

Before Delaney could say anything, the server came to their table. "A bottle of pinot grigio?" Jack asked Delaney. Then he ordered the shrimp salad, their usual lunch at this restaurant. After the server left, he turned back to Delaney, and with a pleading pitch to his voice, said, "I hope I can convince you to feel the same way about this that I do. Please, hear me out before you respond, especially if you are thinking of saying no."

Delaney took a deep breath and leaned forward. The decision was made. She was going to listen to what her husband had to say before telling him anything about the bind she was in. A quick thought passed through her mind as she smiled at Jack. She hoped Detective Holmes didn't walk into the restaurant to interrogate her before she had a chance to tell her husband where she was the night of Jody's murder.

Jack held his wineglass in his right hand; he reached across the table and held Delaney's much smaller hand in his left. He started to say something to her, but hesitated, sipped his wine, and started again. "I guess the best thing to do is to be direct, like ripping off a band-aid." Delaney, intrigued, smiled encouragingly. "Okay, here goes. I want to sell Jack Mac Construction and go back to being a plumber." His eyes, which had been cast downward, now looked fully into Delaney's. He waited for her reaction, but she remained still, showing no emotion to what he had just said. Was she angry? In shock? He couldn't tell, so he went on. "I ran the numbers and it is doable. With the profit from the sale of Jack Mac, plus the money I would make doing plumbing, we would be fine. More than fine. We could maintain the mortgage on the house, but we would probably have to sell the lake house. Or we could rent it and just use it for one or two weeks over the summer." He squeezed her hand and she gave him the faintest hint of a smile. "I've given this a lot of thought, Delaney. This would make me happy, and I haven't been happy with my work for a long time. I want more time with the kids. With you. The money just doesn't matter to me. But if you don't want me to…"

Delaney couldn't talk. She couldn't react. She didn't know what to say. For years she wanted Jack to want more time with her. Not work time, but family time. She wanted to capture the love they had earlier in their marriage when they weren't so busy. For the last few years all they talked about was business, construction and house sales and design. She, too, missed their old life. She never thought Jack would want to go back to it. Hearing him say those words made her feel a surge of warmth inside, a feeling of love so strong that she wanted to climb right over the table and hold him in her arms. But she couldn't just say yes. She couldn't tell him it would all work out until he knew about the money. She had to tell him about the eighty-five thousand dollar kitchen on the Winthrop house, more than double what it should have been. He hadn't allowed for that forty-five thousand dollar overage in his calculations when he reviewed their budget. If that had been the worst of it, she knew they would still be okay. It was a huge chunk of change, but it wasn't going to make or break them, not even when combined with the other work errors. It was the other money that was troubling her. The money from the night Jody was murdered. She had to tell him.

"Jack," she said, her mossy green eyes glistening with tears that were just starting to form. "Before we can decide, there's something you need to know."

Jack saw the concern, no, not concern, fear, on her face, and he slowed his breathing, wondering what she was going to say. Before she could continue, the server arrived with their lunch. The lunch he had been looking forward to now held no interest for him, a knot in his stomach replaced his appetite. Once the food was set before them, Jack looked at his wife. She had dried her tears on her napkin, but there were creases in her forehead that were not there before. She fidgeted with her utensils and avoided his stare. Not able to wait any longer, Jack reached across the table, took her hand, and quietly said, "Go on."

Delaney licked her lips and slowly brought her gaze from her plate to his eyes. "First, let me say I'm sorry. I didn't mean for this to happen. I was trying to make things better. I only made everything worse."

The knot in Jack's stomach turned cold. He could actually feel the fear that he saw on Delaney's face. "Jesus Christ, Delaney. You're scaring the shit out of me. Will you get on with it?"

"It was the night of Jody's murder. I wasn't at

work. I was with Jerry, at his garage. I was there with Jerry and three of his friends--Andy, Carlos, and a guy they called The Buffer. I don't know his real name. We were playing poker. For money. High stakes. I was trying to win back the money that was accidently lost on the Winthrop house. It wasn't my fault but I thought you would be angry. Maybe not angry, but disappointed, if you knew. When I heard about this game, I thought I would jump in and win the money back. Jerry tried to talk me out of it, but I insisted. I wouldn't take no for an answer. He finally let me in the game and I couldn't stop. I kept thinking the next hand would be mine, but it wasn't. I lost. I lost in a big way, and now I have to pay The Buffer a lot of money by the end of the week. I'm going to have to get a loan and I'm so sorry, Jack. I'm so sorry because this might mean you can't change your plans. I want you to sell the business. I want more time with you. I want us to be a family again, but we have this debt you don't know about, and I'm so sorry."

It was Jack's turn to sit quietly. He wasn't sure how to react to Delaney's news that she had been gambling. He thought she was past that. It had been a problem for her seven or eight years ago, but she hadn't gambled at all since then. Not even once, or at least not that he knew of. He picked up his fork and pushed his salad around in his bowl. He took a few bites, although it was more for something to do than for any desire to eat. He just needed a minute to think. Finally, he looked up and asked, "How much?"

"A hundred and ten thousand dollars, plus the

forty-five thousand overage on the Winthrop house, and another thirty from some work issues." Delaney's response was almost a whisper. Jack didn't react. He didn't yell, his face didn't turn angry red, he didn't even gasp. He clenched his hand and took another bite of his salad, his teeth clicking on his fork in a way that made Delaney shudder. Then Delaney stabbed at her food and started to eat, willing her body to chew, swallow and keep the shrimp in her stomach where it belonged. Finally, Jack spoke. His voice was even, his tone measured.

"Other than the night at Jerry's garage, when was the last time you gambled?"

"I haven't, Jack. Honest. It's been years. I don't know what made me do it this time. I overheard Jerry talking about a high stakes game and I had just found out about the Winthrop house and I was so sure I could win. Jerry kept saying no, but I bullied my way in. Believe me, this was the first time since way back when I promised you that I would stop. And it was a mistake. I know that now."

"Once this debt is paid off, how do you feel about my proposal? About my going back to being a plumber?"

Delaney felt a flicker of hope inside. Maybe Jack would forgive her. "Oh, Jack, absolutely. I just want us to be a family again, too. We can sell the lake house if you want. Or rent it. I don't care. Whatever you want."

Jack put his fork down and reached across the table, this time with both hands. He laced Delaney's cold fingers through his. He rubbed his thumbs along her smooth skin. Once again, he stared into her eyes. This time she stared back. The creases in her forehead were gone. She looked younger, happier, hopeful. He felt his own eyes moisten. "I love you, Delaney. We can make this work."

"I love you, too. And I promise, Jack, never again. I will never again gamble our money away. Not one cent."

Soon they were both eating the rest of their lunch with flourish. They were making plans for the future, sounding almost like newlyweds as they discussed the possibilities. There were so many options, so many choices, but when it came right down to it, they realized they both wanted the same thing. They wanted more time to spend with each other and their children.

They finally agreed to keep the lake house but sell the massive house they were currently living in and find something that was more reasonably priced. They could look for a four-bedroom home, maybe even with a pool, but they didn't need mountain views and balconies and a patio with an outdoor kitchen. They could get by with a lot less if it meant more time to be together. Jack would work five days a week instead of six or seven; Delaney would still be a real estate agent, but her time as a designer/house-flipper would come to an end. The thought of going to the kids' school events, having family meals every night and spending weekends together was just too great of a draw. The money was secondary. That was one thing that Jody's death taught them, tomorrow wasn't guaranteed.

Together they sipped their wine and enjoyed their meal as they talked about their future. Delaney was no longer worried about telling Detective Holmes where she was the night of Jody's murder. He didn't need to know the extent of the gambling that took place. She was also no longer concerned about the inheritance. If she received all the money from her mother, great. She would use it to pay off the loan she had to take out to pay off her gambling debt. If she didn't, she would pay it off slowly. It would serve as a constant reminder to what she could have lost with her foolishness.

They both knew it would take some time to adjust to a different lifestyle, both for the two of them and for their children. It wouldn't always be easy, but they would manage. They would all see that the time they would have together would be more valuable than a big house or fancy cars. Delaney could see the happiness on Jack's face as he chatted almost nonstop through their lunch. Her heart was filled with joy and she whispered a silent thank you to the sister she knew she would always love and miss. *Thank you, Jody, for showing me what is truly important in life.*

They finished eating with a renewed appetite for both their lunch and their marriage. There was an aura of happiness surrounding them. Even the server felt the joy in the air when she brought them their check, and especially when she noticed the generous tip that had been added to it. As Delaney and Jack strode hand-in-hand from the restaurant, no one would have ever thought that the one thing on Delaney's mind was that she could borrow an extra ten thousand dollars on the loan to pay off her gambling debt, and if she played her cards right, quite literally, she could double that amount to twenty thousand dollars.

35 HOLMES

Detective Holmes was seated in the farthest booth from the door at the old-fashioned diner that Tony Cardello had chosen for their lunch meeting. He had arrived thirty minutes early so he could choose where they would sit. He didn't like having his back to the door. It was a cop thing. He needed to see what was happening around him at all times.

Ronan recognized Tony as soon as he walked into the diner. Ronan had done a thorough search of both government records and social media. The first thing he noticed was that Tony was short for a man, five feet seven inches. He had a full head of white hair, although it had been jet-black in his youth, and dark brown eyes. His skin was a deep olive-color, but leathery with age. He sported a thick, white chevron mustache, which made him very distinguishable from other patrons in the diner.

Ronan had been seated quietly in his booth,

waiting for Tony to notice him. That had allowed him more time to observe Jody's biological father. He noted that Tony was dressed in a black suit with a gray shirt and a striped tie. It looked expensive. His black shoes were shined to a high gloss. Ronan wondered if Tony always dressed that way or if he wanted to make an impressionable appearance.

As soon as Tony spotted him, he walked over, smiled and extended his hand. With a slight Italian accent he said, "Detective Holmes?"

Without rising from his seat, Ronan grasped the older man's hand and shook it firmly. "Please, have a seat. I'm going to order the club sandwich and a Diet Coke. Join me?"

Tony picked up the menu and appeared to skim over it, but he wasn't reading it. He seemed jittery. "Yes, I'll have the same. Well, a regular Coke for me. I never could get used to that diet stuff. Couldn't adjust to the aftertaste."

They placed their orders and Ronan started right in with his questioning. No use bothering with small talk. They both knew why they were there. "I know you didn't have a chance to know your daughter, Mr. Cardello, but I would still like to offer my condolences. It must be hard to lose your blood under any circumstances."

"Thank you, Detective. I appreciate that. From everything I know, she was a fine woman."

"What did you know about her?" Ronan had a list of specific questions he had planned to ask Tony, but after meeting him, he decided to let Tony talk on his own. He felt there was more to Tony than he had initially been led to believe. Maybe Tony knew more about Jody than anyone had suspected. "Maybe you should start at the beginning," Ronan added.

"I know I was surprised when Caroline first told me she was pregnant. Dumbfounded, you might say." Tony rubbed his fingers together and laughed nervously. He glanced at Ronan. "I didn't know what to do. I didn't know Caroline all that well. We took a class together and had only been out a few times. I was young, not very worldly, and she was so beautiful. She was older than me and I couldn't believe that someone that gorgeous would let someone like me, well, you know. I never even asked her about birth control. I don't suppose it would have mattered at the time if I had. I mean, nothing would have stopped me with the state of mind I was in."

Ronan gently prodded him to continue with his tale. "Go on."

"Like I was saying, I was surprised when she called me to tell me she was pregnant. She said I didn't have to act like the father or anything, but she was going to keep the baby and she needed money. I had, maybe, twenty dollars to my name. I was in school, working part-time, still living at home. I didn't have any money of my own back then. She wasn't happy with me. She got pretty mad on the telephone and started yelling at me."

"What happened next?"

"I think one of her kids came in the room because I could hear crying and Caroline started saying stuff like *it's okay* and *I'll be right there*. Then she just hung up the telephone. She didn't even say goodbye. When my folks got home later that day, I told Papa what happened. I asked him to loan me some money so I could give it to Caroline. After all, this was my baby and I thought it was the least I could do. Instead, he put me on a bus to Virginia. He had a sister in the Roanoke area. I was moved in with Zia Rosa, working at a local diner, and taking college classes at Roanoke College before I knew what hit me. Papa told me to stay away and have nothing to do with Caroline or that baby of hers. He said she was just looking for a meal ticket and it wasn't going to be me. After all, I had my whole life ahead of me."

"So did you stay away?"

"I did for a while. I got caught up in my life in Virginia. I finished school; I got a degree in business and eventually moved to the Richmond area where I opened a little Italian restaurant. I always had a flair for cooking, and with my business degree, I knew how to set things up. I did this for a few years, but I always wondered about my baby. I didn't even know if I had a son or a daughter."

The server brought their food to the table and the two men stopped talking long enough to take a few bites of their sandwiches. It wasn't long before Tony continued with his story. "Finally, I couldn't take the wondering, so I told my staff I was going to take a few days off, something I never did, and I hopped in my car and drove to Maine. I didn't tell anyone where I was heading. I got to Cayne on a Thursday afternoon and I parked down the road from where Caroline and Paul lived. Sure enough, a little after 3:00, I saw three little girls come walking down the street with schoolbags in their hands. I knew immediately the little one was mine. She looked to be about 6-years-old, which was the right age. She was a tiny little thing, dark hair, dark eyes, and cute as a button. And she wasn't just walking, she was hopping and skipping and twirling, giggling as she talked to her sisters. Yes siree, no doubt that sweet little thing was my girl. I was sure of it." Tony blinked back a tear as a shadow crossed his face. Then he continued.

"I wanted to run right over to that little darling and tell her who I was. I longed to give her a hug and claim her as my own, but you know, Detective, I couldn't do it. I was overwhelmed with love. I couldn't do that to her. She looked happy, bouncing down the street with the other two girls. Her sisters. So instead, I watched until she went into Caroline's house, and then I just sat in my car and cried like a baby. I knew I had made the wrong choice all those years ago, but I couldn't let my mistake turn into her problem. It wasn't easy, but the next morning I drove back to Richmond."

Ronan sighed, on the border of being touched by Tony's story. He could feel the remorse he heard in Tony's voice and wondered if he would have had the strength to make the same decision Tony did. He thought of his own daughters and thanked the Lord he never had to spend his life without them. Then he forced his mind to return to the task at hand. "Was that the last time you saw her?" he asked, knowing that his answer was going to be no.

"No. I couldn't disrupt the happy life she had, but I found I couldn't stay completely away. I tried to. Honest I did. But my resolve only lasted about a year. I drove up again when Jody was seven. I didn't know her name until I saw her picture in the local newspaper. She was playing summer league softball and there she was, all smiles, in the front row of her team picture. Jody Peralta. That hurt a little, it should have read Jody Cardello, but to be fair, Paul was more of a father to her than I ever was. Anyway, I went to a couple of her softball games. I stayed away from the other parents, kept my baseball cap low. No one noticed me.

I continued with these rare visits over the next several years. I would try to find out about her from the local newspaper, you know, events she participated in. It wasn't hard. She was always involved with one sport or another. I would go to her games, stay away from everyone, and leave before anyone noticed me. This went on until she was about twelve or thirteen. Then it got more difficult. Damn near impossible."

"Why was that? What changed?"

Tony smiled. "A good change. Probably the best change. I met Olivia. Olivia came to work for me at my restaurant, which was now quite successful. She applied to be a server, but I could see she should be much more than that, so I hired her as a manager. It didn't take long before I asked her out. To make a long story short, we were married a year later. Olivia and I shared everything together. We had the restaurant, our home, two beautiful children, a boy and a girl, everything, except Jody. I can't explain why, I don't know myself, but I never told her about Jody."

"She didn't know you had another daughter?"

"No. Maybe I was ashamed that I gave Jody up. Maybe I thought she would think less of me. I don't know. But I never told her, and I never went to Maine again to see Jody. I would try to read about her in the newspaper. I would see pictures of her from the high school sports page. It was harder after she graduated. Eventually I wasn't able to learn much about her, at least not until social media came about. I missed knowing what she was up to, but instead I focused on Angelo and Cassidy, my children with Olivia. Life was good, mostly. I learned to live with that hollow place in my heart that missed Jody. I pushed it down deep inside of me and tried to ignore it. Overall, Detective, I had a good life. Probably better than I deserved."

Ronan finished the last of his sandwich and drained his Diet Coke. Then he stared thoughtfully at his notepad before closing it and putting it back in his pocket. He leaned forward and looked into Tony's brown eyes. His gaze was intense. "So why were you in Maine only a week before Jody was murdered?"

When Tony met his stare, his eyes were open wide, his face was sincere. He did not hesitate or look away when he replied. "Two reasons, Detective Holmes. I came back for two reasons. First, Olivia was the love of my life. We were married for almost thirty years. The first twenty-seven years were pure joy. Not that we didn't have our ups-and-downs. Like any married couple, we did. But the love, it was always there. Then, three years ago, the disease came that changed everything." Tony took a moment to wipe a tear from his eye. He took a few deep breaths and continued. "Not cancer, Detective. Everyone always thinks it was cancer. But for Olivia, it wasn't. It was a rare autoimmune disease that caused her muscles to deteriorate until they simply stopped functioning. She couldn't walk. Then she couldn't breathe. It was a slow, painful death. As much as I loved her, it was a blessing when she was gone. She was finally out of the pain she had lived with for the last year of her life."

Ronan stayed quiet, knowing that nothing he could say would comfort the man sitting across from him, the man who looked like he had aged ten years in the last few minutes as he sat there telling his story.

"The second thing is, of course, Jody. You see, Detective, both Angelo and Cassidy are married and on their own. I am all alone. They are good children. They call and visit often, but I am still alone. And now I have time to deal with the thoughts I have pushed aside for so many years. These thoughts always turn to Jody. I wanted to see her again. I've wondered about her so many times over the years. Olivia is gone, and I knew this was my chance to see my Jody. So, I did something I never thought I would do."

Ronan sat a bit straighter in his chair, curious what Tony would say next.

"I called Angelo and Cassidy and had them come

to my house. I told them I had news for them. Big news. Life-changing news. They are good children, Detective. They came right away. And then," Tony twisted his hands together as he took several deep breaths in a row. "I told them about Jody. I thought they would be angry, or disgusted. I even thought they might tell me they never wanted to see me again. But they didn't do those things. They told me I needed to find her. To see her. And if the time was right, to tell her about me." Tony was openly crying now, the tears sliding down his face with such force that he was powerless to stop them. "They supported me one hundred percent. They said they understood and that they loved me. With their blessing, I drove to Cayne to find Jody.

I was going to ask Caroline if Jody knew I was her father, but once I got here, I learned that Caroline and her husband, David, had been killed in a car crash. I had planned to visit with Paul next to see what Jody knew. I wanted to see her, to tell her I was her biological father, that she had siblings she didn't know about. But I didn't want to ruin the life she had. You see, Detective, I was never much of a father to her, but I was still a father, and I loved her enough to not want to hurt her. Before I could call Paul, Jody was killed. My girl was killed and I never had the chance…"

With those words Tony sat in the booth and cried. He made no attempt to hide the tears that were flowing freely down his cheeks and bouncing off his hands that were now clasped together on his lap. Ronan noticed that the server, who had started toward their table to refill drinks, made an abrupt U-turn when she got close enough to see the condition Tony was in. Ronan remained quiet, staring down at his empty plate, giving Tony a chance to work through his pain. He let him collect himself before asking him any additional questions. He could tell that Tony's pain was real and he was feeling confident that Tony was no longer a suspect in Jody's murder. Finally, Tony picked up his napkin, dried his eyes, made a few loud sobbing sounds, and smiled weakly at Ronan.

"I apologize. I promised myself I wouldn't do that. It's just that I was so close to seeing her. I know it wasn't much, Detective, but I was hoping to make amends with her. In addition to coming to visit with Jody, to getting to know her, I had another motive for being here."

Ronan waited for Tony to continue.

"At the insistence of both of my children, I wanted to include her in my will. I'm not getting any younger, and my health is precipitous, to say the least. My restaurant has been very successful, and my investments even more so. I was hoping to make up for my lack of being a good father by including her in my will. I know money can't make up for my absence, but I believe that Paul took care of that. I just wanted to show her that I did care about her. I was here to tell her that upon my death she would receive a sum of money—five hundred thousand dollars. I know it can't make up for the mistakes of the past, but I was hoping it would provide her some happiness. But now it's too late. I lost my chance." Tony raised his eyes, now filled with sorrow, and looked at Ronan. "I have changed my will to include my grandson, Hunter, instead of Jody now. I guess I should have asked Paul if that's acceptable, but I was afraid he was going to tell me no, so I just did it. I hope the money brings Hunter joy and not pain. That is truly my intention. And I hope that someday he will meet his other aunt and uncle, and perhaps even cousins by then. I do this out of love, Detective. Only out of love."

Eventually the two men shook hands and parted company. Ronan felt a sadness for Tony that he hadn't anticipated. One decision of a 20-year-old man had changed the course of his entire life. It saddened him to think of the burden that Tony had carried with him for over forty years, and how he would carry it with him until the day he died. Then Ronan paid the check, tipped the server well over the mandatory twenty percent, and left the diner. Tony was no longer a suspect in the Jody Terrel murder case.

36 THE VISITOR

Just one more night. I kept telling myself that, but God, it was going to be the longest fucking twenty-four hours of my life. I was so ready. I just wanted to get this over with.

I still needed to make a few more last-minute decisions. The biggest one was picking the food to add the poison to. I had to be careful because strychnine, while odorless, has a bitter, metallic taste. I wondered what would be best to hide that taste. Maybe sprinkling it on Grey's serving of Mexican casserole. All that spice would cover up the metallic flavor. I also thought about letting him enjoy his meal and instead putting a bit in his dessert. Or in his beer. Then it came to me. I decided to put it in that gross bean salad he always ate. Grey makes three-bean salad for every party, and then he goes on and on about it, claiming how it is so tasty and so healthy. It is so gross is what it is. That would be perfect, and I knew for sure it was a food he always ate. Once I had made that decision, I was relieved. Grey was going to be served strychnine-laced three-bean salad.

I remembered reading that strychnine worked fast, but I wondered exactly how long it would take from the time Grey ingested it to the time the convulsions would begin. I didn't think it was long, maybe as little as fifteen minutes. If I understood what I read correctly, the first sign would be seeing fear in Grey's eyes as he realized something was wrong. He would be restless, apprehensive. Then he would experience involuntary skeletal muscle spasms. Unfortunately, those were going to be painful. Next, there would be severe arching of his neck and back. He was going to look like the girl in *The Exorcist*.

God, I hope I can control my emotions. I know it sounds ridiculous, but I'm terrified I'm going to laugh while everything is happening. It's not that I'll think it's funny. Quite the opposite. I just get so fucking nervous. I hope my family understands that when I get nervous, or anytime I get overly emotional, I laugh.

Thinking ahead, on the off-chance that Grey decides to make a deathbed confession, I'm hoping I can use my nervous laughter to become hysterical and draw attention away from what Grey is saying. I know that's a longshot, but I'm trying to have a contingency plan in place since I don't know what's going to happen. I mean, I can't have Grey sharing his secret before he dies. And he must know the secret. I mean, it makes sense that he, of all people, would know. I need to be prepared so I can protect the person I love. I will do anything, and I do mean anything, to save her from feeling any more pain than she has already suffered.

Anyway, I hope I have done my homework and the strychnine will act fast enough so none of that is a problem. Respiratory failure should occur quickly and Grey should die relatively fast, so the suffering should be short-lived. It bothers me that I have to kill him, but I can't see any other way to guarantee that he won't say or do anything to cause her pain down the road. She is my only real concern. She is the one I must protect. I'm sorry for Grey, and sorrier for leaving Hunter without parents, but what else can I do? I just don't have a choice.

It will be hard for Hunter at first, but he will eventually move on. There will be others to fill the void. They say time heals all wounds. Hunter is young. He has lots of time. As long as Jody and Grey have never shared the secret with him, Hunter has all the time in the world.

37 GRACE

Grace flung herself across her bed and cried. This wasn't a gentle cry where the tears just trickled down her cheeks, but a loud, heart-wrenching cry that was releasing years of pain that had been bottled up inside of her. For as long as she could remember, her mother loved Gage more than she loved her. Tonight, Grace finally had the nerve to confront her mother with that fact. Her mother denied it, but it didn't matter. Grace knew it was true. So, she cried. She cried for the years of pain, the years of being second best, the years of not having the mother she deserved.

Eventually her room went from light to the gray of dusk to the black of night. Grace didn't bother to turn on a light. She preferred the darkness. It matched her mood. Her crying finally stopped and all that remained were occasional shudders and involuntary sobs. She grabbed a tee-shirt from the foot of her bed and wiped her eyes and nose. She could see light coming in from the hall under the crack of her door. She knew there were other people in the house but she didn't hear any noise. No one was talking. She didn't even hear the sound of a distant television playing. She wondered if her parents were discussing what was said. Probably not. Her mother would be far more concerned with how Gage was doing.

Slowly she rolled to her side and sat up, untangling herself from her oversized sweatshirt that had wrapped itself every-which-way around her. She dangled her feet off the side of her bed and pushed her long hair away from her face. Her breathing was now steady. It was after 7:00. She had been in her room all day, alone, but now she noticed a shadow under her door. Then she heard a gentle knock.

"Grace, Honey, can I come in? Please?"

It was her mother. She waited a moment before answering. Did she want to talk to her right now? Did she want to hear whatever lame excuse her mother was going to provide? Or even worse, was her mother going to deny that she loved Gage more? On the other hand, what choice did she have? She couldn't very well never speak to her mother again. At some point they were going to have to talk. Might as well get it over with. She picked up her pillow and clutched it to her chest, almost like it was armor protecting her heart. "Come in," she whispered.

Beth opened the door slowly and stood at the entrance to the room, a mere silhouette, before finally daring to speak. "Can we talk?"

"Sure, Mom. We probably should."

"Honey, I'm so sorry that you feel the way you do. I want you to know that deep down, I don't feel like you think I do. I love you every bit as much as I love Gage. You both mean the world to me. I'm so sorry if I haven't shown you that over the years. I never meant to hurt you."

"I know you never meant to, Mom, but you did. You do. Over and over. It's always Gage this and Gage that. It's never about me."

Beth tucked a stray hair behind her ear and sighed. "You can't mean that. We do so many things together."

"Like what?"

"We bake together. I always try to make things for when your school's drama club has a bake sale. And I offered to take you shopping for a prom dress. And just last week, didn't I bring you to the hair studio so you could get highlights?"

Grace leaned over and turned the light on next to her bed. She wanted to see her mother's face without all the shadows from the dark room. "Are you serious? Is that the best you have? Yes, you made cookies for the bake sale, but did you go to any of the plays I was in? Even when I would rehearse night and day for months? Or when I worked behind the scenes designing sets? Or how about when I was the director? Did you ever bother to show up in the audience? No, you couldn't go. Why? Because Gage had a game or a match or some other event on those nights so you went to see him instead. And a prom dress? Sure, you offered to bring me to get a dress, but that was only because you didn't bother to ask if I was even going. If you had, you would have known that Jaxon asked Katie Carson to the prom and not me. Not me, Mom. I sat alone in my room and cried for two nights in a row and you didn't even know. You never bothered to find out. You did bring me to get my hair done. I've got to give you that one. I wanted to bring myself. I wanted to go with my friends to get my hair done and then go to the mall, but I couldn't. You know why? Because Gage wanted to use the car that day. That's why. So you pacified me by taking me to the hair salon instead. Big deal. Gage got what he wanted and I got the consolation prize. As usual. It's like I said, it's always about Gage."

Beth was flustered. She swept her hair back with both hands before clasping them together. Then she turned to face her daughter, one foot on the floor, the other tucked up on the bed. "Grace, no, that's not true. Sometimes it may seem like he gets more attention, but that's only because he's not as capable as you are. You have always been the more independent one. You are so much more responsible than he is. You always have been. Please believe me, that doesn't mean I love you less. I promise you. And…"

Grace looked up. "And what?"

Beth glanced over her shoulder to assure no one was standing near the open door. She didn't want Jerry or Gage to hear what she was about to tell Grace. She made a half-hearted attempt to smile at her daughter before saying in a low voice, "Grace, Honey, it's not that

I love Gage more than I love you. That's just not true. I love you both so much. I would give my life for either of you. You are both my whole world. Both of you. It's your father, Grace. He always favored you over Gage. Surely you can see that. You have always been his baby girl. I was trying to protect Gage. To make him feel special. I didn't want him to feel left out. Maybe I over-compensated and for that I am truly sorry. I never meant to hurt you. But please know, I never loved Gage more than you. You are both everything to me."

Grace remained quiet, staring down at her hands that were now folded on her lap. Could her mother's words be true? Could her mother focus more on Gage because he needed her more than she did? Because she was trying to balance the love of their father? Grace couldn't deny that her dad did seem to favor her over Gage. He was always there for her. He went to her high school plays. He let her use the car if she asked him. He would share a special wink from across the table, or hug her when she was down. Now that she was thinking about it, she didn't recall him doing that with Gage. Maybe it was true. Maybe her mom was just trying to make sure Gage didn't feel neglected by her dad by being extra nice to him. It was possible.

Grace looked at her mother who was sitting on the bed, close enough that she could reach over and touch her. Her mom looked hopeful that Grace would understand. She looked desperate that Grace was hearing her words. Grace moved her hand over just a few inches until her fingers touched Beth's hand. She could feel how cold her mother's fingertips were as they reached around and clenched Grace's warm hand. They sat there in silence, clutching each other, trying to reconnect. Grace could feel her mother's love flowing through their joined hands and it felt good. For the first time in years, maybe ever, Grace felt like she was the most important person in her mother's life. She wanted this moment to last forever.

Slowly, she could feel Beth pull her closer. Beth's arms wrapped around her. When was the last time her mother held her like this? Sure, she had given her lots of hugs over the years. Hundreds of them. But none ever felt quite so sincere. Grace rested her head on Beth's shoulder and it felt right. Her mom did love her. She had been silly thinking she didn't. All those wasted years feeling like her mother cared more about Gage. No mother could hug her like this if she didn't love her like her life depended on it. Grace could feel a tear slide down her cheek, even though she was smiling. She was at peace.

Grace wasn't sure how long they sat together. It could have been a minute, or an hour. She only knew that it felt right. Then she heard a door at the other end of the hallway open and her brother yell, "Mom, can I borrow the car? I'm hungry and I want to go get something to eat."

Beth kissed Grace on the top of her head and quickly scurried out of their hug. "Of course, Honey. Let me get my keys for you."

38 BETH

Beth was both excited and sad; excited because it was finely time for the family get-together she had been planning, sad because it was the first one without Jody. Sometimes she was surprised at how much she missed her younger sister, especially now when the family was coming together for a party. Jody was definitely the cook of the family. Whatever she brought would have been exquisite. Beth would tell her how delicious everything was, Jody would give her recipes that she would never use, and they would laugh over the silliest things. It was hard to believe that these times were never going to happen again.

Beth wanted to sit at the table, put her head in her hands, and cry. Instead, she looked around the kitchen and realized that she needed to get to work if she wanted to have everything ready in time for the party. The roasted turkey casserole was already in the oven, but she still had to toss the salad and bake both blondies and brownies. Then she would pack everything in her car to bring to Delaney's house. Plus, she still had to shower and find something decent to wear. Hopefully, Jerry and the kids would be home soon.

She worked quickly and by 4:00 everything was ready to go. Jerry still wouldn't be home for another hour, but both Gage and Grace were upstairs in their rooms getting dressed. Beth had made a big deal out of asking Grace to ride to Delaney's with her, even suggesting that Gage could wait and ride over later with Jerry. It seemed silly that they all hurry, so she didn't mind.

She took one last look in the mirror to make sure she looked presentable. She wore dark jeans paired with a royal blue sweater and a silver chain necklace. She ran her fingers through her short blond hair and put silver hoop earrings on. Then she stepped into her boots. She was ready to go.

"Grace, are you ready?" Beth called up the stairs. "Let's head to Delaney's."

Together the two of them loaded the car with everything needed for the party. Beth yelled a final goodbye to Gage and she and Grace made the four-mile drive to Delaney's house. Conversation was minimal on the ride over. As planned, they were the first to arrive. Delaney greeted them at the door and within the hour the kitchen and dining areas were covered with food and drink. Everything was ready and Beth, Grace and Delaney were seated on couches in the family room looking out over the mountains. Most of the snow had melted but the trees were still bare, their branches dark and jagged as they reached toward the graying sky. It was a cool night with an even cooler breeze. By the time family members started arriving, they would be clutching their jackets tightly around their bodies as they made their way across the driveway to the front door. As the three women chatted, it didn't take long before the conversation turned to Jody.

Beth's eyes flew open when Delaney asked her, "Were you relieved to find out that it was Jody who was the half-sister and not you?"

"Delaney! Why are you talking about that now?" Beth looked shocked as she stared at her youngest sister while trying to nod her head in the direction of Grace.

"It's alright, Mom," Grace added. "I already know about Aunt Jody being your half-sister. News like that tends to get around this family rather quickly."

Beth looked at Grace. "You know?"

"Of course I know. We all know. Geesh, Mom. Did you think no one was going to talk about it? Anyway, it's not a big deal. So what. Nana got around. Who cares?"

"Grace! Stop that. That's no way to talk about your grandmother!"

Delaney could not hold back her laughter. "I don't know, Beth. Sounds pretty accurate to me."

Beth tried to look stern, but seeing her sister and her daughter sitting together and laughing like co-conspirators wore away her resolve. Soon the three of them were giggling like school girls. Finally, Beth asked, "So who all knows?"

"God, Mom. Everyone. We all know. The whole family. And honestly, no one cares."

"Who told you?"

"I don't know. I don't remember. And it really doesn't matter. A bunch of us cousins did the same thing you and your sisters did. It's no big deal. Let it go."

"You did what?"

"We sent our DNA into GeneScreen. It looked like fun, to see our family heritage."

Beth sat quietly on the couch trying to decide if this was a good thing or a bad thing. Before she could ponder it further, the front door opened and other family members started arriving. First in was Samantha, Derek, Chelsie and Raegan. Before they even closed the door, Grey and Hunter arrived. Then came Paul and Adeline, followed shortly by Jerry and Gage. Delaney's children, Wyatt and Roxie, were now downstairs, excited to see their cousins. Delaney announced that Jack would be home in a few minutes.

Ten minutes later, Beth smiled as she looked around the large island in the kitchen. It was covered with platters of food--casseroles, salads, breads, a cheese board and a veggie tray. On the counter next to the six-burner Jenn-Air cooktop were at least four or five different kinds of desserts. There was a cooler on the floor filled with soda for the kids and beer and hard cider for the adults. There was also a fully stocked bar available. Then the door between the house and the garage opened and in came Jack. The party was officially underway.

Beth sipped her wine, watching as everyone stood around the kitchen, most with drinks in hand. It was good to see her family laughing and talking, especially Grey and Hunter. She thought about banging two pots together to get everyone to be quiet so they could make a toast to Jody, but then decided against it. After all, the whole point of the party was to reunite the family, to help them cope with Jody's death. It appeared to her that was exactly what they were doing. Why mess with perfection? Instead, she picked up a plate and yelled, "Let's eat!"

It didn't take long before people were digging into the food that was spread around the kitchen. Once plates were filled, some family members wandered into the family room and sat on the beige couches, balancing their plates on their laps to eat. Others stood in the kitchen. A few went outside on the deck. It was cold, but the big stone fireplace was burning wood at full force, so the chairs closest to it were nice and toasty. There was also space in the front living room for people to spread out and eat. Fortunately, Delaney didn't have any rules about where people could bring food in her house.

Jack was helping his children fill their plates, insisting they choose dinner entrees and not desserts for their meals. Samantha and Delaney were both hovering around Paul, making sure he was getting enough to eat. A few others were assuring everyone had what they needed during dinner, whether it was food, drink or a place to sit. For the first time in weeks, Grey felt his appetite come back. He filled his plate, making sure he had a healthy portion of his favorite bean salad. Just as he turned to go in search of Hunter, he awkwardly bumped into another family member. It wasn't his fault, but he set his plate on the table and apologized profusely as he helped them to their feet where they had stumbled. He was surprised that he received a hug for his kindness, and even more surprised at how long the hug lasted. Finally, he accepted his plate that had been retrieved from the table and handed to him. Then he laughed, said thank you, and made his way across the room to Hunter.

Even though his son was 16-years-old, he couldn't help but coddle the boy, especially now that he had just lost his mother. "Hunter," Grey said, "have you gotten anything to eat yet?"

Hunter rolled his eyes, the movement so subtle that it was oblivious to Grey. "Not yet," he replied.

"Here, you take my plate. I'll go fix myself another." With those words that Grey would later come to regret, he passed his dinner plate to Hunter, along with a fork neatly wrapped in a napkin, and hesitated before going off in search of a clean plate to prepare for himself.

"Thanks, Dad," Hunter said, accepting his father's plate because that was easier than arguing with him that he would rather get his own later. Although he wasn't hungry, he scooped up a big bite of his dad's three-bean salad and stuffed it in his mouth for no other reason than to make his father happy. It was just the two of them now and Hunter understood the importance of them sticking together as much as possible.

Grey beamed before walking away. He filled a new plate with food and joined his father-in-law, now in the kitchen, where they quickly engaged in a conversation about the odds of the Red Sox making it to the World Series. Music could be heard from the adjoining family room and laughter was coming from the sisters on the other side of the island near the sink. And that's when the jovial atmosphere of the party suddenly changed.

Beth was standing in the kitchen when the scream came from the family room. She instinctively knew it wasn't the kids playing around. It was Grace, and it was serious. Although she didn't hesitate before dropping her plate on the counter and rushing into the other room, Delaney, Jack and Grey had all arrived before her. Delaney, immediately resuming her role of nurse, was yelling at Jack to call nine-one-one. Grey was on his knees next to Hunter trying his best to comfort him, but doing a rather poor job of it, since his words were rapid and unsure sounding. Hunter was lying on his back, face pale, eyes looking from one person to another, clearly terrified.

Beth could see other people enter the room but they stood back, forming a semi-circle around Hunter, Grey and Delaney. She didn't pay any attention to those family members. She only watched Jack to make sure he got through to nine-one-one. She felt a small touch of relief when he advised that an ambulance was on the way.

"He's seizing," Delaney announced. "Everyone,

stand back. Give us room. Jack, how long before the ambulance gets here?"

"Ten minutes," Jack stated as he pushed his way next to Delaney while simultaneously indicating to everyone else to take a few steps back. He looked across the room where Samantha and Raegan were clinging protectively to each other. Next to them he saw Derek, who was huddled in the corner with Chelsie. "Derek," he yelled, "can you open the front door? Watch for the ambulance. Make sure they don't miss us."

Derek nodded and immediately went to the front of the house. He grabbed his coat and went out the door into the cold evening air, turning on all outside lights along the way.

Inside, Delaney's days as an emergency department nurse were coming back to her like they were yesterday, muscle memory for nursing. Something was dancing around the outskirts of her mind and she was trying her damnedest to focus on what her brain was trying to tell her. It was something important. Something about Hunter's symptoms. She assessed Hunter, whom she now considered her patient. He was restless, terrified. He said his arms and legs hurt. And his jaw. His jaw. That was definitely triggering something in her mind. What the fuck was it? Then he had another seizure. He arched his back. At one point he lifted so high off the floor he appeared to be resting on only his head and feet. Son-of-a-bitch, Delaney thought. He's been poisoned. "Hunter, Hunter, can you hear me? Hunter, did you eat or drink anything tonight? Hunter?"

Grace appeared from in back of Delaney. "We ate dinner together. We sat on the couch and ate together."

"How long ago?" Delaney practically screamed the words at Grace, who took a step back, as if in fear.

"I'm not exactly sure. Maybe twenty minutes ago. It wasn't long. We ate and then we were just sitting here. He started acting weird. He got all nervous and shaky and then he had one of those convulsions like you just saw. That's when I screamed."

Delaney looked back at Hunter. He was now lying quietly on the floor. Suddenly what her mind had been circling around hit her. She knew what she was dealing with. "Jack, Jack, where the fuck are you?"

"I'm right here. What do you need?"

"Listen, run up to my bathroom. In my medicine cabinet, there's Valium. Get it to me. Hurry!"

Jack took off without question. Over the years he had learned to trust Delaney's instinct, especially when it came to nursing matters. She may have been out of the field for a long time, but in her day, she had been one of the best E.D. nurses Cayne Medical Center had ever seen. He wasn't about to argue medicine with her now.

Less than a minute later, Jack was back in the family room with the Valium. Delaney removed the cap and had him help raise Hunter to give him some of the medication. At the same time the wail of an ambulance could be heard. Quickly, Jerry started clearing the room. "Everyone, move into the kitchen. Make way for the paramedics. Let's go, move!"

Beth jumped up to help him. "Yes, everyone, step away. Let's make sure the paramedics have room to work." She waved her arms around and herded everyone into the next room with such efficiency that not one single person noticed when she nonchalantly picked up the bottle of Valium from the table near Delaney and stuffed it, unseen, into her pants pocket.

With the exception of Delaney, Jack, Grey, and Derek, who was still outside, the family members went into the kitchen, but remained hovering by the doorway as much as possible. They were remarkably quiet for such a large crowd. They were obviously trying to listen to everything happening in the family room.

Once the paramedics arrived, they were quick to place an IV line in Hunter and get fluids started on him. There was talk of activated charcoal, but Delaney explained she had already given him Diazepam, plus Hunter was now in and out of consciousness, so that plan of treatment was immediately discarded. They put him on hi-flow oxygen and strapped him to a stretcher. One paramedic was on the radio to the hospital calling in suspected strychnine poisoning. Several gasps could be heard from family members in the kitchen. Grace started to cry. Raegan said 'fuck,' which got her a stern look from Samantha. Even Gage, who didn't usually get riled up by anything, turned pale and had to sit on the closest bar stool. Minutes later, Hunter, Grey and the paramedics left for the hospital, red lights flashing and siren blaring. Looks of fear remained on the faces of all family members left behind. At least, all family members except one. One was working hard to make sure their face didn't show disappointment.

Oh my God. I can't believe I hurt Hunter again. I never meant to hurt Hunter. It was supposed to be Grey. How did Hunter end up with Grey's plate? I mean, I put the fucking plate in Grey's hands. And I can't believe that Delaney figured out what was wrong so fast. I'm glad she did. I didn't want to hurt Hunter, but what am I supposed to do now? Grey is going to be suspicious, and that detective guy will be hanging around. What if I never get another chance to get rid of Grey? I am trying so hard to stop her pain, and now I've made things worse than ever. This is bad.

39 SAMANTHA

Samantha needed a friend right now, but she didn't have anyone to turn to. Too many things were building up in her life and she couldn't handle them. She was pacing from the living room to the kitchen and back to the living room. She walked around the island, across the hardwood floor past the recliner, around the sofa, past the bookshelf, toward the island, repeat. Her footsteps were hard and fast. Her hands were clenched into fists as she walked. Her mind was jumping from one issue to another. Jody was dead. Murdered. Her throat slashed. Someone had tried to kill Hunter. Twice. And Derek. Derek was cheating on her. He was having an affair with that slut from his office. Krystal. For all she knew, he was with her right now. He could be in her bed this very minute instead of home where he belonged. Her stomach wrenched as she made another lap. What was she going to do?

She tried to think back to what she did the last time Derek was having an affair. It was with the little dark-haired woman from the coffee shop. Callie or Carrie or something like that. She was surprised she couldn't remember the woman's name. It had only been a year ago. She swore then that it was going to be the last time. She had even talked to Delaney about what she should do. Now that she was thinking about it, she wondered why she told Delaney. That was so unlike her. She remembered the phone conversation they had. Chelsie and Raegan were both upstairs in their rooms, Derek was golfing. Delaney had called, something about a fund raiser for Wyatt, and Samantha had just found a receipt in Derek's pants for coffee at the shop where Callie/Carrie worked. She was crying when she answered the phone. Delaney had asked what was wrong and it all came pouring out. Samantha couldn't control herself. She told Delaney about the affair and how she couldn't take it anymore and she didn't know what to do. She cried and wailed into the phone for what seemed like hours, at times sobbing like a 5-year-old.

Delaney was so good to her during that call. She didn't judge her or lose patience with her. She let her talk and then she let her cry. After Samantha had settled down, Delaney suggested that she stop hiding from Derek and talk to him. She should tell him that she knows what he's up to and that he has to stop. Samantha explained to Delaney that she couldn't do that. Next, Delaney only half-jokingly suggested that Samantha go to Callie/Carrie and tell her to leave her husband alone or else she would beat the living shit out of her. Hearing Delaney talk like that actually made Samantha laugh.

They talked for hours that day, which was unusual for the two of them. As sisters, they weren't that close. Samantha remembered thinking it was nice, that Delaney was there for her. But after they hung up, she didn't follow any of the advice Delaney had given her. She didn't confront Derek or Callie/Carrie. Eventually the affair fizzled out, like they always did. Samantha stopped crying and life returned to normal. Until now. Now it was starting all over again.

Realizing that she couldn't continue walking in circles around the house, Samantha sat down and pulled out her cell phone. As usual, Derek was gone, Chelsie was back at school for a few more weeks, and Raegan was upstairs in her room. Luckily, Raegan's door was closed. Her computer was on so she couldn't hear her mother cry.

Samantha needed to talk to someone. She thought about calling Delaney but quickly ruled her out. After all, she didn't take Delaney's advice the last time she talked about Derek's affairs, why would Delaney want to talk to her about them again? Plus, she would probably have to hear about how Delaney saved Hunter's life the other night and she wasn't in the mood to listen to how wonderful Delaney was right now. And she knew she was wrong for this, but she also didn't feel like getting an update on Hunter. She had her own issues to deal with; she didn't have it in her to act interested in anyone else.

Then she thought about calling Daddy. He was always nice to her when she called. Of course, there was a chance that Adeline would answer the phone. Adeline would be nice, but Samantha wasn't stupid, she knew that it was just an act. Adeline was always trying to turn her father against her. No, she didn't want to deal with her tonight, either.

She finally decided to call Beth. She didn't know if Beth would have great advice for her, but Beth would have kind words and she would listen. Maybe that's what she needed the most right now.

Beth's phone only rang twice before her voice came across in a cheerful pitch. "Hello."

"Hi, it's me. Samantha. I have to talk to you." Samantha barely got the words out before her tears started to fall. She tried to keep her voice even so she wouldn't disturb Raegan, but as soon as she started telling Beth about the affair Derek was having with Krystal, the sobs got louder. She could no longer sit still and she began pacing again. Without hesitation, she told Beth everything. She told her that Krystal was Derek's secretary, a petite blond with big blue eyes and an exaggerated interest in Derek. She told her about sneaking out and seeing his car at the office when the only other person who was working was Krystal. Since then, she also snuck by Krystal's house. She knew where she lived because at the company Christmas party Krystal had said she lived on Redstone Drive in the yellow house—yellow, just like her hair. Ugh. How lame. Anyway, she hadn't seen Derek's car there, but she thinks he parks in the garage when he goes over. She's absolutely sure about the affair. She went on for almost an hour before she finally gave Beth a chance to respond. By then she was practically in hysterics. "What do I do?" she cried before falling silent.

"Samantha. I'm so sorry. I know how hard this must be for you."

"How can you possibly know? It's not like Jerry ever cheated on you."

"No, but I can hear in your voice the hurt you are feeling. I do want to help."

"You can't help. Nobody can."

"I want to. Just tell me what I can do."

"You can kill that home-wrecking bitch. That's what you can do."

"Samantha, stop. Talking like that isn't going to help. Have you tried talking to Derek?"

"You know I can't. What am I going to say? Stop cheating on me? He'll just deny it. Or worse, he'll leave. I can't risk it, Beth. I can't risk him leaving. What would I do without him?"

At that thought, Samantha started crying all over again. The conversation continued this way for another hour, with Beth trying to find the right words to comfort Samantha, and Samantha not seeing any way out of her situation. Both women were feeling lost when Samantha heard the sound of a garage door being raised. "Beth, listen, I've got to go. Derek's home."

"Are you going to talk to him?"

"No, I can't. But I've got to run. I'm going to jump in the shower so he won't know I've been crying. I've got to go."

"Samantha, I love you."

"Ya, love you too, Beth. Bye." Samantha clicked off her phone as she ran up the stairs and headed to her bedroom. As she ran by Raegan's room, she noticed her door was open just a crack. Shit. She hoped her youngest daughter hadn't been able to hear what she had said to Beth. It's bad enough that Chelsie was aware of her father's shortcomings, she didn't need for Raegan to know about them, too. She wanted to stop and listen at the door to see if she was gaming on her computer, but she didn't have time. She had to get in the shower so Derek wouldn't see the redness around her eyes from her crying.

She wished she was stronger, that she could confront him and tell him to stop or she would leave him. She just didn't think she was ready to say those words. What would she do without him? She would be alone, broke, and solely responsible for their two daughters. No, it would be better to pretend everything was alright, just like she had been doing. She stepped into the steamy shower as he opened the door into the kitchen.

40 GREY

The hum of machinery could be heard nonstop in the background of the hospital room. Although the lights were dimmed, Grey could clearly make out the shape of his son lying in the bed. Hunter's head was elevated and he was surrounded by bags of IV fluids, along with oxygen tubing, monitors and various other machinery. Grey sat quietly in the dark at the side of the bed. He was exhausted as he sat there, feeling like a lone sentinel over his son.

As the nurses came into the room and glanced at Grey, the only movement they saw was the slow rise and fall of his chest. They might have thought he was sleeping, except for his eyes. They were open wide, the light from the monitors reflecting off their dark centers as he stared straight ahead. They tried to get him to go home and rest, but he wouldn't leave. He hadn't shaved or showered. When he was hungry, he waited until a family member brought him something to eat. But not just any family member; he would only accept food from

Delaney, Paul or Samantha. If anyone else brought it, he tossed it in the trash as soon as they left. When he was tired, he slept in the chair alongside Hunter's bed. The nursing staff had been kind; they brought him pillows and warm blankets. He wouldn't even leave the room long enough to use the adjoining bathroom unless there was a nurse in the room tending to Hunter. He wouldn't leave his son alone.

Grey feared for Hunter's life, even though he knew that Hunter was not the killer's target. He was well aware that the plate of tainted food was meant for him, not Hunter. Grey also realized that whoever tried to run Hunter over the night he walked home from math club thought they were aiming the car at Grey. It was usually Grey that walked home. It was a fluke that it was Hunter walking that night. That night, when Hunter was wearing Grey's jacket. But even knowing that Hunter wasn't the target didn't mean he could stop worrying. Twice now, Hunter almost lost his life. Whether he was the target and Hunter was merely a victim of circumstances was irrelevant. Grey would not give the killer another chance to harm his son.

As he sat in the darkness, he thought about the night of the party. Everything was fine when they arrived at Delaney's house. Grey was sure of that. The only guests at the house were family--Jody's dad and his girlfriend, Adeline, and Jody's sisters and their families. That was it. No one else was there. As difficult as it was to accept, one of those family members tried to kill him. Grey also realized that whoever that person was, more than likely, they were the one who killed Jody. He couldn't understand who would do that. Who would hate Jody and him enough to kill them? Or maybe it wasn't Jody. Maybe they were trying to hurt him from the beginning. That thought was even more terrible than believing that they wanted him dead—that Jody died as an innocent bystander. And now, that same fate almost happened to Hunter. Try as he might, he could not think of who could hate him enough to want to kill him.

He ran his hand through his hair. He could only think of one mistake that he had made that could cause someone to despise him that much. But how could something that happened so many years ago come back to haunt him now? Especially since only one other person knew about it. Surely that couldn't be the cause of all this.

Then his mind switched back to the party. He knew that whoever attempted to poison him had to have access to his food shortly before he sat down to eat. After all, he brought the bean salad with him and that is where the police found traces of strychnine, in the bean salad on Hunter's plate. It was not in any other food; clearly he was targeted. But who could have sprinkled it on his plate? Grey wracked his brain. Who did he see that night? Where was everyone? He had to be certain, he couldn't make any mistakes. Try as he might, other than himself and Hunter, he could only eliminate three people from all the people who were at the party. Paul, Samantha and Delaney. The three of them were talking right next to him; they had all been engaged in an intense discussion for at least ten or fifteen minutes before Grace screamed. None of them would have had time to poison Hunter's food. He could eliminate those three, but that left an entire roomful of family members as suspects. As much as he pondered who would want to hurt him, none of it made any sense.

Then he thought about what Hunter's doctor told him. She stressed what an incredibly lucky young man Hunter was, under the circumstances. First, the odds of having someone in the room who recognized the signs of strychnine poisoning was a miracle in itself, and knowing how to treat it was even more amazing. Delaney surely saved the boy's life with her quick thinking. Grey would be forever grateful to his sister-in-law for her actions that night.

Dr. Evans also explained that the person who poisoned Hunter chose the wrong food to use as a conduit. They chose to use Grey's special bean salad that contained legumes, peas, and a variety of both green vegetables and nuts. All of those ingredients contain tannins. Tannins, by chance, neutralize strychnine. That, and the fact that they didn't give him a fatal dose, allowed Hunter to survive what is usually a lethal murder attempt. More often than not, someone poisoned with strychnine will die within an hour or two of ingesting it. It's a quick-acting poison, usually killing its victim before medical staff can figure out what happened. Luckily, in Hunter's case, everything fell into place, and since he survived the first twenty-four hours, the strychnine poisoning won't be fatal.

Hunter needed to remain hospitalized until Dr. Evans ruled out any long-term side effects. She explained to Grey that she was mostly concerned with kidney failure. She wasn't worried about brain damage because Hunter never went into respiratory arrest, so his brain was never oxygen deprived.

Again, it is difficult to look at a 16-year-old boy who just lost his mother to a gruesome murder, and who had someone try to kill him on two separate occasions, and consider him to be lucky. But when Grey gazed at his son, he did. He realized that Hunter must have his own special guardian angel. *Thank you, Jody,* he whispered as he continued his silent vigilance late into the night.

41 THE VISITOR

"Fuck you, Grey. Fuck you and the horse you rode in on." I couldn't believe I said that right out loud, which was okay because I was home alone. Then I laughed. What did that expression mean, anyway? Who rode a horse these days, and even if someone did, why did the horse have to get fucked? What did the horse do other than be forced to carry some fat-ass person who was too lazy to walk or too stupid to drive? Sounds like the horse was already fucked, as far as I could tell. I decided not to use that expression again. It was only derogatory to the poor horse. Instead, a simple "Fuck you, Grey" would have to suffice.

Because of Grey, the poisoning didn't go as planned. I was so disappointed, I didn't know what to do. I never imagined Grey would give his plate of food to Hunter. I couldn't believe it when I realized that he did that. He found out Hunter hadn't eaten anything so he gave him his plate and he fixed himself another. Unfuckingbelievable! Who does that for a 16-year-old?

Why couldn't he just let Hunter get his own plate? Not that it would have made any difference. Delaney still would have figured out what was happening and saved the day. Even if it had been Grey who ingested the poison like he was supposed to, she still would have ruined everything. I mean, shit, she hasn't even been a nurse for like, ten years, and she knew exactly what to do. How the fuck does that even happen? No wonder there's so much tension between the sisters in this family. How can anyone get along with a know-it-all like Delaney?

And to top it off, what the hell got into Jack? He was running around the night of the party barking orders and telling everyone what to do. He swept all of us into the other room like we were cattle. Like Delaney was the only one who was important. Who died and put him in charge? No one, I thought glumly. No one died, thanks to his wife. Then the ambulance arrived and took Hunter away and boom, just like that, it was over.

At first, I was devastated by this--Grey still being alive and all. But later, after serious contemplation, I realized that it wasn't so bad. Hunter was in the intensive care unit at the hospital, so Grey wouldn't be thinking about anything except that. I would have time to come up with a new plan. Rumor is that Hunter was stable, but not completely out of the woods. He could still develop kidney failure and die--or live with the consequences of being poisoned. I hope Hunter doesn't die. After all, we are closely related. As long as he doesn't know the truth, I don't have to worry about him causing any problems.

I shook my head, trying to clear it of these thoughts that never seem to stop, and walked to my closet. Still wrapped in a flannel shirt was the dagger I used to kill Jody. I initially thought it would be safe there, but now that people know a family member is behind everything, that was no longer the case. As much as I hated to, I knew I had to find another home for it.

I considered lots of different options--the river, the lake, a dumpster, the choices were plentiful. Then I had the most brilliant idea of all. What if I hid the dagger on the land that surrounds Delaney's house? The blade has been cleaned so carefully, there wasn't a fingerprint on it. I'm sure of it. I could sneak it into the woods where it wouldn't be found, unless someday I chose to call the police and anonymously tell them about it. Yes, that would be the best place for the dagger to be hidden. That is what I must do, and very soon, before that detective starts snooping around with a search warrant.

42 HOLMES

Ronan was pissed. He had a limited number of suspects, but not a murderer. Worse, he wasn't sure which one of them was the guilty one. Sure, he had it narrowed down to just a few, but a few isn't one. If he could convince a judge to give him a couple of search warrants, that would probably clinch it for him, but no, not enough evidence. He needed more. Come back when you have one suspect, not three. Well, I would have one suspect if the judge would give me the damn search warrant, he thought. The irony of the situation was giving him an ulcer.

Or maybe it was the scotch that he was drinking that was giving him an ulcer. He knew it was not quite the quality of the drink he had at Paul Peralta's house, but it would have to do. He picked up the glass and held it between his thumb and middle finger, swirling its contents. He held it up to the light, but the amber liquid held no secrets. Then he drank it quickly, noting how it warmed him in a way the gas fireplace he was sitting next to hadn't been able to accomplish.

He searched through his notepad making sure he didn't miss any clues, any hint that might help him narrow down his suspect list from three to one. His rough, handwritten notes were etched in his mind from the many times he had read through them. Nothing escaped him. Next, he searched through the financial records, phone records, lab reports and every bit of information that he had collected. He read and reread the documents Wes had sent over. He scanned Jody's autopsy report. He studied everything on this case until his eyes blurred and he was having trouble keeping his head up. He had the evidence in this case practically memorized. There was nothing he was missing. Yet, he still had three suspects, not one.

Ronan glanced at the clock. It was almost 2:00. Jody was dead and Hunter was in the hospital. He was wondering if it would be good detective work to narrow down his suspect list with a quick round of eeny, meeny, miny, moe, when it hit him. He didn't need to worry about three suspects right now. He only needed to take the least likely one off the list. Once she was gone, he could go back to the court for a search warrant. The other two were living in the same house. Finally, he had a concrete plan.

Right now, he was going to finish his scotch and go to bed. Tomorrow, when he woke up, he would shower, eat a full-on Irish breakfast, put on a clean suit, and then pay a visit to one Beth Magnolia Lennox, aka, Suspect Number Three.

43 DELANEY

It had been a busy day, but now the dinner dishes were done. Jack had taken the kids to Thunder Circle where they would enjoy a few rounds of go karts and bumper cars. Delaney sat in a comfortable rocking chair in the quiet little alcove of her bedroom, appreciating the solitude of the empty house. It was just starting to get dark outside, but she hadn't bothered to turn on any lights. There was no reason to. She could relax as well in the graying dusk as she could in a fully lit house.

As she gently rocked by the window, she thought of how her day had gone. She got up early to make breakfast. At least, she made her version of breakfast—oatmeal from little packets out of a box, cinnamon rolls from the freezer, and hot chocolate from pods that worked in the Keurig. After the abrupt end to the party last night, she thought the kids might need to talk. She wondered if they would have questions about what happened. She didn't want to give them too much information, but she made up her mind to honestly answer anything they asked.

Roxie had come down the stairs first, still in her flannel pajamas and fuzzy purple slippers. She looked sleepy when she wandered into the kitchen, so Delaney led her to one of the recliners in the family room, picked her up, and together they rocked quietly for a good thirty minutes. At first, they didn't talk, they just cuddled. Eventually, Roxie asked her how Hunter was and what happened. As gently as possible, Delaney explained that Hunter ate something that was bad and it made him terribly sick. He was now in the hospital where the doctors and nurses were taking very good care of him. Uncle Grey was with him, too. They thought Hunter would be fine in a few days, but he would have to stay in the hospital until they were sure. Roxie seemed content with that explanation.

Shortly after, Delaney headed to the kitchen to slice fresh bananas and pour glasses of orange juice, while Roxie went upstairs to call Wyatt and Jack to breakfast. Soon the four of them were seated around the large farmhouse table. It was rare that they all shared breakfast together, and Delaney, looking at Jack and her children, appreciated just how lucky she was.

After breakfast, the family played games and watched television together. No one even bothered getting dressed until almost noon. Shortly after 3:00, Delaney announced that she had to run to the hospital to bring Grey something to eat. She explained that he didn't want to leave Hunter's side, although she left out the part that it was because he was fearful that someone might sneak into Hunter's room and try to kill him. Delaney changed into jeans and a charcoal sweatshirt and left Jack to watch the kids, announcing that she would be back in an hour.

By the time she returned, everyone was dressed and Jack had made dinner. For the third time that day, the four of them sat around the table for a family meal. Knowing how close they came to losing Hunter, they all clung a little more to each other than they would have under normal circumstances. During dinner, Jack laughingly told Delaney that he promised to take the kids to Thunder Circle for a couple of hours since they whooped him on one of the video games they played. Although they invited Delaney to go with them, she opted to stay at home and relax. Well, relax after she took care of the supper dishes, she thought.

With hoots and hollers, Jack and the two children grabbed their coats and headed out the door, each claiming that they would be the victor of both go-karts and bumper cars. As she watched them go, Delaney's heart was filled with love for this family of hers.

She cleared the table and loaded the dishwasher. Once the kitchen was taken care of, she left only a small light on and went upstairs to her bedroom. Instead of taking a shower like she planned, she collapsed on the rocking chair next to the window and just sat there, enjoying the solitude that only comes at dusk with an empty house. She did love this house with its spacious rooms and spa bathroom, but after today, she knew she could let it go. It wasn't nearly as important to her as her family was. Watching Jack playing with the children, seeing their faces light up during game time today, that's what mattered to her. She realized that she was finally ready to sell the house and move to something smaller and more reasonably priced.

She would miss this view, though. With that thought in mind, she glanced through the window to the darkening night. It was still gray outside, but soon the only light would be from the full moon that was rapidly taking its place in the blackening sky. Then something caught her eye on the small dirt road that was used as a right-of-way from the main street through the back line of their property. Usually, the only time they saw traffic on that road was when a utility company needed to access the cables that ran through their property to their neighbors. That almost never occurred this late in the day.

Not wanting to disrupt the peacefulness that surrounded her, she stayed in her chair and watched the vehicle as it drove slowly down the dirt road. Odd, she thought, that it wasn't a white utility truck. Odder still was that it didn't have its headlights on. True, it wasn't yet nightfall, but it was dark enough to turn on its lights.

Then the vehicle pulled over and backed into a flat area where there were no trees. She tried to see what kind of vehicle it was. If I didn't know better, she thought, I would say that was Samantha's car. She chuckled at the thought of Samantha being in the woods this late in the day. Samantha, who didn't even like driving to the mall at night, sure as hell wouldn't be traipsing alone in the three acres of woods behind Delaney's house.

Curious, Delaney kept watching the vehicle to see what would happen next. She wasn't fearful, but she was careful not to move or attract any attention to the window where she was sitting. She was certain it was better that whoever was out there didn't realize they were being watched. She saw a person emerge from the driver's side of the vehicle. She waited, but no one else got out. Either the driver was alone, or if they had a passenger, the passenger elected to stay inside. Delaney tried to see if she could recognize who was now walking toward the tree line, but they were wearing a dark coat and watch cap. She couldn't make out if it was a man or a woman, let alone any facial features. They were carrying something. Not something big, not a body was actually the thought that went through her mind, but something that they could hold in one hand. Then they disappeared in the trees.

Delaney was unsure what to do. What if this person tried to enter her home. Should she hide? Call the police? What could she use to protect herself? The more she thought about it, the more she understood that she could be in real danger. This was not her imagination running away with silly thoughts. Someone killed Jody. Someone made two attempts to kill Hunter. And that someone was a member of her family. The same family that was in this very house, eating and drinking and laughing like everything was fine, just last night. What if they were coming back right now to kill her? After all, she did prevent them from finishing the job they started with Hunter.

Suddenly she was afraid. Terrified might be a better word. She sat motionless, her hand clinging so tightly to her cell phone that her knuckles were turning white. She was listening for the slightest noise that someone might be entering her house. What should she do? Even if she called nine-one-one at the first sound of a door opening or a window breaking, it would take them at least ten minutes to arrive. Could she fight off whoever it was for that long?

Should she hide? Should she try to slide under the bed right now, before whoever was out there even tried to get into the house? They probably didn't know she was home. They wouldn't think to look under the bed. Then she could just stay quiet until, until what? Until Jack got home with the children? No, that wasn't a good plan. She couldn't risk them hurting Jack or her kids. No, whatever was going to happen, had to happen now.

She peered out the window again, not rocking, not moving her body. She slowly turned her head to see if the vehicle had changed its position. There was movement. It was darker outside and more difficult to make out what was happening, but she was sure she saw movement. Yes, there it was again. Someone was walking near the vehicle. Then she saw the front door of the car open. The figure dressed in dark clothing got in, closed the door, and started the car. This time the headlights came on. The car reversed direction and headed back down the dirt road the same way it came in. Delaney let out a long, deep breath. How incredibly strange, she thought. Someone came here to put something on our land. She wondered what it was. She was curious; she couldn't imagine what was so important that someone would actually sneak onto her land when they thought no one was home to leave it there. A chill ran down her spine. She reassured herself that whatever it was, it was too small to be a body. She would cling to that bit of knowledge because there was no way in hell she was going out there tonight to see what it was.

She finally loosened her grip on her cell phone. It would be at least another hour before Jack returned with the kids. She knew one thing for sure, she wasn't taking a shower now. She wasn't moving from this chair until she heard his car pull into the garage and the sound of him and their children fill the house. Only then would she stop her vigilance to make sure no one was trying to enter her home. Suddenly, she understood how Grey felt as he sat in the hospital room watching over Hunter. What, exactly, was happening to this family?

44 BETH

Detective Holmes wanted to talk to Beth. Beth wanted to talk to Grace. Jerry didn't want to talk to anybody. This was not the way Beth thought the day after the family get-together was going to go. She had envisioned her family sharing breakfast this morning, chatting happily about the lovely time they had last night. Instead, she was sitting alone at the kitchen table pushing her cereal around in her bowl, wondering how everything had gone so wrong. Someone tried to kill Hunter. And not just anyone, but someone in the family. How could that be? How could a person in their own family hate him enough to want to kill him? Especially after his mother had just been murdered.

She pulled the heavy brown sweater she was wearing tighter around her shoulders as she felt a chill shudder through her body. She couldn't think of anyone in the family that disliked Hunter, except for Gage. Hunter and Gage never seemed to click. She always thought it was because Gage was so much more, well, more everything. Gage was taller, more muscular and definitely better looking. He was an athlete and liked to spend time at the gym. And Lord knows he was popular and the girls all loved him. Hunter, on the other hand, was, what's the word, a nerd. Was that word still used? Hunter was small and wore thick glasses and his hair was always too long and hung too far over his forehead. He never dressed as stylishly as Gage and he didn't seem to have any friends. Beth assumed that Hunter had to be jealous of Gage. After all, why wouldn't he be? Gage was everything that Hunter was not. But that wouldn't make Gage want to harm Hunter. If anything, it would be the other way around. No, Gage would never hurt someone who was clearly weaker than himself. Whoever tried to hurt Hunter, it could not have been Gage.

Then who could it be? She thought of each member of the family, but not one person seemed capable of doing this horrible thing. Even more so, it was likely that whoever tried to kill Hunter was the same person who killed Jody. Who could possibly have done that?

She sat there for another twenty minutes watching her Cheerios get soggy before finally giving up and dumping them down the drain. Her mind spinning and she longed to take a second gummy, but she didn't dare. She had to keep her mind sharp. Instead, she stretched and walked into the living room. She was hoping Grace would come downstairs. She wanted to talk to her before Detective Holmes arrived. She would like to get something sorted out today.

"Hi, Mom." As if hearing her wish, Grace's voice came to her from the staircase. "You're up early."

"Yes, I couldn't sleep with everything going on."

"Any word on Hunter?"

"Not much other than he's holding his own."

Grace sat down across from her mother and pulled her robe over her legs. The house wasn't cold but the events of last night were on the minds of both women, causing them to seek security by wrapping themselves in their clothing.

"Do you want breakfast?"

"No, I'm not hungry. I don't think I could eat anything right now."

"Me neither. I tried, but no luck." Beth fidgeted with the hem of her sweater. She looked at Grace. "Honey, I have to ask you something. You said you and some others sent your DNA to GeneScreen? When? Why didn't you tell me?"

"Back on that, Mom? It's really no big deal about Aunt Jody being your half-sister. None of us care. She is still just Aunt Jody to us."

"I know. She is, she was, still just my sister to me. But I don't remember seeing any of your names in my family tree. That's why I was wondering."

"We didn't use our real names. You have to be 18-years-old to submit your DNA. Since none of us are eighteen yet, we used fake names. We didn't want to get in trouble, plus, it was kind of funny. You should see the names we used." Grace smiled as she thought back to the day that she and her cousins got together with their own GeneScreen kits.

"That makes sense. Who sent DNA samples in? What names did you use?"

"Are you sure you're not going to get mad if I tell you? I don't want to get anyone in trouble."

"I'm sure. With everything that's going on right now, I don't think a simple DNA test with a funny name is going to be a problem."

Grace laughed. "Okay then, but first, you have to promise you won't get mad. And you won't tell your sisters. Deal?"

Beth smiled. "Deal."

"Okay, here's what we did. Hunter did his first. He used Leonard Hofstadter as his name. You know, after that nerdy genius guy on that television show, *The Big Bang Theory*. He said they were both little and smart and they both wore glasses. It was pretty funny, and not all that far from the truth."

Beth laughed. She was familiar with the show and could see the resemblance. "Who else?"

"I was Cinderella."

"Because she's beautiful?"

"Remember, you promised you wouldn't get mad."

Beth twisted a strand of hair around her finger, anxious as she wondered what Grace was going to say next. "I remember."

"Actually, because Cinderella is the stepsister that always comes in second."

Beth flinched but didn't say anything other than,

"Keep going."

"Chelsie signed up as Sarah Chandler. She said that was a woman from the 1800s who escaped from prison after committing a petty crime. That's how she felt living at home. She always had to listen to her mom complain about her dad and going to college was like escaping from prison."

Beth tried to control her giggle but it came out before she could stop it, causing Grace to laugh right out loud. Then Grace continued. "Raegan picked Sloane Sutherland because one of her friends thinks she looks like her. You know, they both have dark hair and freckles over their cheeks. Although honestly, I think Raegan just likes her because she's a dark character with a lot of piercings, and you know Aunt Samantha, she won't let Raegan even get her nose pierced. And Gage was Elton John. And that's it. That's all five of us." Grace nervously bit on the side of her index finger while watching Beth to see how she took the last name she was given. At first Beth didn't react, a smile still frozen on her face from the previous comments. Then, slowly, a questioning look appeared in her eyes. Her lips turned into a frown and she looked directly at Grace.

"Did you say Elton John?"

Grace returned her gaze and mumbled, "Yes."

Beth looked confused. "But Gage doesn't play the piano. He doesn't sing. He's not the least bit musically inclined."

"No, Mom, he isn't."

"But, the only other thing Elton John is known

for is…" Beth stopped talking. What she was thinking could not be true. Her tall, strapping son who had a following of girls could not be, oh God, she couldn't bring herself to even think the word, let alone say it.

"Gay, Mom. The word is gay. And yes, it's true. Gage is gay. He prefers men to women."

Beth shuddered. "No. How can you say that?"

"Because it's true. Think about it. When has Gage ever brought a girlfriend home? When have you ever met a girl he's dating? Really, Mom, you should have known."

Beth stared at her hands clenched tightly together on her lap. Her mind was racing. Now that Grace mentioned it, she couldn't think of a time that Gage talked about a girl he had a crush on. He never brought a girlfriend home. "But, what about the times he would go to the movies with a friend?"

"That was Tyler, Mom. He was meeting Tyler."

Beth sat back, drawing her legs under her. She wrapped her arms around them and rocked back and forth. Her son was gay. Her tall, handsome, athletic son, her pride and joy, the one person she thought she knew everything about, was gay. She wasn't sure what upset her more, that he wasn't the man she thought he was, or that he kept this secret from her. She rocked harder. Where had she gone wrong? Had she babied him too much? Had she not let him spend enough time with his father? Was it her fault he turned out like this? She didn't understand. How was he going to get through life? Oh God. She closed her eyes and let her tears fall. After a few minutes, she could feel someone tapping her leg. "Mom, stop. See why he never told you?"

Beth opened her eyes to see Grace looking crossly at her."

"What?"

"This is exactly why Gage never told you. He knew how you would react, acting like it's a big deal. Let me tell you. It's not. He's happy with who he is. Why can't you be?"

"It's just that, people will make fun, they'll…"

"People won't do shit. He'll be fine. No one cares. I don't care that he's gay. Dad doesn't care. No one cares. So maybe you shouldn't care, either."

"People know?"

"Of course people know. People see him for who he is, not as some imaginary idol, like you treat him. And by the way, they love him and appreciate him for who he is. He doesn't have to pretend with other people." With that, Grace stood up and stomped across the floor. "I'm going upstairs to get dressed. I want to visit Hunter in the hospital today. Oh, and Mom, just so you know. Hunter's not gay. He has a girlfriend." Then Grace turned and ran up the stairs, slamming her door once she got to her room.

Beth sat alone in the living room for a very long time. She barely spoke an hour later when Gage and Grace came down the stairs together and said they were going to visit Hunter. She couldn't meet Gage's eyes as she passed him her car keys. Jerry left the house shortly after. She wasn't even sure where he said he was going.

She was still in shock. How could Gage have kept this from her for all these years?

Alone in the house, Beth finally realized she could cry no more. She pulled herself off the couch, went upstairs, washed up and fixed her hair. Detective Holmes would be here shortly and she needed to make herself presentable. She went back into the kitchen and sipped on a glass of Merlot while she made a batch of chocolate-chip cookies, from a package, not from scratch. Then she mixed up a pitcher of lemonade. As much as she was tired of being interrogated by the detective, she still needed to be a good hostess and offer him refreshments. Then she grabbed a pen and a pad of paper and went back into the living room to wait for the doorbell to ring.

While she was sitting there, she thought about the names the kids had used for the DNA testing. She wanted to write them down before she forgot so she could check them against her family tree. She wasn't upset with them, some of the names they chose were kind of funny. Let's see, what were they again? She quickly jotted down the following list, unsure of Raegan's name, vowing to herself that she would have to look it up later:

Grace:	Cinderella
Gage:	Elton John
Hunter:	Leonard Hoftstadter (sp?)
Chelsie:	Sarah Chandler
Raegan:	Sloane Sutherland

Beth stared at the paper for a few more minutes. Just as she pulled out her cell phone to look up the last two names, the doorbell rang. Detective Holmes must be here for yet another question-and-answer period. She put the pad on the coffee table, tucked in her blouse, and opened the front door.

"Hello, Detective. Please, come in."

"Hello, Mrs. Lennox. Thank you for agreeing to see me on such short notice. Especially with all that you have been going through."

"Please, it's Beth. And of course. Anything I can do to help you find out who is doing this to our family."

Beth took Ronan's jacket and placed it on one of the five brass hooks that hung to the left of the front door. Then she escorted him into the living room, indicating he should be seated on the chair directly across from the sofa. Instead, he flipped through his notebook until he found the page of handwritten notes he was looking for. He skimmed through Beth's previous responses to his questions. Then he turned to Beth and said, "I'm sorry to repeat myself, but let me get this question out of the way. The night that your sister was killed, you said you were home alone?"

"Yes."

"Can you tell me what you did that night?"

"Yes. As I told you before, I cleaned up the kitchen and turned in early for the night. I read for about twenty minutes. Then I turned on television and watched until I heard the children get home. I can never fall asleep until I know they are both home safe and sound."

"Ah, yes, the definitive sign of a good mother." Ronan glanced up and gave Beth a reassuring look. "Do you remember what you watched on television?"

"Of course, Detective. Every detail of that night is engraved in my mind. I doubt if I will ever forget." Beth went on to list not only the shows she watched, but also what each episode was about. She then told him what time each of her children arrived home, as well as when her husband got home. Ronan had already compared these times to phone records and when the family's Ring camera had shown people coming into the house. The alarm system also indicated that Beth had not left her home all evening, as neither the garage nor any of the exterior doors opened from the time the kids left until they returned home several hours later. It was looking more and more like Beth could be removed from Ronan's suspect list for the night of Jody's murder.

"Detective, why don't you have a seat. Let me bring out some refreshments that I made. You wouldn't want me to be a bad hostess now, would you?"

"No ma'am." Ronan sat in the chair where Beth had previously indicated he should be seated and relaxed. He was all but sure that Beth was not the guilty party; the rest of the interview would be a mere formality. After this he could approach the judge for a search warrant since the last two suspects lived in the same house. He was confident that would not be a problem, because even though there were two suspects, only one seemed to be a likely choice.

As he waited for Beth to return, wondering what delicious treat she would bestow upon him this time, he glanced around the room. As usual, everything was neatly arranged and comfortable. While the house wasn't exactly something out of *Modern Home and Gardens*, it certainly looked like the perfect place to raise a happy, middle-class American family.

Then he glanced at the notepad that was lying open on the table. He scanned the list of names in front of him. Each of the names belonged to a cousin with an alias listed after their name. Cinderella for Grace? He didn't think her position in the family was quite that drastic, but he remembered how his own daughters felt when they were teenagers. He laughed. Maybe Cinderella worked after all. Then he saw Elton John after Gage. He wondered if Beth finally understood the reason why that name was chosen for her son. Leonard Hoftstadter for Hunter, that made perfect sense. Sarah Chandler, he wasn't sure who that was. Then he saw the last name. Sloane Sutherland for Raegan. His blood ran cold. He jumped to his feet and headed to the front door. He grabbed his coat and yelled, "Thank you, Mrs. Lennox, but I need to leave." He ran to his car to telephone Wes about getting a search warrant for the Anderson residence. Beth Lennox was definitely no longer a suspect.

45 SISTERS

Detective Holmes was barely out of the house when Beth's cell phone buzzed. She was standing in the kitchen, still holding the tray of cookies and glasses of lemonade, staring at the door when she heard it. She put the tray on the bar and pulled the phone from her pocket. "Hello."

"Beth, it's Samantha. Can you meet Delaney and me at The Growler right away? I need you." Samantha sounded desperate; her voice was a mixture of tears and anger.

"Sure. Detective Holmes just left. I can be there in fifteen minutes."

"Thank you, Beth. We'll be there. In the back."

Beth disconnected and looked at her phone. What a strange call, she thought. She couldn't imagine what was going on with Samantha. It must be pretty bad if she wanted to see both her and Delaney. Without taking time to leave a note for Jerry, she grabbed her purse and her jacket and started for the garage. Then she remembered that the kids took her car. She called Samantha back and made arrangements for her to swing by and pick her up. Ten minutes later, she was sitting in the front seat of Samantha's car heading to the bar to meet with Delaney.

The Growler was an older pub in downtown Cayne. It had brown paneled walls and a concrete floor that gave it an industrial vibe. The walls were lined with pictures of old movie posters, famous sports shots, and various military paraphernalia, making the theme of the bar difficult to determine. All of this went unnoticed by the two sisters as they made their way to the booth in the back of the pub where Delaney was already seated. Beth scooted into the seat first and Samantha sat next to her, signaling to the server before she was all the way seated. Once they placed their first drink order, Samantha could feel her tears start to slide down her cheeks. She reached out and grabbed both Delaney's hand and Beth's hand.

"I don't know what to do anymore. It's Derek. He's at it again. He's having another affair. I'm sure of it. I've ignored it so many times in the past, but I can't this time. I can't let him get away with it again."

Beth and Delaney gave each other a knowing look indicating they were not surprised. After all, they had seen this scenario between Samantha and Derek play out several times before. The only difference was, this time Samantha was choosing not to look the other way. This time she was asking what she should do, like she meant it. They sensed it was not like in the past when she would ask what to do, when they both knew full well that she wasn't going to do a damn thing. Delaney spoke first. "I'm so sorry, Samantha. This must be hard for you. Are you sure? How do you know?"

Samantha went into great detail explaining all the ways she knew Derek was cheating on her. She told them about his late nights at work, the mysterious phone calls, the missed dinners, and finally, how she went to his office and saw the cars parked there when he was supposed to be alone. She told them about driving by Krystal's house, and while she didn't see his car there the first few times, the last time it was in the driveway. Lastly, she told them about finding a receipt for plane tickets for a weekend in San Diego. Plane tickets, as in two. He told her he was going to California for a business trip. There was no doubt he was cheating. She was sure. And this time, she wasn't going to let him get away with it. She was done.

The three sisters drank and talked for hours about Derek and Samantha, covering the years of problems the two of them had. Derek's affairs started soon after Chelsie was born, and yes, Samantha had made a pretty big mistake herself, but at least she learned from it. Derek never did. He just kept carrying on. Of course, he never had any consequences—Samantha blamed herself for that. Her own guilt, combined with a fear of being left alone and having to raise the two girls on her own, caused her to stay quiet all these years. Now she could see that he never had any reason to stop. He could have his affairs and keep his home life, too.

"Well, no more. Those days are done. He is

going to end it with this Krystal bitch or we are through. That's it." Samantha spoke with an authoritarian tone that both Delaney and Beth were sure Derek had never heard come out of her before. They were both encouraging her to deal with him in this manner.

It could have been the years of anger, or perhaps the many rounds of drinks, but as the night wore on, Samantha, Beth and Delaney left their tears behind and started in on an entire evening of man-bashing that finally dissolved into absolute silliness and laughter. All three turned their cell phones off and stuffed them into their pocketbooks. Let the men go on without them for one night, they decided. And then they clinked their glasses together and drank to woman power.

46 HOLMES

Ronan had his suspect list down to only three names: Beth Lennox, Derek Anderson and Raegan Anderson. He was relatively sure Beth was not Jody's killer. Although she didn't have a solid alibi, she also didn't have a motive. Sure, there was the half-sister thing. He knew that she and Jody discovered one of them was a half-sister, but it didn't take long before they realized that it was Jody who wasn't Paul's daughter, not Beth. Even if they didn't know Paul was already aware of this and wasn't going to write Jody out of the will, it didn't matter. Beth's inheritance was safe. She was Paul's biological child. Financially, she had no motive to kill Jody.

Ronan also knew there was bad blood between Beth's son, Gage, and Jody's son, Hunter. The cousins didn't get along. He talked to both boys about it, and while he could tell there was something between the two of them, it never felt strong enough to cause a family rift. It felt more like they just didn't hang in the same circles.

They didn't enjoy the same things. There wasn't any real animosity between the two of them, certainly not enough to cause Beth to kill Jody. Plus, try as he might, he could not picture cookie-baking, muffin-mixing, 105-pound Beth slashing anyone's throat. It was preposterous.

As far as his last two suspects, Derek and Raegan Anderson, that should be easy. Raegan was a child. What reason would she have to kill her aunt? None that Ronan could come up with. Initially, he didn't look at her too seriously, but then he saw that list at Beth's house. What was that all about? The list contained five cousins' names next to five alias names. It seemed that each cousin had chosen an alias to describe themself. Hunter was the kid off that television show, *The Big Bang Theory*. They were both the brainy, nerdy type. Gage was easy to figure out, too. Gage was gay, so was Elton John. The other three weren't as obvious.

Grace chose Cinderella. Ronan finally concluded that she chose that name because Gage was the apple of his mother's eye, not Grace. Ronan didn't know who Sarah Chandler was. When he looked that name up. He learned that Sarah Chandler was a young woman sentenced to death for a petty crime in the early 1800s. She managed to escape from prison, thereby escaping the death penalty. Ronan laughed at the thought of Chelsie comparing her life at home to that of being in prison. That left Raegan, one of the final suspects in Jody's murder case. At first, he didn't seriously consider her a suspect. After all, she was only 17-years-old. But then he saw the name she selected was Sloane

Sutherland, the name of a serial killer in a popular book called *Butcher and Blackbird*. That choice startled him. That's why he left Beth's house suddenly. He had to dig into this further. Why would she choose the name of a female serial killer?

But then Ronan looked to his prime suspect, Derek Anderson. Derek had lots of secrets he was keeping. The more Ronan looked into Derek's background, the more he found. Almost from the beginning of his marriage to Samantha, Derek had a wandering eye. He liked adventure. He was never content to be just a family man. When Samantha could share adventures with him, their marriage was fine, but as soon as their first daughter came along, everything changed. Samantha became a responsible parent and Derek got his kicks by running around with other women. Lots of other women. Most recently, he was having an affair with his secretary, Krystal Maynard. It had been going on for several months. Derek's financials indicated that it started sometime before the holidays. Ronan wondered if Samantha knew about it.

Of course, all that meant was that Derek was a scumbag. It didn't mean he was a killer. It also didn't give him a reason to kill Jody, unless somehow Jody found out about his affair with Krystal. That could be a reason.

Ronan turned to his computer and brought up Krystal's social media account. She was the same age as Delaney, not Jody. He compared her friends list with both Jody's and Delaney's, but there were no matches.

None of these women seemed to run in the same circles.

Ronan glanced at the clock. What was taking that judge so long to make up his mind? Was he going to grant the warrant for the Anderson household or not? Whether the killer was Derek or Raegan, it didn't matter. Either way he wanted to search their house to see if he could find the murder weapon, or at least something with a trace of blood on it. He still didn't understand why either one of them would want to kill Jody or Hunter, but a bloody knife would go a long way to helping him find out.

47 DEREK

Things went too far this time, no doubt about it. He could still picture Samantha's face as she stood in their bedroom holding the receipt for not one, but two airplane tickets to San Diego. How could he have been so stupid? Did he think she wouldn't check the Visa bill?

She looked so small, standing there in her tight jeans and oversized sweatshirt. Small and angry. Her face was actually red with rage. Her hands were clenched in fists, and she was yelling. Not speaking loudly. Not being sarcastic. Actually yelling. Something in her had changed. Maybe it was Jody's death. Maybe it had been the night out with her sisters, but ever since then, she seemed different. And right now, different meant angry.

Usually, his first instinct would be to protect himself, but this time was different. This time he knew he couldn't lie his way out of it. She knew what he was up to. He knew it, and she knew he knew it. Instead of trying to be deceitful, he felt something he didn't usually feel. He felt guilt. She was his wife, the mother of his children, and he was a shit. He had been lying and cheating on her almost since the beginning. He always justified it because she had made a mistake, but looking at her now, he realized that she had made a mistake. One. He had made so many. He couldn't continue. It had to stop, and it had to stop now.

"I'm sorry, Samantha. I don't know what else to say. I am so sorry."

"Sorry? For what, Derek? For being nothing but a cheater? Or for finally having to admit to it? What are you really sorry for?"

"I never meant to hurt you." Derek stared at the floor, unable to look at the hurt in his wife's eyes. She had made it so easy on him. He knew she was aware of his cheating, but she never said anything about it. She let him get away with it. He figured she didn't care. He never thought about the pain he was causing her. Now, seeing her standing there waving the Visa bill in front of him, tears spilling out from her eyes and running down her cheeks, he could see he was wrong. It wasn't that she didn't care, it was because she cared too much.

"For someone who never meant to hurt me, you did a fine job of it."

Derek looked up. Her fingers were still clenched around the bill. Otherwise, she hadn't moved. If it wasn't for her chest heaving and her tears still flowing, she would look almost like a statue. He took a step toward her and reached his hand out. He wanted to hold her. He wanted to tell her he would stop the affairs and be a better husband. Instead, he stopped dead in his tracks when she glared up at him. "Don't you dare come near me. Not one inch closer, do you understand? I don't want you anywhere near me. We are done."

Her words, icy cold and filled with hatred, hit him like a ton of bricks. She didn't want him anymore. He could feel his stomach flipflop, nausea spewing across his body. "Samantha, no. You can't be serious. I'll change. I promise."

Samantha stared into his eyes. She didn't falter. She didn't even blink. "I have never been more serious in my life. Your bag is packed. It's on the bed. Pick it up and get the hell out."

Derek continued to stand there, shocked. He wanted to be angry. To yell back. To say that he wasn't going to leave. That it was his house, too. But he couldn't. Samantha was right. He had been nothing but shit all these years and it was finally catching up to him. This is what he deserved and it was time he man up and take what was coming to him. Still, he didn't want to go. "Samantha, please."

"Now, Derek. Get out now."

Derek walked to the bed and picked up the small black carrying case that Samantha had filled with enough clothing and toiletries to last him for a couple of days. That would give him time to meet with his attorney and figure out what to do next. He turned and started toward the door when she called his name. He stopped and a flicker of hope crossed his mind.

"Derek, when your attorney contacts mine, it would be best if it was to agree to the settlement we will offer. Under the circumstances, it will be fair. It will be what we both deserve. You owe me that much. And for once, put your daughters ahead of yourself. You owe them, too."

Derek was crushed. Not only did she not want him, but she made sure he knew that he was more than just a shitty husband. He was a shitty father, too. Sure, he supported his family over the years, but had he ever stepped up and taken care of them the way they deserved to be taken care of? Obviously, he wasn't there for Samantha, but he never thought about the fact that he wasn't there for Chelsie or Raegan, either.

They say that when you die, a movie of your life plays before your eyes. Derek wasn't dying, per se, but suddenly that same movie played in his mind. He realized he wasn't there when his daughters were infants. He didn't change diapers or give them baths or teach them to crawl or walk or talk. How many school events did he miss because he had to sneak off with whatever woman he was seeing when they were younger? He thought about the time both girls wanted to go on a camping weekend with some of the families from their softball team. He said he couldn't go because of work. Actually, he went to Seattle with Megan or Morgan or some woman whose name began with an M. Samantha took the girls alone.

Samantha was right. He wasn't there for his girls. He spent his entire marriage chasing what was fun for him at the moment, never caring what he missed or who he hurt along the way. What had he done? It didn't matter. It was too late. He quickly reached for the door, not turning back to look at Samantha. He didn't want her to see his face, to see the regret that he was sure would show. As he left the room he muttered, "Have your lawyer draw up the paperwork. We won't contest it. I'm sorry, Samantha, for everything." Then he closed the door behind him and left the house for what he knew would be the final time.

Once he got to his car, he didn't know where to go. He had never felt so alone in his life. He didn't feel like going on an adventure like he usually did. What he wanted was to go home to his wife and children, but he knew that was no longer an option. Instead, he drove around aimlessly. He thought about checking into a hotel, but that seemed depressing. Sitting in a hotel room by himself was more than he could take. Plus, he knew an empty hotel room would equate to drowning his misery at the hotel bar, and that sounded like an even worse fate than crying alone in his room. Instead, he opted for what was an equally poor choice, but one that would at least be several hundred dollars less expensive.

He decided to go to his office for an hour or two. From there he would make arrangements about where to stay for the night, or perhaps for several nights. Of course, he would need to pick up flowers and a bottle of wine. Then he would head over to a little yellow house on Redstone Drive.

48 THE VISITOR

Krystal. That was the name of the woman my so-called father was having an affair with. It wasn't the first affair he ever had, but it was going to be the last.

When I had first learned about her, I looked her up on social media. In her picture, she was blond, but I already knew that. I heard my parents say something about her yellow car and her yellow house matching her yellow hair. Pretty fucking stupid, if you ask me. Her picture also showed that she's little, one would say petite. I guess she's pretty. She has big blue eyes. She appears to be fit and trim. Mostly what I saw when I looked at her pictures, though, was someone who made my mother cry. This Krystal chick may have thought it was okay to run around with my father, but what wasn't okay was the way their affair was hurting my mother. Didn't she realize that my mom was sitting at home every night crying because my dad was cheating on her again? Didn't she know how many nights I had to listen to my mother suffer while he was out fucking around? If she did know, didn't she care?

Well, no more. I decided that I had to put a stop to it. I may not have been able to alleviate the issue with Grey yet, but I sure as hell could take care of this one.

I learned where Krystal lived by listening to my parents. I knew it was the yellow house on Redstone Drive. Redstone Drive isn't very long and this was the only yellow house. I had driven by a few weeks ago and found it. I had even parked down the street and watched it a few times. It didn't take long before I saw my dad's car pull into the driveway. At the time I wasn't sure what I should do, but after hearing my parents fighting earlier tonight, it was an easy decision. This affair needed to end. My mother may have sounded strong when she kicked my father out, but I knew better. She was only putting on an act. Inside she was hurting.

After my dad left, I wondered if he would go to Krystal's house. I knew I had to get here first. I drove over and watched for him, but when he didn't show up, I figured he found someplace else to go for the night. Good. That gave me time to do what I had to do. I figured if I could take care of Krystal, maybe Dad would learn his lesson. Just maybe he would stop with the affair and beg Mom for forgiveness. Then he could move back in and they could be together again. I think that's what Mom needs to be happy. Oh, I know she kicked him out, but I don't think that's what she wants. I think what she wants most is for him to love her again.

I left my car down the street and walked to Krystal's house. Her street was dark and quiet and because I wore dark clothing, I blended right in. When I first approached her house, I didn't go on the front porch, instead I stood behind a thick evergreen bush near a side window. Her shades were open so I could easily see right inside.

I watched for a while as she set her dining room table with shiny black plates and gold tableware on top of a crimson-red tablecloth. She put crystal wine glasses just to the right of each plate. All I could think was, tacky. Even more disgusting was the outfit she was wearing. Her shiny purple blouse was virtually see-through; nothing was left to the imagination. She had paired it with black pants that were so tight I doubted if she could even sit down in them. She looked like the whore I knew her to be.

I watched her for a minute longer as she stood in front of a mirror running her fingers through her long, wavy hair. As she gave her cheeks a quick pinch and ran her pinky finger around her lips, I suddenly realized I needed to hurry. This wasn't the scene of a woman planning a quiet evening at home. This was a woman getting ready for company. My father must be on his way over. I needed to act quickly.

After I checked to make sure the street was empty, I scurried around to the front porch. I wished I had kept the knife that I had used to kill Jody instead of dumping it at Delaney's, but I didn't have time to worry about that. I would have to ad lib once I was inside.

As quickly as possible, I made my way up the four porch stairs and rang her doorbell. I made sure I stood in the shadows in case she looked out the window before she opened the door. Fortunately, she didn't bother since she was obviously expecting someone. Instead, she jerked open the door and said, "Darling, come in."

The words were out of her mouth before she noticed who was standing in front of her. She took a step back when she saw it was me and not my dad, unsure what she should do. She stumbled over her words before she finally settled on a simple hello.

"I guess you're not going to invite me in, so I'll have to do that myself," I said as I pushed past her. She closed the door in back of me, clearly struggling with what to do next. Since I walked down the short hall into the main part of the house, she didn't have much choice. She closed the door and followed me. I turned to face her, sneering at the ridiculous way she was dressed. "Expecting someone special, or do you always dress like that?"

Krystal was taken aback by that comment. I bet she was thinking that my father said his daughters are such nice young women. I saw the confusion on her face. Finally, she uttered her brilliant comeback.

"I'm sorry. What did you say?"

"You heard me."

Krystal took a step back. Clearly she didn't want to have this conversation with me, not when she was expecting my father to arrive any minute. I needed to hurry. I looked around the small space. It was a combination living room, dining area and kitchen.

Behind me she said, "I think it would be best if you leave."

"You think I should leave? Guess what. I think you should stop fucking my father. Or better yet, I think you should have never started. What do you think of that?"

Krystal's hand, with its painted red fingernails, went up to her mouth in shock. She didn't know what to make of me. I figured I wasn't at all who my father described. Then she repeated her request. "Please, I think you should leave, and perhaps we can talk about this when you are a bit calmer. More rational."

"So now you think I'm not rational. Let me tell you something. I'm not leaving, and I'm not the one who needs to be more rational." With those words, I turned and walked through the living room, past the blue-flowered couch and into the small dining area. "Did I interrupt your dinner plans? What a shame. Hope you're not hungry." Then I raised my arm and with one fell swoop I shoved both place settings off the table, causing them to crash to the floor. "Change of plans," I said in a voice that was much deeper, much huskier than it was when I first walked through the front door.

Cognizant of the time, I now made my way into the kitchen with Krystal following closely behind. She was angry. I think those were her best dishes. She was yelling something about how I had no right to break her things. I was standing at her counter now. Krystal walked up close behind me and in her sternest voice she said, "You need to leave my house right now or I am going to call the police. Do you understand? Right now?"

For a few seconds, I didn't move. Then, when I sensed Krystal so close to me that I could touch her, I turned. My right-hand darted out and latched on to the largest knife in the cutlery block on her counter. I whipped around, and without hesitation, I plunged the knife deep into Krystal's midsection. It slid in easily, the only resistance I felt was at the very beginning, before it popped through her skin. I sensed the clean knife wound wouldn't do the damage I longed for. I didn't pull the knife out to plunge it in again. Instead, I jerked the knife in an upward motion, splicing through Krystal's diaphragm, cutting into her lung. She tried to call out to her Alexa to call nine-one-one, but she was too late. My knife had found her aortic artery. Blood was gushing out of the hole in her midsection, spurting with every heartbeat. Until it didn't. Then it just flowed.

I pulled the knife out and watched as Krystal crumpled to the floor. *Guess who won't be fucking Daddy tonight.* Then I walked to the sink, opened the cabinet doors and pulled out the bleach. I was standing at the sink washing the knife when a male voice from behind me made me jump. Startled, I picked up the knife and turned around. "Dad, what are you doing here?"

49 DEREK

Derek could not believe what he was looking at. Krystal was dead. It didn't take a medical person to know that. It was obvious by the amount of blood that was spreading from her body across the kitchen floor. He slowly made his way to her through the massive red puddle, holding onto the bar so he wouldn't slip, but it was a wasted effort. He knew he wasn't going to find a pulse. No one could survive that much blood loss and be alive.

Once his suspicion was confirmed, he stood up and walked toward the sink. Raegan was standing there, still cleaning the knife. He reached over, carefully easing the blade away from her, and turned off the water. Slowly, he put his hands on her shoulders and turned her around so she was facing him. Ignoring the blood that covered so much of her body, he pulled her to his chest and gently pushed her hair away from her face. He held her and rocked her back and forth, all the while maintaining an eerie calm. He smoothed her hair, and with his lips barely moving against the top of her head, he asked, "What did you do?"

"I killed her, Dad. I had to. She was making Mom cry. It was her fault that you were lying. Mom followed you and knew you weren't working late. Mom knew you were here with the blond lady in the yellow house. Krystal. Krystal was the reason you were always gone. Krystal was the reason you lied to Mom and made her cry. Mom didn't know what to do, so I had to do something. I couldn't let Mom keep getting hurt. Don't you understand?"

"But why did you have to kill her?"

"Because you wouldn't stop seeing her and she was going to keep inviting you over. She was never going to stop." Raegan was quiet for a moment, comforted by the gentle rocking in Derek's arms. Just when Derek thought she was not going to say anything else, she added, "I had to kill Krystal. Now she can't hurt Mom anymore."

Derek thought he was going to throw up. The blood. The fact that his daughter killed his lover. He had been on edge when he arrived, and now this. All because of him. He was to blame, and he knew it. He was the reason Samantha was so unhappy. It was his fault that Krystal was dead. And Raegan. What the hell had he done to Raegan? He looked at his daughter, covered in blood, but still looking so young. She was a child, practically a baby.

He hugged her tighter; together they stood in the blood-filled kitchen and rocked. Then, another thought filled his mind. It was terrifying, but he had to know.

Without loosening his grip, he continued to stroke Raegan's hair and he asked, "Raegan, what about Aunt Jody? Did you also have to kill Aunt Jody?"

"I think you know the answer to that. I didn't plan to kill her. Honest. I just wanted to talk to her. I went over that night to see what she was going to do. At first she just started yelling about Mom, about she better keep her mouth shut or else. She was raving like a lunatic! But as we kept talking, I found out she didn't know why I was there. She was surprised when I told her, but then it was too late and I couldn't take it back. She got angry. She said she was going to tell Hunter, that he deserved to know. I tried to talk to her but she wouldn't listen. She threatened to tell everyone! I told her that she shouldn't make Mom cry. I tried to explain that to her, Dad. I tried, but she didn't care. She told me to mind my own business. She was going to call Mom right away. So I had to kill her. I didn't want to, Dad, but I didn't have a choice. I couldn't let her ruin everything, especially since it was all my fault. I had to take care of Mom. I had to protect her, didn't I, Dad?"

Derek stood there, frozen in place. Hearing those words pour out of Raegan's mouth stung because of the harsh truth in them. If he had been a better husband, a better father, than none of this would have happened. His sister-in law would not be dead. His lover would not be lying in a pool of blood at his feet, and his baby girl would not be guilty of murdering the both of them. He was devastated, drowning in an endless chasm of guilt. Still, he had to press a little further. "And Hunter?"

"I never wanted to hurt Hunter. The first time with the car, I thought it was Grey walking home. Grey always walked home from the school. He is the one with the royal blue coat. Not Hunter. How was I supposed to know that they traded that night? Grey was the one who knew the secret. He was the one that I was afraid would tell. Not Hunter."

"And the second time? The poison? The night of the party?"

"Same thing. I added the poison to Grey's food, not Hunter's. I sprinkled the tiniest amount of strychnine to Grey's stupid three-bean salad after I bumped into him. It was easy. He helped me up and I hugged him as a thank you. His plate was on the table, and when we hugged, I reached behind him and added the poison to his plate. He never knew. No one did. I was very secretive. But then he gave his plate to Hunter. He shouldn't have done that."

Derek only managed to put some of the pieces together. Raegan killed Jody because she knew a secret and she was going to tell everyone. Raegan tried to kill Grey because he also knew the secret. She never tried to kill Hunter. The two attempts on his life were simply mistaken identities. Both times she was after Grey. Derek wondered what the secret was, but that wasn't his main concern. What he was most concerned about was whether or not Raegan was going to try to kill Grey again. He turned to his daughter and asked her this very question.

Raegan looked deeply into Derek's eyes as she

pondered this. She appeared to be giving it intense thought before she finally answered. "No. It doesn't matter anymore. I figured it out. There were two secrets. One is already out there and it can't hurt Mom. I don't have to worry about that one. And the other one, well, Grey is not going to tell. He is too afraid that Hunter will get hurt. He is just happy that Hunter is alive and he will never risk anything happening to him."

Derek's mind was spinning. He didn't understand anything except that his baby girl had killed two people and had almost killed a third. She had tried twice to kill Grey. Fortunately, she missed both times, and it now sounded like she didn't need to make any further attempts on his life.

And it was all his fault. All this time he thought he was being so careful, that his dalliances weren't hurting anyone, when in fact they were hurting everyone he loved. He could just die. All he had done was cause those around him to suffer. And for what? So he could end up alone with no one to care about him? Samantha hated him. No doubt Chelsie would hate him. And Raegan, poor little Raegan. Look what his actions had driven her to. Still, he had one more question to ask her. "Raegan, is there anyone else who knows the secret?"

"No. No one else. Everything will be okay now. I took care of everything. Mom can be happy now. We can all be happy."

Despite the fact that Derek didn't have a clue what this secret was that Raegan was talking about, or the knowledge that his daughter had killed two people,

Derek felt a small sliver of relief. The killing was done. Raegan would never kill another person again. She would be alright. Somehow, he understood that. He also knew that he had failed her. All the years he chose different women over his wife, work over his family, time away over time at home, had come back to haunt him. Not only was he paying the price for his selfishness, but so were Samantha and Chelsie, and most of all, Raegan. Derek understood that the further away from all of them he was, the better off they would be. It was then he knew what he had to do.

"Raegan, listen carefully. We have to get this place cleaned up. Do you understand me? We have to make sure no one knows you were here."

"What do you mean, that I was never here?"

"Let's get this place cleaned up and I'll explain."

"I'm very good at the cleanup part. No one found a trace of me at Aunt Jody's." Raegan smiled when she said that, so proud of herself for outsmarting the police.

"Yes, you did an excellent job. Now let's get busy. And while we work, I want you to tell me all about that night at Aunt Jody's. Tell me every detail."

The two of them worked diligently until every trace of Raegan had been removed. Derek didn't care about the blood pool on the floor. There was no way they were going to hide the fact that Krystal had been murdered. He wasn't even going to try. He just wanted to make sure there was no trace of Raegan.

Derek asked Raegan to describe every detail

about Jody's murder. He needed to know what was said and how the murder was committed and where the murder weapon was. In Delaney's yard. Really? He also asked Raegan about the night she almost ran over Hunter. He knew where she got the car and why no one realized she took it. Then she told him about the shed with the rat poison and how she used that to add to Grey's food on the night of the party. She explained all of her plans and her actions to Derek in great detail. All that was left was for her to have an alibi. He didn't think she would need one, but it was better to be cautious.

"I understand, Dad. Are you sure about this?"

"Yes, Raegan. I'm sure. Very sure. I haven't been much of a father to you for most of your life. It's about time I stepped up, don't you think?"

Raegan looked up at Derek and smiled. "I love you, Dad. I won't let you down." Then she wrapped her arms around him and hugged him tightly, almost as if she was trying to make up for an entire lifetime of hugs she would never have again.

Derek opened the backdoor for his daughter and in the darkness of the night, she crept out of the house. She would be back home and in bed before the police even knew there had been another murder, a murder that Derek was fully ready to confess to committing.

50 HOLMES

It would be daylight soon and Ronan was just getting home. It had been one hell of a night. Blood and bodies and blue lights flashing in every direction. The little yellow house on Redstone Drive was lit up like the Devil's Christmas tree. He was glad to be out of there.

Ronan was tempted to pour himself a shot of whiskey, but settled for a glass of orange juice instead. He wasn't ready to eat anything yet, although his stomach would be happier if it had some nourishment. He downed the juice and hoped he wouldn't pay for it with a bout of heartburn.

Initially, last night started with him being unhappy with the judge for again delaying the search warrant for the Anderson residence. In retrospect, he guessed it no longer mattered. The murder of Jody Terrel had been solved, as had the attempts on Hunter Terrel's life and the murder of Krystal Maynard. As he had suspected for quite some time, it was Jody's brother-in-law, Derek Anderson. He knew Derek had been a scoundrel. Early on, Ronan had discovered that Derek cheated on Samantha with many women, including a brief stint with his own sister-in-law, Jody Terrel. Ronan figured that Jody wasn't able to live with the guilt any longer and was going to tell Samantha. That's why Derek killed her. At least, that's what Derek's suicide note stated. The note also explained that Derek had never tried to kill Hunter. The first time it looked like there was an attempt on Hunter's life, it was actually an error of mistaken identity. Derek explained that he thought it was Grey walking down the street wearing the blue ski parka. He was shocked when he heard it was Hunter. The second time, the night of the party, he had poisoned Grey's dinner. He was devastated when he discovered that Grey gave his plate to Hunter. He never wanted to hurt Hunter. This was also clearly outlined in his suicide note.

But Derek definitely did try to kill Grey. Grey learned about the affair between Jody and Derek, and he wanted to keep him quiet. It seemed like such a waste that Jody had to die over one mistake she had made sixteen years ago. Especially when Samantha had finally grown a backbone and thrown her bum of a husband out.

Ronan had a little difficulty understanding why Derek killed Krystal. Derek's note said that he blamed her for the end of his marriage. Samantha threw him out because she found out about their affair. That also seemed unfair. After all, it wasn't Krystal who was cheating, it was Derek. Even at the very end he couldn't take responsibility for his own actions. Krystal wasn't the reason Derek's marriage ended. He did that to himself.

Derek was nothing more than a weak, sniveling excuse of a man, and that weakness caused the end of so many lives. Jody. Krystal. And Derek himself. He couldn't even man up and go to prison. Instead, he chose to slit his wrists and die at his lover's house. Now, who knew how long it would take for those he left behind to recover from his mistakes. What a terrible state of affairs that family was forced to contend with. Samantha, Chelsie, Raegan, Grey, Hunter, all the others. How could one man cause so many so much hurt?

Ronan threw his coat on the couch and kicked off his shoes. He sank into his living room chair. After being up all night, it felt good to finally relax. He was glad to have this case closed. It had been gnawing at him for far too many weeks. It was almost a relief that there wouldn't be a trial. They had Derek's suicide letter with all the information they needed--how he committed the murders, why he did them, even where he hid the murder weapon he used on Jody. It was all there, every detail. Couldn't be wrapped up any tighter. Still, something was nagging at him. It seemed silly in the context of things, but he kept flashing back to the list of names he found on Beth's table. Each name meant something to the one that chose it. So why did Raegan choose Sloane Sutherland? Sloane, the name of a serial killer.

Ronan shook his head. He was just being silly.

There was no way Raegan was involved with these murders. She was just a kid. Anyway, they caught the murderer. They had a full confession. Plus, there wasn't a judge or jury alive that would convict that sweet girl. Time to drop it and move on. Case closed.

EPILOGUE

ONE YEAR LATER

Raegan was happy, and it wasn't just the pretend happy she used to be. It was genuine. She no longer heard her mother crying in her bed at night. She no longer saw her dad sneaking into his study to talk on his phone. He wasn't missing her school events to spend time at the office or running off on business trips. He was dead. That should have been harder than having him away on business, but it turns out it wasn't. She finally knew that her dad loved her. Well, that statement wasn't quite true. What she should have said is that she knew Derek loved her. Because he's not really her dad, now, is he? Raegan has a secret of her own. It is her secret and hers alone, and she will never tell a soul. That's what one should do with a secret.

Last year when all the cousins decided to do the GeneScreen testing, she did it, too. It was going to be fun, learning all about their family history. Just like

Chelsie, Gage, Grace and Hunter, she submitted her DNA. She had been so excited that she checked her computer every day for the results. She would even get up in the middle of the night to see if GeneScreen had sent her an update. Then it came, just after midnight. She was sure no one else had seen it yet. Imagine her surprise when she saw that she and Chelsie were not sisters, but half-sisters. If her aunts were shocked about Jody being a half-sister, they weren't nearly as surprised as she was about Chelsie. But that was only half the surprise. The real shock was Hunter. Hunter was her half-brother. Not her cousin. Her half-brother. It didn't take long to figure out what happened.

Her dad, or perhaps she should call him Derek, had a long history of affairs. Everyone knew that. By sneaking around and listening when she wasn't supposed to, Raegan had learned that Derek even had an affair with Jody. It was short-lived, but that was pretty low. Seriously, her mom's sister? Yuck! What she hadn't realized until recently was that her mom and Grey did the whole retaliation thing. When her mom had first found out about Derek's affair, Grey had shown up on her doorstep. Samantha had been crying. He comforted her, and one thing led to another. It was never planned. It was a mistake, but they got more than they bargained for. They got Raegan. Derek wasn't Raegan's dad. Grey was.

When Raegan heard Samantha on the telephone with Jody, she was able to put together that Jody was upset about a DNA test. Raegan was devastated. She assumed Jody had figured out that Raegan and Hunter were half-sister and brother. If only she had known then that it was Jody finding out that she and Beth were half-sisters that was upsetting her. But Raegan didn't know that, she thought Jody found out about Raegan and Hunter being siblings. That's why she went to see Jody, to convince her not to tell anyone what she had learned. Samantha had managed to keep that secret for seventeen years. It would devastate her if anyone found out about it now.

So Raegan went to visit Jody on a cold night in March. Once she had started talking to Jody that night, she was surprised to find out that Jody didn't know that Grey was Raegan's father. Samantha and Grey never told her the truth. Only then, it was too late. Raegan had revealed the secret herself. And once Jody did know, she was furious. She said she had to tell Hunter. It was only fair that he knew he had a sister. Raegan pleaded with her. "Can you imagine what that will do to my mother? After all, she and Grey had kept that secret for so many years. It would only hurt everyone to tell now!" But Jody wouldn't listen. She said she didn't care who it hurt. She had screamed something about Samantha wasn't willing to keep her secret--she was going to make sure Daddy knew that Jody wasn't his daughter, so why should she keep Samantha's. Raegan knew then that she had to take immediate action. She couldn't let the fact that she and Hunter were half-siblings come out, especially because it would have been all her fault. That's when she knew she had to kill Jody.

Afterwards, when Raegan had more time to think about what she had done, she started to worry that Grey might decide to open his mouth and tell people that Raegan was his daughter. That was why she tried to run him over with the car, only, it wasn't Grey. It was Hunter wearing Grey's jacket. What a mistake that would have been. Then she tried again, the whole strychnine fiasco. Unfortunately, that didn't work, either.

But then she realized that Grey had kept that secret since she was born; it was unlikely he would ever tell anyone. The biggest threat to it being revealed was Jody. Raegan knew that Jody was going to try to use it as leverage to have Samantha never reveal that she was not Paul's daughter. Typical Jody, worrying about her share of Paul's inheritance. That was the telephone conversation between Jody and Samantha—Jody pleading with Samantha to not tell Paul that he was not her father. Of course, Samantha refused. Once Raegan had inadvertently told Jody about Raegan being Grey's daughter, part of Jody's plan was to blackmail Samantha. *If you tell Daddy I'm not his real daughter, I will tell everyone that Derek is not Raegan's real father.* Clearly, that is no longer important. So for right now, Raegan doesn't think she has to worry. Plus, Grey is so focused on Hunter's recovery that he isn't able to think about anything else.

Hunter is doing quite well and should make a full recovery. Both he and Grey are relieved that Derek is dead and they no longer have to worry about anyone trying to kill them. They mostly tend to stay away from the family now. They need time to heal from their wounds, and not just the physical ones.

So it looks like no one else will ever find out that Jody and Derek had an affair, or that Raegan is the child of Samantha and Grey. As soon as Raegan saw the results on GeneScreen, she closed her account and all of her records were disabled. No one will ever see them.

Tonight, Raegan sits alone in her room. The house is quiet. Chelsie is back at school and her mom is out with her sisters. Raegan is happy, but she does like to be careful. She likes to be prepared. With that in mind, she walks into her closet and goes to the far back corner. Wrapped in a fleece blanket is a brand new, hand forged, steel blade hunting knife. Chances are she will never need it, but it's there just in case Grey, or possibly even Hunter if Grey ever tells him, decides to tell the secret that will cause her mother to cry.

ABOUT THE AUTHOR

Shary Caya Lavoie is a registered nurse and a veteran of the U. S. Navy. She has a Bachelor of Arts Degree in Psychology and a Master of Arts Degree in Human Services with a Focus on Health and Wellness. Shary was born in Connecticut, grew up in Maine, and now lives in the heart of the Blue Ridge Mountains with her husband, Bert. Together they have six children and eight grandchildren. And let's not forget the other grands: Boone, Science, Top, Zeus and Zoey.

****

Other books by Shary Caya Lavoie:

- ***The Bell Deception*** – *a cozy murder mystery: Kylie and Michael Bell have it all, until Michael is arrested for murder on the night they are celebrating their first wedding anniversary. A mystery unresolved until the book's final page.*

- ***Nine Lies and a Truth: Ten Tales of Terror*** – *Ten scary stories (ages 10+): Can you figure out which one is based on an encounter that the author actually experienced?*

- ***Clementine and the Gold: The Wayward Wabble*** – *a magical fantasy chapter book for ages 7-13+: Help Clementine as she visits the magical world of Obies when she receives a special request from Izzi Orange and Essy Saffron. When the wabble goes wayward, will Clementine get home in time for Christmas?*

- ***Lenny and the Gold*** – *a magical fantasy chapter book for ages 7-13+: Help Lenny and his two best friends as they travel on a perilous quest; the fate of an entire magical realm rests in their hands!*

Made in the USA
Columbia, SC
15 December 2024